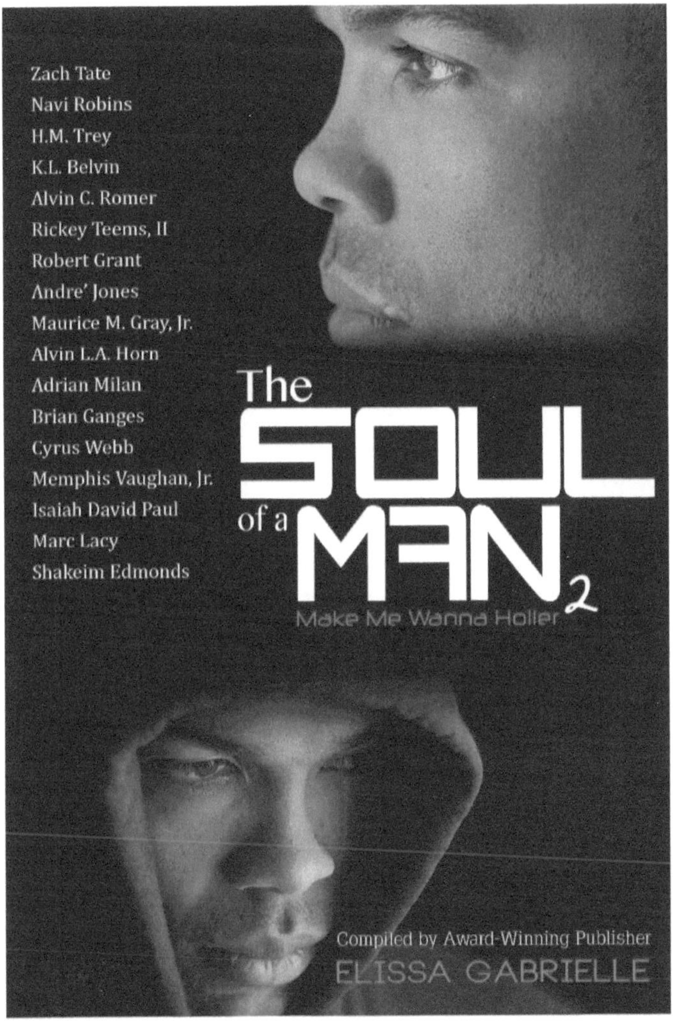

Zach Tate
Navi Robins
H.M. Trey
K.L. Belvin
Alvin C. Romer
Rickey Teems, II
Robert Grant
Andre' Jones
Maurice M. Gray, Jr.
Alvin L.A. Horn
Adrian Milan
Brian Ganges
Cyrus Webb
Memphis Vaughan, Jr.
Isaiah David Paul
Marc Lacy
Shakeim Edmonds

The SOUL of a MAN 2

Make Me Wanna Holler

Compiled by Award-Winning Publisher
ELISSA GABRIELLE

Giving Your Soul a Rise...One Page at a Time

ISBN-13: 978-0692590768

ISBN-10: 0692590765

Publisher's Note

Peace In The Storm Publishing, LLC.
P.O. Box 1152
Pocono Summit, PA 18346
Visit our Web site at:
www.PeaceInTheStormPublishing.com
www.TheSoulofaMan.org

Publisher's Note

Dear Beloveds,

I've been asked on numerous occasions why the need to herald the plight of the Black male, and why the publishing of two books on the subject. My answer has never wavered, for in my mind it's mere simplicity to justify whatever means that manifest change in how my Black men are seen in the eyes from those who judge them.

*It goes deeper than that, though. As a publisher with designs on giving them voices, why not let them speak for themselves? Thus, my intent was to come up with thought-provoking sentiments to enlighten the world why men of color has something to say about revealing the source of their angst. Truth and affirmation are always the best anecdote to elicit wellness and redeeming value. **The Soul Of A Man 2: Make Me Wanna Holler** captures the essence of real life experiences, applying proven principles to help restore pride, solve problems and overcome challenges. As an achieving Black woman observing over the years of how lowered standards has affected the men I know...it permeated me across the pantheon of diaspora to see how far or near I could be if I gave a few good authors a platform for accountability. I wanted to make a difference, and I wanted to see differences in how change would affect them. You would want to agree with me when I say that lowered standards affects us all when it comes to how Kingdom men are not being dominion to their families. It shows up negatively at times in our storied culture. Just observe how it has been In the economical downside of women trying to run households without their men just trying to make it. It doesn't take much more than a cursory glance around our disenfranchised neighborhoods, our churches to discover that men—not all, but many have missed the goal to live to be respected by those who feel that they should be elevated anew. Why wouldn't I want to see better days for our Black men?*

If you feel that I'm on a mission, well...I am! I feel too, that we have everything going for us but too little coming together. Our men seemed to have been shoved into a race they didn't choose and whose finish line they can't picture...it's like they feel that they are doing the right things at the wrong time; some are doing the wrong things all the time. In this uplifting and riveting collection of stories, readers will find wonderful examples of hope and encouragement as they are touched

by the words straight from the depths of their souls about the need to change. Change that got them through difficult times, change that saved family crises, change that mended broken relationships, change that turned their businesses around, change that influenced entire mindsets of people of another persuasion to see them in new prisms of light. THIS is what I wanted you to see and understand. Whether you have read the previous Soul Of A Man installment that I published, both of these books has such powerful declarations of commitment that will enthrall and inspire you to be

better men, and better women understanding your man better. It's no coincidence that I talk about change.

To live with change, to optimize change, you need principles that don't change. I cannot fully describe the respect and reverence I have for every author who has contributed a story in this volume for their willingness to share their inward struggles. I want you to be able to see that all of them are rich human beings who should be respected for what they represent, and what they are trying to accomplish. This book may not change the world, but I'm hoping it will change YOU. I would like for you to see a picture hanging on the wall straight, with a new vantage point with keen insight in what lies in the hearts of souls of real men! Their stories are splendid illustrations of profound change. I feel humbled by their humanity and deeply grateful for them sharing. **Peace in the Storm Publishing** has always given the reading public excellent choices to enhance their page-turning delight. This effort is within the same realm. Add this book to your collection!

Always and in All Ways,
I remain,

Elissa Gabrielle

President & CEO
Peace In The Storm Publishing, LLC

TABLE OF CONTENTS

INTRODUCTION

Elissa Gabrielle has unearthed another gem! As the publisher of this book, she will tell you that, "All men of color are not rapists, convicts, drug dealers and deadbeat dads who are only good for their sexual prowess. All men of color are not the devil incarnate plotting on how to destroy the world. They are not the boogeyman. As a matter of fact, our men of color are kings, rocks to our families, inventors, teachers, scholars, healers, our leaders, our heroes. I have a unique responsibility to not only entertain, but to enlighten, and educate and I take that responsibility seriously to REWRITE THE NARRATIVE by giving you influential storytellers affecting positive change." As one of the authors therein, I echo her sentiments as well as my peers. In life we all embark on journeys that tend to shape our lives one way or another. Because we're individuals we deal with the consequences and hope that we come out unscathed...but for every ordeal based on those journeys there are stories being told where testaments and testimonies are par for the course.

The key to all of the angst is being able to rise above mediocrity to become magnificent, or allow corruptness to be corrected. My plight may not be any different from others who may want to tell their version of how they got over. Going from tragedy to triumph is not just a one-man show, nor is it exclusive to the voices that cry out to be heard. Who are we? We've been used, misused and abused in many facets of our Diasporas... we're men and we want you to be part of what we bring in the stories we want to tell. Often society gets it wrong, but we want to tell it the way WE see it. In the beginning of our journey was the first installment of voices down deep depicted in the seminal and award-winning original anthology 'The Soul Of A Man,' where a few good men gave it to you straight up with no chaser, holding nothing back as we delved deep within to disclose what were prevalent for accountability. We yearned for that second chance to prove our worth, and to allow us to regain lost horizons. Well, we're back!

Now six years later, and no less daunting comes 'The Soul Of A Man 2' with more stories catapulting to the surface not wanting to be left out. It's often said that the second time around is always better. The publisher heard the hue and cry and gave reason to provide more colors to enhance the canvases we continue to paint on. We wanted those colors to be resplendent with all of the shades that give rise to not only make you wanna holler, but to validate whispers to screams! We've *aligned ourselves again for more page-turning delights, all 17 of us…and when you DO holler, make sure you tell someone else why you're doing it! Are you ready for us? The soul of this man, welcomes you. Each story is poignant and precious with enough verve to take us serious. We are vociferous and valued. I invite you to delve into the hearts and souls of* **Adrian Milan, Marc Lacy, Alvin L. A. Horn, Alvin C. Romer, Maurice M. Gray Jr, Zach Tate, Pastor Andre Jones, Gospel Recording Artist Robert Grant, Shakeim Edmonds, H. M. Trey, Memphis Vaughan Jr, KL Belvin, Isaiah David Paul, Rickey Teems II, Brian Ganges, and talk show host, Cyrus Webb.**

Editor/Founder of
The Romer Review

Warriors of the Blues

Alvin L.A. Horn

"Black Men - we penned whispers and hollers
Black Men - writing with and purpose and direction
Black Men - offering a mental lift, and knocking out lack of knowledge with words
of intellect
Black Men - make you wanna holler…"
~Alvin L.A. Horn

First Stanza of the Blues

A Black Man's Blues —

Our Bond that Binds us Together

Red white and the blues

Woven into pain and pride that we are still alive

Forced onto human cargo ships and sold off on the block of Roots Avenue, Lynched

Black Men Place, Emmett Till Boulevard, Trayvon Martin Cul-De-Sac, Eric

Garner-I Can't Breathe Ave at the end of Dead Man's Corner

We are living through the blues that binds us that bonds us

The blues makes it so we can't be torn apart although it appears at times we don't stand

for the same things

We got the same blues in different hues of blackness

The same thing - the blues of being Black in America is our source of pride that we

have endured

Remanufactured fake romantic USA flag waving pride of being American

MAKE ME WANNA HOLLER

Don't trip, I'm glad and proud to be American because my people died on this land

while building a nation for the ruling class

Like apple pie and Chevrolet

Shit gets eaten and shit keeps breaking down

By' American and die for being a profiled Black American from 8 to 80

Living a Black Man Blues

Where daily racist actions are labeled isolated incidents

Making me a warrior of isolated incidents

When I just want to love my woman, spiritually, and financially, and be fatherly to

my children

I just want to be unchained from the way it has been

I want to see my brother's free and not jailed for the same crime others are free from,

because they have mo-money and less melatonin

That money came from my ancestors' back pain of being stepped on and over in

manpower uses

Get your hands out of my pockets money - I want my just-due from the stealing of

Black ideas

I want our royalties, from then and now

Now American manufactures make money on Black asses thrown in private jails

The blues, our bonding glue black men live and sing to ease, or hide the pain

The blues even turned into Last Poets, Def Poets and Tupac and Public Enemies

shouting hard truths

But the man drowned and killed or helped to kill dreamers and thinkers, and found and

paid for fake wanna-be ghetto boyz to shout Bitch come dance on my pole beside my

rented pool and Benz

THE SOUL OF A MAN 2

Our women, our sisters, our mothers have endured the blues, and now live with the
insult of boyz they tried to raise, but those boyz call other women names that they are
related to through the DNA of the blues
The blues is corporate incorporated deals to divide and conquer my people
Yet that part of the blues we live has not cooked my people to death despite the fact some
minds are fried and greasy

For the record
The blues has kept us alive and enduring as the needle keeps droppin'and pinin' our soul
to shit spinnin' that will never change
Damn shame
I got the blues and proud to have them, soul-to-keep, my love, and our will to survive
Despite a cold-cold world burning hot with no respect for a Black men's soul
I live with an intravenous drip of the blues of repeated racist history
The blues that are cast on me and were meant to destroy me, but actually they have
kept my drive alive to bind to bond with my brothers to survive
My brothers are living and surviving blues, I tip my fedora to you, I love you in all
the shade of blues we are in as we will always and forever be bonded by the blues

Second Stanza of the Blues

What keeps me sane - the tremendous strength and courage of the soul of the Black man in America that cannot be matched by any man from any culture at any time since the creation of man. The Blues is our badge, our shield, our fisted glove, and our intellect on how to deal and survive.

From Biblical times, people suffered and were set free allowing them thrive and prosper. In those times, man has absolutely saturated himself on power, greed and immoral wanting's and acted unquestionable. Man had choices all through history to be the best man or fall into sinning against another man. These men would be Africans, Middle Eastern, Asiatic backgrounds men and eastern and western Europe male.

As civilizations learned and had access to the gun power and metals and used advanced weaponry for gains, many African cultures and all religions warned of coveting they neighbor's possessions. Power, greed and immoral wanting's, is a powerful drug that pollutes the soul of any man. Corrupt beliefs of the rich to take more than needed was done with hopes of passing on power and controls to a chosen sec of people, which then has created wars of epic proportions. In so, men have chosen darker skin men to be on the lowest rung of society as a way of not sharing the earth's riches.

This is where the African man, the Black man started feeling the blues and surviving those blues which became our badge of honor. Europeans came to the African continent of seemly never-ending resources, with evil intent to control the continent. The Black man's back, legs and broad shoulders - his physical strength, and willingness to live through all, has made him an unlimited milk and honey, the black pearl and black coal. Along with the Black woman the Black man was a resource more valuable than gold.

First, the Europeans used diabolical verbiage casting dark skin men, as to be, less value than other men, and then came the new nation America to further immoral evil. From evil speak came plots and plans, used through governmental rules and laws, economics, and from bondage and born into incarcerations, and killings to murder the souls of Black men, and yet we live. Our blues has bonded us, and in that bond, we have lived to see another day.

The conquer and divide, the tearing of brothers from mothers, the Queens of African soil and separating those brothers on ships bound for soils of the Americas has left us wandering in the wilderness.

Unlike the Jews wanting to leave for the land of milk and honey, there was no parting of the Red Sea to swallow up our captures. Unlike the Jew again, there has been no recusing for the Black man as in an American D-Day to push back and shut down the genocide of the German ovens of the stopping the holocaust. Unlike the A bomb that put horrifying fear to stop the immoral enslaving and Japanese rule of the pacific, there has been no American A-bomb to stop racist actions and laws used against the Black man. Unlike reparations paid for the wrong doing to the American Japanese held against their will in internment camps and some Native Americans for the stealing lands and breaking treaties, no such payments to Blacks have been paid for the free labor that built this country's wealth. Even apologies have turned into political battles for the enslavement of Black people, and the lasting legacy attached. The souls of the Black man has endured no matter the battle or the length of the wars, we have survived. A Black Man's Blues is our pride in continuing to be Black and alive.

We know the story of the Black Holocaust, and the untold millions who died crossing an ocean shackled as live cargo and we are still living the legacy of separation and the butchering of cultures. The untold story of Black genocide; most slaves when they became old and near or past the average living age of a white man, we were treated like an old dog and put down. Yeah, so much for the master being good to his slaves. If you were no longer able to contribute as a useful servant, such as break a back, tear ligaments, rupture discs in your back, lose a limb, become useless, and it became the end of your life from that good old slave masters. Don't think for one moment it was a movie, *Roots* don't hold a candle to how it really was. For sure, it wasn't some old slave with gray hair looking happy and singing, Glory, Glory, Glory. A broken slave was a dead slave; no sitting on your ass and letting a big happy colored woman come to you and take care of you after she had let the master's babies suck on her tits.

The souls of black men crossing over the Atlantic was a training ground for the battles to come. Survival of the fittest was a mental and physical ordeal, and here we, in 2015 Black men are feared for the most part, because we have survived. We have survived the blues of being in America!

Now battles to live are weekly as we are killed by the police and their backers. Now Black boys pull triggers from guns loaded from political machines and bankers laundering money from drugs shipments into low-income hoods. Now the battles Black men find themselves in, is the number of funeral services at mortuaries of murdered Black bodies. The fact is the troubled Black man is remarkable in displaying grit and resolution in being prideful to be a surviving Black man in America. When Black men look into each other's eyes, it's a code we know, saying, I'm proud to see you Black man and know we are bonded by our suffering and existence, but we cry.

THE SOUL OF A MAN 2

Cry Man

Why would your eyes be dry

Your soul has been an aquifer for the ugly the world flushes

Your soul, from the shed blood of your elders has absorbed the worst the world has
dished out and you stand

Shot you while unarmed, and THEY say you are superhuman, you're almost animal
like, sounds like a bad movie, but it is not a bad movie

The Blues you live is real

They strangle you because you look dangerous as you are accused of selling untaxed
cigarettes, as THEY finance weed shops in hoods, as they sell, 40oz's in the hoods

Cry my brother as I know you do behind closed doors

Cry as THEY protest an elephant going to another zoo

Cry as Yuppie-ville wants more police protection for the electric cars parked on their
white picket fenced hoods

Yeah THEY want protection from their youthful white teens blowing off steam, but
don't kill them just send them home with a fine

Yep, THEY have more concern about the poor whites that live amongst them to stop
stealing their Amazon package that was delivered to their doors, and THEY want
Black boys profiled as thugs to keep them away their daughters

My brother, throw up from being force-fed so much disrespect

I know you're sick as you worry will your sons make it home

Cry as we – well, some of us are trying to live together

As many white parents, and grandparents now have blended families, they have the
same worry that related Black men will be profiled and jailed ... and maybe killed

Cry when you wake and smell the coffee of a new day, knowing at any point of the day you will witness a racial injustice through the national news or right in your face

as a backhanded slap

But you act so beautiful in the face of another isolated incident

Being effervescent in the face of a long history

Because you have survived

No genocide has taken your soul

Yet my soul brother, go ahead and cry

Let those tears rain like the rains of God that lifted Noah's ark to float to a new

beginning

You see, those tears, they fertilize never giving up and trying in every way to live with

the blues

Cry my soul brother, as you are your own promise when you see the rainbow of brown

hues of your people still standing erect.

Third Stanza of the Blues

The souls of Black men in suits in these modern times know the blues. Black men wake-up prepared for heartache to the fact they have to be warriors of isolated incidents. That backhanded slap, when a Black person recounts a negative race based situation they had to deal with is often referred to as an isolated incident. The person most often telling us it is an isolated incident is a white person. With just a little bit of conciseness of awareness, one can see race based problems here in America are not isolated incidents. Black in America for our brothers is going to sleep with certain worries that we are used to that few other American know about, and much less understand, or care to comprehend the full scope. Otherwise said, it is simply disrespect.

Integration of schools from Kindergarten on up to higher learning, and jobs and careers, neighborhoods, and social settings often masks the strife a Black man's walk as compared to our counterparts that we mix with. Race mixing has cloaked the dark side of amalgamation of the races.

The struggle is real, although we thrive in so many areas of manhood, yet on the surface of non-in-depth analysis of statics, there are slants of good and bad fitting into perfect boxes to meet agendas. Often the news is imbalanced for a destruction of blackness by the main stream media and in the social media arena; it leaves blackness appearing as we are failed or dangerous.

That first look in the mirror a Black man sees in whatever shade of brown he may be is what may come with an encounter of that day, all because he is non-white. A mini-movie plays in Black man's soul as fresh sequences or continuations of races based on negative situations. Black men wake and wish the mirror reflected our existence in society as a valued soul with no less and no more than any other man.

Conversely, what is thrown into our faces is we are looking for a handout, or an advantage and we take a deep sigh knowing that lie is told to great successes to use us and abuse us economically and administering unfairly judicially. The augment we are then faced with in trying to get some understanding is, *when did we ever have an advantage, and when was it ever close to being equal?* It is a debate with white society that tries to act as if they are a current day victim for the sins of their forefathers.

MAKE ME WANNA HOLLER

Public discussions turn quickly against Blacks as we are told not to play the race card when we are dealt the race card when the slightest mention of race is in the air. Basically it's being told to hold your pain for my comfort of my entitlement to deny any responsibility of simply comprehending or having empathy...Move on, is a slogan of denial and acceptance of history and the long lasting effects. I heard it said in different tones and revaluations from the likes of W. E. B." Du Bois, Marcus Garvey, Richard Wright, Ralph Ellison, Chester Himes, James Baldwin, Gwendolyn Brooks, Lorraine Hansberry, Alexis Haley, Jim Brown, Malcolm X and Martin Luther King. The voices of today, although they often leave us confused when it comes to internal views of each other, but they are voices: Sister Souljah, Reverend Al Sharpton, Dr. Boyce Watkins, Wendell Pierce, Spike Lee, Harold Ford, Jr, Touré, Melissa Harris Perry, and Kareem Abdul-Jabbar; but the theme of the blues still resonates in what is happening to Black souls.

ഇഇഇഇഇ

Today's Blues: How do we move on from the from the slaves of the 1600's to now while the souls of Black folk are hurt and angry and wanting to talk about it, but often we are told don't play the race card when are still suffering through racist systems from the first slaves.

As many Black souls know, in one way or another,

"If issues of inequality doesn't affect you...don't tell others who are affected by historical bias how to interpret their plight." The most comedic thing that tears at the soul of Black folk sis that we hear racism is over, and it's not about race. That is so flippant, it ain't funny! It's not funny, but we laugh when it hurts, and we laugh to get by.

How do *THEY* see us? Criminal minded, violent, less civil under their standards, lazy, baby makers, and baby killers, and on and on negative slogans History shows long before slaves ever touched this land we had love amongst us, building alliances (the village) to produce children to be proud of. We had an educational system that taught us well, and lead the world in creativity. History showed we knew how to be neighbors with people of not our kind.

After slavery we built towns and areas within the United States where we thrived as a community only to have, once again, White hatred with guns and destructive mind-sets of burning crosses bring down our functional walls. Black Wall Street is not a myth; there were thriving self-sustaining Black communities across America that were destroyed by jealous hateful white power structures.

Got A Black-Eye

Not from a punch ... even though we in a fight

And no damn door knob ... even though I have seen more damn closed doors and tight asses than a gated community has fake smiles

Got a black-eye

Born with it

Living in America

I see through a Black-Eye

I speak with a Black mind and mouth

I make no excuse to not to conform and accept the status quo

I'm relevant to my period in time

Looking through my Black-Eye

I see you

America

Forth Stanza of the Blues

A life experience one of those isolated I experienced: 1994, my beautiful daughter, at the age 7 is out for a ride in daddy's old classic truck on a Sunday afternoon. Ice cream is on our mind as we cruise down a country road. We're doing the all-American thing that all fathers want to cherish in the memory.

As I pass an old church and actually going below the speed limit, I see a police car coming from the opposite direction. The first thing that comes to most Black males, is it Black Tax time? Will he turn around and pull me over. Although we wish it was *Never Never Land*, but we are Black Americans and history from 400 years and on up to 4 hours and on down to 4 minutes ago, our souls has had that thought, is it Black Tax time.

Many times before and since I had been pulled over and harassed, but this time, it was in front of my daughter and the cop made her cry. She had seen and heard the disrespect thrown at her protector. Her father could not show anger and she sensed my constraints, which brought fear to her safety. How much of an isolated incident was that? Well my father experienced the same exact treatment in front of me when I was a child in the 60's. Now my son and nephews experiences are the very same. Then we see on the news, "Black man shot in Walmart for holding a toy gun," when white men walk in the same store with assault rifles carefree. It's hard pressed to find a Black man who has not experienced racism several times, if not many times, in their life from the light verbal to the hardcore violent.

Just like the first look in the mirror, almost every day we see encounters of when the police are near. We go through the, *ifs* and what to do *if*… often we are prepared, in so that we don't lose our cool. When racists speak, or when they stare at us with that look, we know the look, and we know the tone. We know the code words. We know.

White hatred toward Black men quickly brings out their guns to point at us along with destructive mind-sets of mental cross-burning as a clear and present danger to our sons and daughters. It leaves the souls of modern Black men feeling helpless, as runaway slaves were with the hounds tearing at skin and bone. Maybe that sounds dramatic, but wait, think for just a moment.

Whether you like the Black Presidents politics or not, we have watched the right/conservative mostly republican racist politicians and commentaries, and actions of different objectionable fractions bite like hounds on the heels. The other component often is whites that appear to be friendly with us at work or socially will turn on us. Most of us have experienced that. The same democrats who sided with Obama ran from him when it came to being re-elected and lost anyway.

Visions of the cop driving behind you and whether it's from the profiling harassment of a traffic stop, or a warrant search, and a trumped up ticket you have reflection that can turn to anger. Oh, those "Black Taxes." The Black tax is paying a cost on top of what most others are not paying. Black Taxes take money from you, your family, and your community, and brings your buying power down (credit scores) and cheat your savings, and over a lifetime, your retirement nest egg.

Too few Black men don't know of the encounter with law enforcement that leads to you being late to a job you're trying to hang onto. Black Tax. Maybe an encounter with police leads to being thrown in jail on bogus charges, or by false witness. No man is perfect, so maybe the offense is minor, but the outcome can be deadly. We pray bullets or a beating to death is not levied as the worst part of the Black Taxes. But yes, we are angered by the fact weekly an unarmed Black male is gunned down, and rarely is there retribution of justice of a positive verdict in the court of law for the unarmed Black victim.

The soul of the Black man is stronger and more hardened allowing him to never die, never, although he knows he is always in a world war. Isolated incidents are battles he loses in what feels like 99 to 1. We have been a struggle so long we don't give ourselves hardly enough credit for surviving in America. It's almost as if we have become desensitized to the pain we feel. Strangely, as it maybe, we come to an elder's funeral, and feel somewhat happy and thankful that we are coming to celebrate an elder's long-life of surviving the blues for so long.

Our souls are tired, but far from beaten down. We are tired from decades and centuries of being sick and tired of a repeated history. We are always hearing about change and hope, yet when you read this, ask yourself, *will it change in your lifetime?*

Let's get really-real, as it is said on the streets:

This country cannot rid itself of the race issue; it has too much nasty history and its legacy.

America! America!

God shed His grace on thee,

And crowned thy good with brotherhood

From sea to shining sea!

Old and new Europeans and American rule annexed the rest of the world. They subjugated, by military domination and called it liberation by massacring, only later to add further damage by ghettoization, and the sexual rape of darker skinned peoples of the world. Old and new Europeans and American rule appropriated and embezzled properties, wealth, and culture. Old and new Europeans and American rule abolished and annihilated dark skinned peoples narration and description of their past. Old and new Europeans and American rule concealed and censored the faiths and beliefs through torment and oppression. Now we see in America, the passing of laws, and school districts banning the teaching of the recognition of the people's history if it doesn't make America look favorable. The old saying *pull yourself up by your bootstraps* is a crock of bullshit if you don't believe we are still feeling the after effects of it all.

Our ancestors here in America and now our parents had hopes that it would be different for you and us as a people. Now, are you saying the same about those born after you? Are your prayers going out to a couple of generations ahead, and thinking that their world is the one that race is not the problem of the day. Our elder's prayed that same prayer for you.

How can we get to change, I mean really, how do we when we are perceived as scary, violent, aggressors, a vision painted in their psyche by boogieman tales. We were kings in a beautiful history prior to being American property. We were born with intellect, drive, and love, but now we are warriors of isolated incidents, and it makes some fight with wrong or right intentions; and either way, the outcome is scary for us, our young Black males, and black families suffer the most.

The news, *is there ever any good news about black men?* Let's be clear, most black men don't produce bad news, they are simply burned in character assassination at work, or in the public arena and from the hands of our own, or imprisoned by prosecuting suited agendas or murdered the old-fashioned way, from men with badges.

What does that mean? On one side of the coin, the personal responsibility that Malcolm X spoke of until his death is that many of our best tools and weapons are missing. On top of that list that used to make us more prepared is, we were armed with survival knowledge. Black men were once given mental awareness of mental shovels and axes and mental guns as weapons to fight in a world that will never love and respect us. Like Malcolm X made clear, we can't ask them to love us until we love ourselves, and end even then, *they* will never respect us, but they will have a real reason to fear us. That is the best tool we can have to move forward. Told to us by fathers, grandfather, and even women elders prior to the seventies and for sure in the sixties and before, we were told, *you must work twice as hard, and think three times smarter, and always be one-step ahead of the hounds of trouble.* We were told that if a man wasn't busy, he is subject to giving up his freedom.

Fifth Stanza of the Blues

The blues solo:

For the Black man who looks in the mirror and don't see black, the blues can turn a docile man to militant in one isolated incident. That Black quickly finds himself in line with other Black men even if he chooses not to vocally express it. If a Black man has, or had not lived the common/stereotypical life of Black man's awareness, he lives in the shadows of the same colored-folk who passed for white throughout history. *They lived in fear.* Strangely all Black men live in fear just different kinds and degrees all associated to how we came to this country and how each family and man have integrated into standards that we had no hands in setting since slavery ended.

Different kinds and degrees of fear is a Black Tax on the heart and soul and mind. Being Black is scary no matter your wealth or status in life and for sure no matter how poor you may be. Christian or Muslim or non-believing of any faith, if you're Black in America, you have fears.

I share the bonds of the blues with Charles Barkley who lives in fear, although he's in public denial. His blues is in the hue of lonely with self-hatred and ignorance of a lost soul. A man such as him with no basketball skills and from the background he came from would most likely be like the Black men he hates. All through history we have had some Black men turn on their Black women and other Black men to rise above in white society acceptance. If he only understood, *THEY* don't like him either.

Jim Brown, I gladly share the bonds of the blues with him. He lives in fear, but he used his masculine exterior and High-IQ and verbal skills to fight off approaching ignorance. Whether he is liked or not, America respected him from a distance.

Ali's blues is mixed with so many shades of the blues, and all of us are tied to each variation at some point and time in our lives. Ali lived in fear, and now may only fear for other Black people as he has sacrificed so much for.

Blues for Obama is theme of a fake picture of a warm, cozy community without conflict associating itself with that foreign-sounding word Kumbaya's. These blues are a total confusion of twisting of the soul of the Black man of was it good or bad. All through history we have found certain things we wanted; but when we achieved them, it brought other problems to the forefront that no one thought would happen. Hardcore racism has risen like burning crosses for Black men and women in the workforce, and with police matters. Our souls feel the lashes of look and listen to the hatred so freely exhibited in politics, that news media, and in the social media.

THE SOUL OF A MAN 2

The attacks on Obama that are not political based have for sure made him a Black man now if he wasn't before. He has the blues and his family sees and hears the blues in tones of hurt that will affect their souls forever, much like any of our family have endured. The brother has not transcended race, as most Black folks knew from the beginning.

Obama, being a man of color, has all but shut down a functional debate and governance. What he has endured is the very same damn thing most black men have dealt with while on the job to feed their families for decades. Long before white women hit the glass ceiling, Black men didn't have or see a glass ceiling to bump their heads on, but knocks upside the head from doors being shut in a black man's face have been laced with stitches of anger threaded by the leaded pipes of integration that busted open with venomous words

Obama may have changed some policies that will help Black people in the future we all hope. As of now the economics of America has improved despite a Republican congress that had no problem displaying its hate for a Black man in charge. But the good, the bad, the ugly: just like the lessening of segregation may have hurt the soul of our Black communities that the flip side integration let us live in communities of better schools and housing. Sometimes you have to be careful for what you ask for, because of the blues that comes with, *change has come.*

Black is blue. Or is the blues black as we live in fear. T.D. Jakes lives in fear. Prince lives in fear. Michael Jordan lives in fear along with Russell Wilson, Richard Sherman, LeBron James, Denzel Washington, they all lives in fear. Spike Lee lives in fear. Colin Powell lives in fear, Will Smith lives in fear, and Jay Z, and conservative Black men who deny that we live in fear, when they do live in fear. The Black man who has never been in trouble, always worked hard, and led a decent life, and even goes to church as he has for the last 30 years, and he lives in fear. That would be the majority of Black men although you'll never see that on TV or read about it. We are blue, but it the soul of the blues that has kept us alive.

Sixth Stanza of the Blues

More on the Black Tax: We witnessed our elder relations work for the *man* and in many cases; we saw Black men and woman who worked for themselves in what we called a hustle, even when they had a mainstream job. Black men all know about that position where you're doing the work of others, but are not recognized with the correct monetary levels and name, i.e. Black Tax. Your counterparts would say, it's an isolated incident. The hustle was used to help offset the Black Tax of higher interest rates for loans of any kind, or no banks loan in red-lining practices from banks. Often we put our money in banks that would not loan money to Black communities, and Black owned banks were rare.

Many of our elders worked multiple jobs to not only get ahead, but mostly to keep up. The blues of lack of earning power brought less property holdings, less to borrow against, less to furnish higher education, less business ownership, fewer laws to protect, and less legal representation. Many nationalities have worked as such, and whites, but for Black American's, it was Black Tax time. Because we were not allowed to be on the same earning levels, we relegated to living conditions based on where we were allowed to live and how we were policed.

To the outside world, and even when we see and judge our own, Black men are often deemed or evaluated as, cool, smiling and happy, hip and slick, shuffling or uneducated, frustrated and angry, non-trusting and guilty without a trial. The problem is, when pre-judged before a personal interaction that can lead into hate and racist acts against the Black man.

Of course each Black man knows the so-called isolated incident, which is choice of words to diminish your existence and your situation, Black men and women have all had to turn the other cheek while dealing with an unquestionable -undeniable racist situation. To react any other way, and maybe you lose your job, or it puts you in or keeps you in negative treatments, and can cause you to lose your life.

Last Stanza of the Blues

We have,

Protested

Voted

Banded together

Thrived in education

Became dominate in physical achievements

Even burn baby burn has had a way of keeping us alive

Then beat down: being stolen in 1600s did not eradicate us

Then becoming the most valuable crop helping create a nation in the 1700s did not

exterminate us

The building of a nation in the 1800's made white men kill each other over us

Although set-free, we were then free to be used and abused and conned, and imprisoned

and lynched, and our women raped

Our boys stood little chance as a master plan was in place by a system not designed

for us, but designed against us, but we lived

After each storm has passed, we look in the mirror at our wounded souls, and go back

out in the chill of America

We reinvent our ways and see if that works

But evil is so dominant as it tears at us as if we were gator bait

Yet, I see your smile and hear your laughter, Black man

It hurts so badly at times, all you can do is laugh

Our blues that binds us is a sweet solace, because they don't understand that

Discarding varying hues of hostility or

Our blues leaves THEM perplexed and crawling with insecurities

Madness to many, but,

We are still vibrant despite THEIR issues

We are forever extraordinary

Despite it all, we are a living legacy

The murder of our babies, and the police who give us the blues; there is an untold story of many of these officers killing black men, and beating Black women with fists are veterans of the Iraq and Afghanistan wars. They are used to killing or becoming very aggressive with short tempers, and challenging, with a trust no one attitude. Black people know all too well how threatening police can be as an ass-backwards way of gaining respect. Many of their actions and reactions are by-products of how they survived in wars. The police in sophisticated SUV squad trucks and cars are men who have killed before, hundreds and maybe thousands of times, in violent video games of their generation. The killing games are equal to the Killing Fields of mass mental and physical destruction. From the eighties and nineties going into the 2000's, a lot of officers were playing violent video games in where the suspects were dark and they hunted killed them. A high percentage of police officers have played those games and are veterans of the Middle East wars and the people they killed in those wars were dark skinned.

So it is no wonder, that we see police in military gear acting aggressive in military battlefield techniques, because so many were in the armed services and now they are police on the street.

e/oe/oe/oe/o

How to fight back: What is missing greatly from our protests of today is our elders are not in the fight as they were in the 50's, 60's, and 70's. We want to blame our young people for what they do-do wrong, and they need to take responsibility for their actions, but the elder next door neighbor is missing from the marches, the protests, the fight. Some things can't be helped as they are what they are as in, a higher percentage of grandma's and granddad's is now younger and not the 60's and 70's years of age as it was in the 1950's and 1960's

If we the nation saw 50-60-70 year olds out their protesting in big numbers saying don't shoot my grandchildren, and great grandkids, it would be the same effect as when the nation saw for the first time fire hoses being used on elders and kids in the 60's. Soon after the vision of that in American living rooms, civil rights became important. We also need our Black church leaders to go to their white church leaders, and ask them why are they on the sidelines, and come join in. We can't let the white churches who sat on their holier-than-thou pews as in the 60's. We need our elders to do more than get on their knees and pray, they need to get out in the streets, and be seen and heard once again to help keep the glue that binds us and bonds us as one, as we survive the blues.

The one African, Colored, Negro, Black, African American culture that can't be killed, removed, and outlawed, is our connection to living the blues here in America; it ties our people together forever. Whether an isolated incident, or daily, weekly, or yearly and decades of occurrences, theses blues are ours to celebrate surviving them up until now and forever more.

The Transformation of a Black Man into a Father

Navi Robins

"Tragedy can either shape a man or break a man, but it can also bring resolution and acceptance of our own imperfections as black men in America. "The Transformation of a Black Man to a Father" is a first-hand account of my journey on learning how to become a father and the struggles of attempting to break a vicious cycle that plaques the African American community in America today."

~ Navi Robins

The year was 2002; I was twenty eight years old and believed that I had reached the pinnacle of the American dream. I had a six figure salary, a successful singing and song writing career with a major record deal in the works, a twenty eight hundred square foot condo along Chicago's lakefront, a couple of expensive cars, and a beautiful family. Did you notice the order I placed everything in my description of my life? Did you notice a few things missing? You see back then I thought I had my priorities in order, but fast forward thirteen years and I've learned the hard way that my priorities were all out of whack.

On the surface it appeared I was a great catch and most would believe I had my life planned out for me. But truthfully, I was damaged goods and although I had two beautiful baby boys living with me, I also had a daughter by another woman. Although bothered by the fact all of my children weren't under the same roof, I didn't see it as a major problem. When I reflect on my thought process...I was all screwed up. I believed because of what I "had" I was untouchable and it's always during your time of arrogance and excess that The Creator shows you exactly how "touchable" you really are.

Enter Job on stage left...

It was a Thursday night like any other. I was on my way out to go sing for another crowded room in downtown Chicago. Earlier that evening I was in the living room playing with my three month old son, Kai. Although Mercy, his older brother is my first born. Kai and I shared a special bond because, unlike my other two children, I was there in the delivery room when he was born. When my other two children were born, I was either working or out of town. I wanted to be there, but I felt like my presence wasn't as important as making sure I secured a steady paycheck. But with Kai, I was there from the beginning until he came into this world and our bond was stronger because of it.

His mother had laid him down on our bed right after he fell asleep and I went about getting ready for another late night. Right before I was about to leave, I went into our bedroom to kiss him goodbye and didn't see him in the middle of the bed where his mother laid him down earlier. I looked towards the head of the bed and noticed his tiny feet sticking straight up and I jumped on the bed to find him caught between the headboard and mattress. When I pulled him out, his tiny body just collapsed in my arms and I screamed for his mother to call 911. I started CPR, but he wouldn't open his eyes. Miraculously the ambulance showed up in less than five minutes and they took him away to the hospital that was right around the corner from our condo.

THE SOUL OF A MAN 2

His mother was hysterical, but I maintained my composure as we walked into the hospital and sat in the waiting room. Eventually my parents and my older brother showed up and waited with us and I noticed how everyone was really out of sorts. Not me though. I was confident my baby would pull through because of who his father was. Most say they've had brushes with death or had near death experiences. For me I've had close encounters with death all my life that were sometimes so bizarre most would find it unbelievable. My battles with death started early when it came to take me when I was five years old. I was swept away during high tide in the Atlantic Ocean in Tampa Bay, Florida at night. To this day no one can explain how I survived that ordeal being so far out in the ocean at night, but somehow I fought to stay alive and I survived. Then when I was ten years old, death came with a fully loaded magazine of Malaria. We'd just arrived in Liberia in 1984 and after two weeks I came down with the worst case of Malaria anyone could possibly get. My temperature was so high, I started to hallucinate and lost my ability to see and walk for almost two weeks. Then a few months later death brought an entire army with it and I had my first taste of war when the country of Liberia had its second Coup d'é Tate. I'd gotten up early that morning to go to the outdoor market, and once the shooting started, I was trapped while people were dying all around me. I crawled out of that market through mud and feces to get away and find my way back to the school's compound. After that, for the next seven years while living overseas, death and I battled constantly like Jacob wrestled with the angel. Each time I was victorious, not unscarred, but alive nonetheless. So it wasn't farfetched for me to believe my beautiful baby boy would inherit his father's favor against death. I was so confident that when the doctor walked up to us, I believed he was going to tell us Kai was ok, but instead he told us they were unable to save him after several hours of doing everything they could. I was still in denial until they allowed us to see his tiny lifeless body lying on a bed in an empty room painted in the most hideous shade of yellow I'd ever seen. His mother walked into the room and started begging for Kai to wake up, but I remained silent. I was totally lost and when I saw him there, unable to move, unable to smile back at me and I was unable to look into his beautiful eyes and tell him I loved him…I collapsed on the floor and refused to leave that room.

I lost my baby that night, but I also lost something else and to be honest, I really didn't want it back again. I lost my faith in God and my ability to feel. I didn't curse God, but I decided that he and I wasn't going to rock with each other for a while until I got some answers. I hated myself and was plagued with nightmares of what I imagined Kai suffered through when he was trying to fight to live. How he cried out for me to save him, but I couldn't hear him and because of that he died alone in a dark room. I was supposed to be there. I was supposed to be his protector and savior. I failed and I couldn't find any reason to forgive myself. My guilt caused me to deny myself the time to mourn him as punishment for not being the father I should've been. The fact that Kai's name meant life in Hebrew made my pain and self-hatred even more potent, and after that day, I lost my passion for life.

If you thought my worries were over after burying my three month old baby, you would be sorely mistaken. My troubles were just beginning. Within a year I lost my six figure salary and every material thing I owned. The record deal was also a bust because the record label went belly up, but I'd lost my love for music after Kai's passing and I refused to sing professionally for several years after that.

Because I hated myself, it was impossible for me to love anyone else and soon my relationship suffered until I lost my family as well. Left with nothing but my self-loathing, I was unleashed unto the world and I gravitated to every woman or relationship that was toxic to me healing from the loss of my son and my faith. I was financially unstable and emotionally unavailable, yet I still convinced myself that I was ready to start over and each time, I tried I was either the wrong man for that woman or she was the wrong woman for me. To say I made bad choices is the understatement of the century.

Then one day I received a phone call from my oldest son's mother saying she could no longer care for him and I needed to take him. For a man who'd just lost a son, you would think I would be ecstatic to have one of my babies with me, but actually I wasn't the least bit excited. I love my children but throughout my life I was never exposed to strong black father figures, only strong black men. Men who were revolutionaries, soldiers, educators and men of vision. My mother is a strong woman with a spirit likened to Harriet Tubman or Sojourner Truth, but she was not my father; and no matter how strong she was, the lack of a strong father figure caused me a lot of pain. My stepfather was a revolutionary, Marine and Martial Arts expert and from him I learned how to be a man of strong convictions. I was raised to be a warrior, a soldier, a man that looks his adversary in the eyes and dare them to violate my rights as a man. But when it came to being a strong father figure, he wasn't up to the task. Many men believe just because they are around or teaching something that they are being a good father. Unfortunately, they are mistaken and it scars a child as if the father was never there. A child without a father is a tragedy waiting to happen and the world takes advantage of their lack of protection. Although there are strong mothers in this world that raise their children alone, a child without a father is still easy bait. Because this blue marble in space is driven by testosterone and insecure men of low moral standards; society seems to go out of its way to suppress women. From fashion to contribution, women are not shown the respect they deserve and when a single mother shows up with her male children, the world sees an easy target.

My self-hatred attempted to give me every excuse as to why I wasn't fit or ready to be a single father. I had other things to do and it wasn't fair that I had to put everything on hold for my child. Yeah, I was a real piece of work, but one day as I was alone in my apartment, I reflected on my life and all the times as a young boy I was exposed to the abuse of other adults because I was unprotected by a father figure. With my mother living several hours away and a stepfather who wasn't interested, I found myself the "Oliver Twist" of the boarding school I attended and I have the scars of the physical abuse I endured because I was left defenseless.

It was at that moment of reflection I pictured my son going through the same things and even worse on the deadly streets of the west side of Chicago. I knew if I lost another child I would definitively lose my mind and probably take my own life, so I called his mother back and told her I'll take him. The moment I took my son as my responsibility, everything that could go wrong for us did. We struggled and sometimes found ourselves a week away from being homeless, but no matter what happened, it was me and him against the world. I didn't know it at the time, but Mercy became my anchor and road back to the land of the living. I started making better decisions in life and in relationships because I always thought about how this decision would affect his life. I won't lie and say sometimes it was hard to resist the temptation of dating women I knew couldn't offer me more than a great bedroom experience. But I knew I didn't want my son to make the same mistakes I did so I decided to stay home instead of having a parade of women coming in and out of the apartment at all hours of the night.

It was during these long nights confined to our apartment that I started to study online about computers and software. My initial interest was to learn how to upgrade the DVD drive on my computer, but soon I found myself intrigued by the inner workings of computers and the software that allowed them to run smoothly. Within a year I was able to not only change a DVD drive, but was also able to build an entire computer from scratch. Soon our financial troubles faded away and I started my own computer business when I built computer devices that could be installed and used in vehicles. This was something unheard of in 2004 and my business grew until I was making twice as much money building CARPC's than what I was making at the office.

Things were starting to look up for us, but there can be no victory if change isn't complete. Although I was on the road to recovery, I still wasn't whole and soon things tanked and I lost my business and my job; all within a couple of weeks. Unable to survive on our own, my son and I were forced to move in with my parents in their small two bedroom condo. It was during this time I relapsed in my self-hatred and started behaving like I didn't have a care in the world or a five year old son depending on me to get it together. I was unaware that what was missing couldn't be bought or learned online because my soul was empty and lost, but I'd been that way for so long I thought it was normal. My parents watched me and were heartbroken and one day my mother had enough. We had an argument so bad it still brings tears to my eyes to this day when I reflect on all the horrible things that I said that day. I didn't want to hear her pleas for me to find myself for the sake of my son and daughter because again I thought I was ok. My behavior had gotten so bad my mother believed I was on drugs or an alcoholic, which when you consider I've never had a drink or taken any type of drugs my entire life, sheds light on just how off balance my soul was.

I ignored all the signs that I was becoming the same men that didn't have the strength to be strong fathers in their son's lives. And as I reflect on my behavior today I offer no excuses. The loss of Kai was a horrible experience that still hurts to this day, but it was no excuse to neglect my children that were still alive. As I write this it burns me deep in my soul because of all the years I wasted fighting who I really was; trying to fit into an easier version of me. My descent took years and my ascension wasn't going to be an overnight success either. After that blow up with my mom, a light clicked on in me because after everything she's sacrificed for me to be alive today and seeing her heartbroken and crying, I knew that my destructive behavior was causing a rift between us. There's a saying, "A mother is god in the eyes of a child," and there's no truer statement to a male child who doesn't have an active father figure in their lives. I'd lost enough and I wasn't going to lose my mother who thought I hated her because of everything I went through growing up overseas. She believed that I blamed her for my scars and she ruined my life. This, of course, wasn't how I felt but no matter what I said to her, she wouldn't believe me.

Truth is, regardless of the horrors I experienced I wouldn't change a thing, because it was the strength I gained conquering those things that allowed me to be able to pull myself up from the dirt. Although I had the displeasure of experiencing the worst of mankind, I was also blessed to experience the best. I know had I not experienced all those things, the good and the bad, I would not be sitting at this laptop today with the strength and integrity to reveal the less flattering part of me. Change is a personal journey that happens when our souls have awakened and decided we are tired of being a victim. Prayer can help to cope with the pain, but coping is like aspirin. It only numbs the pain; it doesn't solve the problem that caused it. Only the will to change and action can bring about true victory. This is something I learned when I began my upward ascension back to the land of the living.

So the first thing I had to do was allow myself to mourn the loss of my son. Mourning Kai was a soul cleansing experience, yet forgiving myself will be a life long journey that I must travel one road marker at a time. I then asked my oldest son and daughter for their forgiveness for my failures and started living my life in a manner that revealed to them I meant it. My change was hard and I still made mistakes along the way, but this time I was falling forward and not backwards. I was still without my faith in God, but I felt it was time for Him and me to have a talk. So I fell to my knees and let him know exactly how I felt about everything and I do mean *everything*. I felt if we were going to rock with each other again, I needed to say everything so that there would be no misunderstandings between us.

After that day I found myself paying closer attention to my children and I discovered that although my oldest son was only two years old when his little brother passed, he was also in constant pain from his loss. I was so engulfed in my own pain I had no idea that my son was suffering as well. He constantly watched the home videos of Kai when he thought no one was paying attention. He was a lonely child and found it hard to make friends because he yearned for his little brother. They also had a connection and it was severed by his death, and like me, he never got over it. He needed me and I needed him in order for the both of us to heal and so we embarked on a slow journey to get to that healing. Again, I made mistakes along that journey but they were mistakes, not habits and I started to learn from them so that I never repeated them.

Enter Love and Maturity...

Throughout my life I've learned that The Creator did not create us to live this life alone. We were meant to travel through life with people that enhance the experience and enrich our lives. The miracle of love is that two imperfect people recognizes each other's imperfections and yet find a reason to trust and have enough faith to love each other regardless. I found that love in the most unlikely of places from the most unlikely woman. Had I met my fiancé years earlier, I would've broken her heart and added another scar on a woman that had been through enough on her own. At first things started off very casually, but unlike my previous relationships, there was something inside of me that yearned for this woman to be more than my girlfriend or sexual conquest. It was scary at first that I was willing to give up so much so soon, but something in me said, "It's time". So I trusted it and I am thankful every day that I listened.

THE SOUL OF A MAN 2

As in any relationship, we had some bad times and for my part, I needed to learn how to love her with inclusion. I needed to include her into my life and make decisions that reflected that inclusion. We were both used to doing everything on our own and it was a hard transition trying to navigate this new terrain of unity. Unlike my previous relationships, this woman was a woman of requirements that exceeded just paying bills and occasional date nights. I needed to change from being just a man and become something more. I needed to become a protector of the family and her heart. It wasn't enough to just be there; I needed to be active and I needed to be productive and selfless. She trusted me with her life and the lives of her two daughters and I needed to become more than what I used to be. I had to do more, be more, love more. For someone used to doing for self it was a difficult transition, but she was and is worth it.

After living together for several years one day she asked me to join her in the bathroom and showed me a pregnancy test that was positive. Prior to that day I believed that I was actually cursed and wouldn't have any more children, or if I did, they wouldn't survive very long. So to say I was terrified is an understatement. But unlike before my first response wasn't to run into myself, but to embrace my fear and share it with her. I don't think she understood just how bad it was until I started waking up in the middle of the night screaming. I frightened her because she thought I was having nightmares about my time as a prisoner of war; but the truth is, I was having nightmares of Kai coming to take away my new son from me.

I can't recall a night I didn't have a nightmare during her pregnancy and the loss of sleep enhanced my anxiety. The day she went into labor I refused to do anything or be anywhere else, but at the hospital. As if the cosmos was playing a sick joke on my sanity, she had complications and the baby's heart rate was dropping, so they had to do an emergency C-Section. It took hours of silent prayer and nail biting for me to remain sane during the delivery and then the miracle of Aiden was born. He was beautiful and represented everything that was right and beautiful in our lives. His birth brought two families from different backgrounds and nationalities together. From his birth also awakened something inside of me; Navi' Robins the author. Throughout my life I believed singing and music was my greatest talent and gift. I believed music was the destination, but I was wrong. Music was a marker on the journey to me becoming a wizard of words and by the time Aiden was a year old, I was a published author. The feeling that accomplishment gave me was unlike any other and there wasn't a doubt in my mind Aiden's birth helped make that possible. When Aiden came into my life he changed everything for me and my other two children. Although no one can replace Kai, Aiden was confirmation we would all be alright. Each of my children represents a different stage in my life when they were born. Mercy represents sacrifice, Alexia represents patience, Kai represents forgiveness, Aiden represents redemption and Eden represents joy and a new beginning.

Today I have six beautiful children; two boys and two girls and two more girls that are not physically mines, but I love them as if they were. Becoming a father isn't a drive-thru life event; it's a struggle to find yourself and then learn how to love your children the right way. No one prior to becoming a parent has any experience in sacrificing beyond your own interests. Just like becoming president of the United States for the first time; there's no class or app for that.

THE SOUL OF A MAN 2

Society paints a picture of black fatherhood as if it's not allowed the journey of discovery, while affording everyone else the luxury of a learning curve. No father, regardless of race or background, gets it right on the first try and it's even harder for a child growing up without his father because he has no blueprint to build upon.

What burns my soul to no end is when a black father makes a mistake on his journey and he's painted as unfit or unwilling. I was willing and I loved my babies, but I made mistakes and it wasn't for a lack of love for them. I just didn't know any better and I didn't have anyone to show me the way. Does that make me unfit? Does it mean I should be denied the joy of fatherhood because once upon a time I didn't know how to be anything but selfish? Ask yourself if expecting black men to be perfect fathers as a requirement for recognition and access to their children to be a fair and impartial concept. I've always wanted a family and my children brought me great joy, but I was a man reaching from the depths of pain and denial. Everyone has demons they have to fight and no one is an exception to this reality, but men who *want* to be fathers should not be denied that blessing just because their battles are not relatable to someone else.

୧୬୧୬୧

The difference between myself and a "deadbeat" is I stayed the course just like many black fathers, and although still not where I want to be, I feel confident I will get there eventually. My life is just one example of how black men who grew up without fathers become great fathers through sacrifice and growth. I was blessed to have full access to my children without hindrance from their mothers or the courts, but I can't imagine how fathers deal who never had that opportunity. Those fathers are the real champions and should be honored as such. When I was twenty eight years old, I had no idea how to be a father or a protector and I suffered for it. My priorities should've always been God and family first, but like many I drank the Kool-Aid of an uncaring and materialistic society. I was taught otherwise as a child, but I lost my way and had to relearn what is truly important and what is trivial and fleeting. Faith in God and yourself is paramount in changing into who we were meant to be. I needed to evolve in order to resolve and that journey was painful, but I'm still here. My babies are still here and they have no question today that their father loves them and would lay his life down to protect them. Now, when asked about my life I always begin with God, a beautiful family and a purpose to write my own legacy into history. This is my life now and I love it.

What About ME

H.M. Trey

"Often "mis"ed is the African American man. When I say "mis"ed I am referring to misunderstood and misrepresented. Just like all other races there ARE some good African American Men in this very diverse country. The Soul of a Man 2 brings you a sample of such distinguished African American gentlemen that represent proud voices in their respective communities. It is always refreshing to me to see positive images of African American men doing positive things providing positive messages for the entire world to see. This sort of representation is highly needed to discredit all the negative stereotypes that our men are forced to deal with in these "United" States of America. The change must start somewhere...so why not with us? I am honored and humbled to be in this number!" ~ H. M. Trey

My Passion to Write

Things happen for a reason. I don't think this is a coincidence but rather a blessing. I have been blessed with the opportunity to write under a publisher called Peace in the Storm Publishing. Writing tends to help me through and serves as my "peace" with life struggles and situations. The storms that come in my life often rage with torrential downpours, but my "Peace in the Storm" comes when I write at times. Thankful for my opportunity!

I dedicate this piece to my daddy, Hurley A. Morgan Jr. My daddy went home to be with the angels February 7, 2014. He was there to witness my first breath as I was there to witness his last. Love you much daddy and miss you more than words can ever say!

The Vision of These Brown Eyes of MinE

My brown eyes are usually covered with contacts or glasses that resemble those that the late great Malcolm X graced upon his face. All that simply means is that my vision is far less than 20/20...my physical vision that is. If I remove my corrective lens of choice, my vision would be very blurry. I have to stand basically on top of the desired view to get a clear sight of it. But I am thankful still! Why?! I may be blind but I can see! No, I'm not actually blind. What I actually mean is that my vision is horrible without the assistance of these man-made objects. But the meaning behind this figure of speech is that no matter how bad my sight is (physically) my vision is very strong (mentally). I have been blessed with "mental" vision. I may not be the smartest man in the world but...I'm smart enough!

Born a little over 38 years ago in Statesville, NC to what I can personally say the best parents that a child can be born to, I am a man of vision and hope. Blessed to be able to carry on the name of my father and grandfather (who didn't have the pleasure of meeting) and I carry it like a badge of honor. My outlook of the world usually comes through the lenses of what I believe is common sense. Common sense...you would think that the need to change the criminal mindset within some and the racist mindset in others would be common sense. Saving the world instead of destroying the only place we all have to live in...yep, you guessed it. Staying away from the things that will kill you (i.e. drugs and violence towards one another) is what I believe to be common sense. The idea that we need to work together, no matter what race you are, would be common sense. But what I have learned that I am certain that many already know is that common sense isn't all that common. The term should be changed and pegged the name "rare" sense.

Over the years I have seen with my very own brown eyes that the world is falling apart from the inside out. We still have racial tension in this world. In America, we call ourselves the land of the free, but can easily be called the land of the hate. I'm an African-American and I experience hate from other races and hate from my own race. In America, African-American community's sense of community continues to fade away right along with the image of fatherhood. The news, regular media, and/or social media tend to show me negative images these days that make me fearful for my daughter and the younger generation's future. And that is what I want to take a few minutes of your time to talk about. What is it that these brown eyes of mine really see and what things are important to me. I am always looking out for others and listening to other's problems in life. But then I have to ask myself one question…What About **ME?**

This Skin of MinE

I can recall one moment as a child being at the Iredell County fair with my father. During that moment a white man in one of the game booths yelled out to my father as we were walking by, "Hey Nigger!" This was an attempt to get my father's attention to come play the game to win a prize. That was the first and only time that I ever saw my father give someone the middle finger. Now I heard my father curse, but never had I seen him give anyone the universal gesture. That moment in time stuck with me. Between that time in my life up until this very day, I have learned a lot about this skin of mine. I am an African American male and I have learned that based on the fact that I was born with the skin I'm in that I will have to deal with negative stigmas, stereotypes, and disgust pointed in my direction…not because of my character which deals with abyssal traits that really define me as a person, but rather my skin color which deals with the superficial and has nothing to do with the type of person I am. I have learned that the fact that I bleed the same bodily fluid that everyone walking this Earth bleeds doesn't mean that I will be viewed as an equal part of society. I understand that I may have to fight twice as hard as my Caucasian counterpart at times to have the same success despite having the same qualifications to deserve having that success. I thank God for my parents, however, for instilling in me the determination and drive to get anything in life I want, despite the doors that may shut in my face or the windows of opportunities that may close because of the fact that my skin is a darker shade. It may be hard and I may be faced with roadblocks, but I will not allow that to hold me back. This skin I'm in will not be the reason I fail.

In 2008, history was made in the United States when a witty Senator from Illinois became the 44th president. An African-American president was supposed to indicate that change that our country needed, but instead it revealed what the world already knew…how racially divided our country continues to be despite the fact that this is the so-called land of the free and equal opportunities. On paper that is a true fact, but in actuality…not so much the case. These United States of America! One man, Barrack Obama, has managed to open up old wounds, old feelings across the country making our country look more like it should have the title of The *Divided* States of America. Racial tension is just as high as they were in the 1960's and I thank God that we have enough rights today that on paper appear to protect us from the lynching's, heartless killings, and burning of homes, churches, schools, and establishments that we faced before and during Civil Rights times. Notice I say "appear". Some of the issues that we, we being African-Americans, continue to be faced with in the "land of the free" and "equal opportunities" have turned more mental. We are faced with mental lynchings in the form of unjust treatment in the legal system, police brutality, and glass ceilings in the workforce. The prisons and the lack of resources in our communities that lead to the miseducation of our children puts many African-Americans in that dreaded category of modern day slavery.

African-Americans as a race are hit with many negative stereotypes...lazy people, angry people, criminal minded people, drug dealers, dangerous/violent people, baby mamas/baby daddies, uneducated people. The men are only good at rapping and/or playing sports. The women are only good at having babies and being on welfare. Negative stereotypes simply mean that people have designed a book cover for a race of people with no intention of reading the pages within that book. The media is just as guilty with its portrayal of the African-American people. All you see is the negative pictures painted by society splattered all over every media platform there is. Everywhere you look around, you see images of poor parenting/deadbeat daddy representations, mug shots, murder/crime scenes (mainly black on black), drug dealers/users, sagging pants on the boys/men, scantily clad dressed girls/women, welfare recipients, nappy headed/no teeth representations, uneducated/bad English speaking representations, and/or animalistic portrayals. This is the picture painted by America for the rest of the world to see giving the world the impression that this is all African-Americans. They already say that we all look alike, but to also say that we all act alike is preposterous! That is just as bad as an African-American saying that all white people are racists. We know that racists still exist and to say that they don't would mean that one is naïve, but to put all white people in that category is crazy to me. Besides, every race of people has individuals that fit the negative descriptions that get forced upon African-Americans. We are looked at as the bottom of the totem pole.

Then there are the African-American people...my people. You absolutely cannot point one finger at anyone without four fingers pointing back at you. As a race we are the worst in engaging self-pity, blaming others for our actions, refraining from accepting the consequences of our actions, and coming up with excuse after excuse for our predicaments as a people. As they say, "Excuses are tools of the incompetent, which builds monuments of nothingness." So from the outside looking in, our excuses as a people make us look very incompetent as a whole and according to this quote...simply put, being that we are often looked at as incompetent, it is also believed that we cannot, will not build anything worth anything.

The question now becomes, "What does all this have to do with me?" My answer...*a lot!* No matter how smart I am, how many degrees I have, how many skills/talents I have...no matter how wonderful my character is, how big my heart is, how much of a help that I am to any race I may be...I am still looked at as a black man first. I get judged by my cover without the reader even opening up my book and reading the pages of me.

What exactly is on the pages of ME? Education-wise I have a Bachelor of Arts Degree from the University of North Carolina at Chapel Hill, a Masters of Business Administration and a Masters of Public Administration from Strayer University. I have taken and passed the North Carolina State Exam for Health and Life Insurance.

THE SOUL OF A MAN 2

Career-wise, I have worked in the human services field in some capacity since 1999. I have assisted with the establishment of a Non-profit Organization. I am in the process of having my second novel published and have recently signed on to have that novel published with Peace in the Storm Publishing. Finally, the one accomplishment that I feel is just as important as many of my before mentioned accomplishments is the fact that I don't have a criminal record. That's right! I have never been arrested. I have never sold drugs, I have never shot at anyone, and I have never committed a breaking and entering or a larceny. I have never committed a felony nor a misdemeanor...*NEVER!* I am a gentle giant but when I add a fitted cap, some Jordan's, and some other urban clothing, I am immediately transformed into a thug...at least that is how I am viewed by some. I have experienced the sudden sound of locking doors, which I understand because safety is important. I have also experienced the crossing of the street/sidewalk and the clutching of purses. Not to mention being followed around stores as if I am going to steal something. All because of the skin I am in? Or is it that I exude the characteristics of being a bad person? In any sense, I get prejudged!

I look at movies such as 42, The Help, and The Butler, just to name a few, to get an idea of the struggles people with the same color skin as mine had to endure. This is just a few of the movies of the many that have been filmed that show the plight of African-Americans. These movies allow for the people born post-Civil Rights years to see what people before them had to go through for us to be able to have what we have, even if we have to go through the extra b.s. to get it at times. Seeing these stories often anger me in three ways. It angers me to know that African-Americans had to go through so much heartache, torture, murders, brutality, name calling, disrespect...blood, sweat, and tears when we were forced here in the first place to be pieces of property with no intentions of being able to have those rights listed in the Constitution. What do they call it? Oh yeah...liberty and justice for all. It also angers me to see my people that were born post-Civil Rights years and didn't have to endure all that pain act like the animals that some of America expect them to act like. I mean, the gangs continue to be an issue, drugs and disease continue to spread in our neighborhoods, black-on-black crime continues to be high, we break into people's homes and steal, we drop out of high school, we wear the sagging pants and scantily clad clothing, etc. Lastly, it angers me that no matter what type of person that I am I have to work twice as hard, still, than my Caucasian counterparts. I have never been one to use excuses at getting what I want in life, but I am no fool. I see how the world sees me and how I am treated as a black man.

We often appear to be uneducated, misguided, and separated as a people. No unity is in our neighborhoods. We can't support one another if we are not getting anything out of it. We continue to show that we are unappreciative of those that died, bled, and cried fighting for us. I never get it. Looking at these movies and hearing the stories lead me to struggle with understanding how this is so. How can we not do more as a people to show our pride of the skin we are in? We have to, better yet, we must do more to represent ourselves as the human beings that we are. We may not ever get the equality that is rightfully ours, but we also must take more pride in who we are and do whatever necessary to disprove any stereotypes and negative pictures painted about our race.

THE SOUL OF A MAN 2

A person's perception of things is that person's reality. It's how people see the world and as we all know, there are a multitude of perceptions in the world. I know for fact that how I see the world through these brown eyes of MinE is totally different from many. I suppose that my state of mind comes from how I was raised. The type of people I have been fortunate enough to have become acquainted with. Because no matter how the rest of the world sees my superficial self, no matter how my people represent themselves, I will continue to be the best me I can be. I will work on treating all people fairly and just. I will continue to do right as a human being. I am so proud of this skin of MinE!

The African-American MalE and Fatherhood

I want to start off by saying that I am a very proud father. Now it has not been an easy journey for me as a father these fourteen and a half years that I have been one…not by far. Actually it has been one of the most challenging parts of my life as I have journeyed to where I am now in life. I may stir up a feather or two for this, but it is a part of me, a story that I am now ready to share with the world.

As a father, I believe that I have taken parenting skills from both my parents. Being that we are talking about fatherhood and before I go any further, I want to give a heartfelt thank you to my father who I believe is resting peacefully now in heaven up above. My father was a quiet father that did what was necessary to provide for his family and love his wife, kids, and grandkids while he had them on this Earth. I thank God for both my parents, but most importantly I thank God for providing me with a real father that I was able to use as an example. I lost my father February 7, 2014. It was the hardest day of my life to this date because I was there in the hospital as he took his last breath. Daddy I love you...and I really and truly miss you.

The African-American father. Society tends to portray the African-American father as a dying breed. There are baby daddies or deadbeat daddies to name a few of the titles that we now tend to get a lot. Today, society has a poor image of fatherhood in the African-American community. Remember the images of fatherhood we had on television in the past. TV fathers such as James Evans, Cliff Huxtable, or Carl Winslow showed that fathers were the head of the family and family ties were strong regardless of the economic status of the family. These portrayals of the African-American family on television are now overshadowed by reality television that further damages our image to other races in the country and around the world. Our boys are raised by single mothers and/or the streets, so they tend to lack a true father figure at times, which leads to a vicious cycle in our community. These boys to men don't have examples in their lives of how to be fathers so they can be fathers themselves. It is kind of like on the job training.

The father in the home represents the supervisor and the boys represent the employees that need the training. The training and the job itself are challenging...teaching a boy how to be a respectful, responsible man. The issue now is that there are not enough fathers in our community to be those supervisors to train those boys. Now these fathers also need to be there to be that supervisor for our girls as well. That job entails those fathers showing those girls how a man should treat a woman. A father's role to a daughter is to be that first example of how a man should respect a woman and teach them that a father is there for that daughter so a girl growing into a woman don't need a man for superficial things (the things money buys) because the father can easily be in that role. My current job puts me deep in our community working very closely to our children both boys and girls. I am able to see how the kids are suffering because there are no father figures around. Now don't get me wrong...I do see great examples of fathers in our community but we need more. As an African-American we need to take more pride in the foundation of our community. We need to work harder to unify ourselves and make the role of fatherhood a sacred thing again.

Now...let's switch gears and talk about H. M. Trey and his path as a father. My biggest accomplishment, which is ongoing for the rest of my life, is being a father for my beautiful daughter. As I stated before it has not been an easy road for me...matter-of-fact, my story can easily be made into a Lifetime movie. It can actually be defined as trying, stressful, and painful. This is not due to my daughter and anything that she has done, but instead my daughter's mother who has made every step of the way challenging. I mean so much so that there were times along the way that I honestly felt like giving up. Lots of prayer that went up and lots of tears that came down as I fought to be a part of my daughter's life. I mean I took a lot of mess from her mother in order to see my daughter. I practically have had to fight to do something that a mother would normally be glad that a father would want to do...be a father to their child.

It was in January of 2000 that I visited my daughter in that Augusta Hospital in the PICU. My daughter was premature. I vividly remember that day. My nervousness as I went into that unit was very high. I recall walking in and looking to my left in the corner seeing a nurse attending to one of the babies. I soon came to realize that the baby she was attending to was my little angel. I walked up to the nurse and I could hear that tiny baby crying at the top of her lungs because I guess she didn't like what the nurse was doing. It wasn't a loud cry, but for a preemie she showed that she had some lungs on her. What happened next floored me, forever changed me, took my breath away, and forever stole my heart all at the same time. I peeped around the nurse's shoulder at my angel and she stopped crying and turned her little head towards me and looked me right in the eye. Right then, at that very moment...I knew I was a father. That was the moment that my heart melted and it was stolen by my angel.

Nowadays you often hear about men, particularly black men, being in court for child support. You hear about the number of cases about black men getting locked up due to the lack of payment or getting their checks garnished by their states to pay the child support. My case was and continues to be rather different. I had to call upon the court to help **ME** get visitation due to the fact that her mother wouldn't allow me to see her. Again, all I wanted to do was be able to see my child. I wanted both her mother and I to co-parent without drama, without stress, and with one common goal...to ensure that our daughter had both parents actively in her life to ensure that she has a chance in this crazy world. I even attempted to do mediation to no avail. One thing that I have learned for sure is that my daughter's mother does not like me. I swear to the world that I didn't do anything to justifiably warrant this hate. That is my opinion of the matter...but the proof is in the pudding as I was granted joint custody. Providing for my child was never an issue. I would give my last if my child needed it, but due to the fact that her mother disliked me, for reasons to this day I am still unsure of, she decided to make my journey as a father one of the most difficult things that I have had to endure. To tell you my story as a father and the challenges I have had to be one...you wouldn't believe me if I told you. As I mentioned before, it could easily be made a Lifetime movie. I have provided you just a snapshot and maybe...just maybe one day I will tell the entire story in an autobiography of some sort, but right now I will just say that it was hard. My daughter's mother and I have two totally different recollections of events, but one thing for certain is that my path of fatherhood that I have been on for all these years has forced me to grow as a person, harden my outer shell just a little bit, and be patient...very patient. Despite her mother's dislike for me, my love for my daughter has grown.

My message to all fathers and fathers to be...no matter what never stop loving your child(ren), never allow for anyone or anything to stop you from being in their lives, and teach and guide them to be respectable members of society. The bottom line is that children not only need their fathers in their lives but need fathers in their lives that make a positive difference to those lives. And for the women...yes hold the fathers accountable, but at the same time do not be a barrier to fathers being able to be fathers. You have to remember that no child comes to anyone before people lay down and create the child and ask to be on this Earth, so why punish a child or set a child up for failure all because two grown-ups can't get along or dislike one another. The only way to break a vicious cycle is to take action and do one's part to make the change. The only way for the African-American community to fix the damaged image of fatherhood is to take an active stand and destroy the stereotypes and the vicious cycles that come along with fatherhood. We all know that men and women break up, fail to get married, and/or hate one another after the fact, but just because that relationship ends don't mean relationships with children should end as well. I am one that will sacrifice everything to make sure that I keep a positive relationship with my daughter despite the poor relationship her mother and I have. Why...because fatherhood is just that important to me.

Identity (The Unmasking)

Robert Grant

"Always pray to have eyes that see the best, a heart that forgives the worst, a mind that forgets the bad, and a soul that never loses faith." ~*Robert Grant*

"Who am I?"

It's a question that is asked by millions of people today, but it seems to be the main question that so many men are asking themselves these days. It includes, "Why am I here? What am I here for? Why Me?" We, as men, have been through so much; not just presently, but many of us are still living in our past while being products of our environment, where the world has told us whom we should be, and who we can't be. In many cases, childhood and the environment we were brought up in has shown us whom we have become; but not who we were destined to be. Who we were predestined to be, because God knew us before we were ever born. If you read your bible like I do, you will see that Jeremiah 1:5 states that very thing. God says, "(Robert) before I shaped you in the womb I knew all about you. Before you saw the light of day, I had holy plans for you." That is God telling me that there is nothing that you do (Robert) surprises me. I, and I alone know your destiny (Robert). That also tells me God had/has some great plans for you and I. Now as we stand as adults we have been told that God created us to be great. Created with a purpose and a plan. Which brings us back to the question, "Who am I? " Where and how do I fit in to this great plan?

Many of us have suffered from this question as far back as our early childhood, both men and women alike. Now please excuse me, ladies, if I appear to speak more to the men on this subject than I do to you. It's not my intentions to exclude you or leave you, ladies, out; but, at this point in life, don't you want a man who knows who he is? If we (men) know who we are, then we will not only know how to treat you, protect you; but also, love you with no conditions. We will be able to recognize your heart more than we do your body. Right now many of us are stuck on stupid. Let's just keep it real. The great news though is that we don't have to stay stuck. Ladies, I know you want us to see more of you than how you look in some tight jeans and a mini skirt. Right? Having said that, there are some of you (ladies) who may need to look at yourselves and ask, "Do I know who I am? The treasure and gift I am?" Every photo posted does not have to reveal so much, not every man needs to see your rear view. What you put out there, is what you are going to get back. Stop complaining when the inbox fills up with nonsense. Are the "likes" that important to you that you will compromise your integrity, and assumptions of your character? If you continue to promote to the sexual side of yourself to men, what do you expect to get? I'll tell you; the sexual side of the man looking, and in most cases, that's all. So that's what you are going to attract. I understand that me posting pictures constantly with me shirtless, does not tell my character; but honestly, what does it say to most of you ladies? Am I just eye candy to you? Or does it provoke you to say, "I want to know his heart." Wait! Not where I wanted to go LOL.

Back to the subject at hand. I just have a heart for men because I was once in this place. Please keep reading and you may see some areas that you are dealing with as well, or you may be seeing in your son, husband, father or brother.

My mother raised 3 boys on her own, so I know the importance of you ladies, so I may ask a question or two? You will be surprised at the number of grown men with the need and yearning for their father. You also eventually will see the need of sons for their fathers; not just now, but 20, 30 years from now. We are seeing so much domestic violence, abuse, and death with our men right now. Unfortunately, you see it mostly with our black men. At least that's who the news, sports channels show you. Could you imagine how bad it could really get if we didn't try and reach them now? We could lose so many men to themselves. We hear so many young men say they don't want anything to do with their father, but in most cases....that's me hiding behind a mask, when the truth is, I needed him to tell me who I was. You have grown 30+ men still needing the relationship of their father. Please ladies, don't be fooled by this. Understand we are hurting in ways you probably could never imagine. Men get beat up in the world, and come home and get beat up as well. Our wives and girlfriends are upset for whatever reason, not seeing the pain we are dealing with. Normally we get quiet at this point, saying nothing is wrong. They feel the system has let them down, the church has let them down, and that's not mentioning family members that are no longer there to give any kind of support or encouragement. Here is a question ladies; Does your man, husband, son, father, any man in your life; do you know if he has someone that he is accountable to? Another man that holds him responsible for his actions and thoughts? That other male person who calls and checks on him, whom he can talk to about things when he can't talk to you about them, things he is dealing with? Or does he just try and handle things on his own? Not letting anyone in.

As men, somewhere down the line, we have forgotten who we are, that's if we ever knew. No one seems to recognize us at all. The husbands, the fathers, we were meant to be have been affected by this. How can we help our children know their DNA, their fingerprint that makes them different from everyone else, if we have no clue or idea of our own identity? Knowing who we are helps them to know who they are. Each one of us has been given a different and unique fingerprint pattern that distinguishes us from everyone else. You must understand the pattern, the very things that have molded you into the man you are today. You can't change your DNA, nor can you change your fingerprint, but you can surely change your mindset. Understand who you were meant to be. There really is a king in you.

Do you know who you are? I ask this question again because I want us all to find our true identity. Our children, and our children's children are counting on it. We have let people steal it with their words, and with their silence.

Life has taught me a lot. As the oldest child of 3 boys, it was hard, it was painful, and it was disappointing a lot of that time. Why? Because I really never knew who I was as a kid. I knew I was a son, and a grandson, but that was really the extent of it. I didn't know the plan God had for my life, which I was to be. I was thrust into being the man of the house at an early age when one; I was not ready for such a task and title, and two; I never wanted to be the man of the house. How was I supposed to know how to handle that anyway? Most times, I closed myself off from the world; locking myself in my room for hours. That's never a good thing. I hid myself from disappointments, instead of accepting the challenges, like I did on a football field, or basketball court. I excelled tremendously in sports. I was really good at sports, and I loved the acceptance and love I received from it. I remember having this discussion with my mother once, when she told me that as a baby, she gave me back to God, but that is all I ever really knew about myself pertaining to why I was here. What did that mean, she gave me back to God? What did that entail?   Was there some great secret to all this? Why tell me something that meant absolutely nothing to me at that time? I needed more from her.

Truth of the matter is I didn't know my father very well at that age, so I didn't know my DNA. I didn't have anyone to help me see or read the fine print that could only be seen by my father's eyes on my birth certificate. Yes, I believe there is a fine print just below your name that God gives you, that can only be seen by a father, interpreted by a father, read by a father. Everything created had a name and a purpose. When God made man, He called him Adam; (first man) in Genesis 2. God also named His son, Emmanuel (God with us) in Matt 1:23. Both had a purpose and an identity.

Important to understand, when a father names his son, he is generally calling him by his purpose. Nothing against mothers naming their sons; history has shown they usually name them according to emotions or circumstances. My belief is when a man names his son; he immediately begins to tell his son who he is. Some see the athlete in him, the engineer, the preacher and so on. It's given to him by God, and God only. Some may not see this the way I do, but that's what I see. I think about how the great men of the Bible were who laid hands on their sons, speaking blessing, grace, prosperity, authority, over their lives. Blessing them to be great men for God. The effect that it had. Those men knew who they were at that very moment. I think about if my father had been the one that told me that he laid me at the altar instead of my mother, I probably would have wanted to know more. I would have asked more questions. I just would not have let that be it. I believe it would have made more of an impact on me if it had been told by my father. Every son wants to make his father proud. And every father should want to be proud of his son. Think about it...we have the power to bless our sons, speaking into their lives to be great. Dedicating them back to their creator. Helping mold them into what they are to become. Showing them the fine print on their birth certificate. There are some of you that need to be a father to some nephews. I see a lot of young men with no father at all, so let's not forget about them.

Churches need to step up and recognize some needs of our young men, that generation they like to call the X generation. I so disagree with that term and why they use it. I personally think there should be some kind of program put together and taught on how to reach our young men, and our hurting and lost fathers. If we don't change the minds of our men, nothing is really going to change. The generations of families will continue to suffer. There are some fathers that are really beating themselves up because they made past mistakes, and missed out on so much with their sons. They missed out on raising them. Fathers, sons, listen to me....its never too late to be a son, and it's never too late to be the father you were intended to be, no matter the age. Yes, there are some men that just don't give two cents about connecting with their sons, but that is not who I am talking to right now. I'm talking to the many who have recognized not only who they are but, the mistakes they have made in life. You may have in the past only seen what your father didn't do, but now you see what you didn't do. It's called a generational curse that God has the power to destroy. Recognize that you need help and cannot do it on your own. Don't get discouraged because you don't see the results you would like to see immediately. Know God is working it out for your good.

Again, I never really knew my father as I should have; I never really put forth the effort either, but it wasn't until now, listening to my father speak of his childhood, that I began to fully understand me. Understanding why I did certain things. I learned so much just from spending that time with him, learning to forgive him, and accepting my own faults in the relationship. Yes, sitting down and just listening to my father did help, but the true lesson of learning who I am came from God. A lot of what I heard my father say, whom I have a great relationship with now, I know it helped me tremendously. But like I said, the main revelation of who I was born to be and who I was still to become, came from God. I know there are some of you that don't have a personal relationship with God; but, that's ok. If you are still here, among the living, then it's not too late to develop one. In fact, if you continue to read this, I am believing God will tug at your heart, and there will be no resisting of His love for you. The truth is, He is the only one who can truly tell you who you are and give you the complete story of who you are. He designed you. He formed you before you were ever born. (Jeremiah 1:5) Your

DNA, your fingerprint is His, and His alone. Our parents raise us to fear God, speak life into that in a way we can understand, but when its time for God to take over, He does. Part of our job as a parent is to know when to move out the way and allow God to take over. The whole entire book, the chapters of your life get revealed to you each day as you spend that time with your Creator.

✐✐✐✐✐✐

    In getting to know God, the Creator, I learned who I am and whose I am. Once you learn that guys, so much peace will come to you. True fact! A lot of times, as men, we do not wish to be seen. We wear a mask. Not wanting to be seen as sensitive and vulnerable, or as some of you would say, a wimp or a punk. We feel we have to show strength all the time. We do not wish to appear weak to our family, friends, and acquaintances. We believe there is a high price to pay if we do. We believe taking off our mask gives away too much power and vulnerability, believing it will be used against us. Our minds can truly be our kryptonite. Crippling us at the unexpected time. Our mind tells us we've done too much wrong to ever be forgiven, that our children will never forgive us, or our fathers never loved us. Our mind tells us we are not good enough for that person we find ourselves attracted to, or to even have. Our mind tells us, God does not care about me, love me, or hear my prayers. Our mind tells us we should just take our own life because no one really cares. Kryptonite! Just like it was deadly to a comic book hero named "Superman," it can also be deadly to you and I. What makes us different from Superman, we have a greater power and strength to fight off this effect. To break the stronghold it may have on us. Superman fought most of his battles alone, but we don't have to. We can help each other. You hear so much about mental illness today where more and more men are taking their lives. I have witnessed pastor's sons, actors, athletes, and just the ordinary man who looks to have everything take their lives because of the battle in their mind. If this is a battle you are dealing with, please talk to someone; don't let this take your voice. Don't let this take your life, God has so much more for you.

We have seen our fellow man looked down upon, disrespected, and torn down. Not just by society, but by our women, families and churches. And yes, parents in a lot of cases, too. You've been called stupid, useless, that you would never amount to anything. These are extremely harmful words to a young man who does not know who or what he is. No man wants to be that man without the "S" on his chest. He wants to be the hero. He wants to feel needed. He wants to fix everything. He wants to be the "Savior," if you will. Saving the day. The loss of a job has KO'D so many men, which leads to a feeling of abandonment. No longer feeling the respect he once had with his peers, his family, and especially his wife. It's that *what are doing for me right now*, rather than what you did yesterday that hurts the man today. This is where you have to grab on to your Creator, knowing he has the finisher of His work.

Life is hard trying to do things without God; it can be downright deadly if you don't know your Father in heaven. We are seeing suicide rising at an alarming rate with our men. It's not a black thing, white thing, rich or poor thing. It's an "I don't know who I am" thing, and that starts in your mind. A life without God has seemingly taken the very life out you. Something is standing on your chest forcing the breath that it takes to live, out of you. No longer able to take long easy breaths but you are gasping for air. This is how it normally happens for many; the feeling of being buried alive until all your life is gone, wishing you would just die. No longer feeling you could survive this. Buried alive until all the air to your brain is gone. If the mind dies, the body follows right along with it. Remember, God breathed that life into you from the very beginning, so keep breathing until your lungs are free and strong again, pumping the oxygen to your mind. There is nothing like the breath of life. I'm not trying to be so religious that I don't understand; I just want you to know the truth. I want you ladies to know what could possibly be happening to your husbands, your brothers, you sons, and even your fathers. The pressure of life is real.

Men…the enemy is trying to kill you, it's been that way before Christ, and after Christ was born. Word of your greatness has gotten out, so there is a hit out on your life. A target has been placed on your back. Think about it; before Christ there was Moses' greatness. There was a target on his life, so they set out to kill all the male children to put a halt to Gods plans. And when Christ was born, King Herod sent word out to have all the boys less than 2 years of age to be killed. The word got out about their greatness and the great things they would do and accomplish. This time is no different. Look at the world. Still trying to kill our men, our young men; but the weapon being used now is your own mind being used against you. Attacks don't seem to stop. There is only one solution for what you're dealing with. Knowing your identity! One of my greatest examples I love to use is Tupac. Why Tupac? I believe we saw greatness in this young man, whom left too soon. His knowledge spoke to me more than his music did; he had the ability to reach millions. He had the ability to change the world. I believe this young man really didn't know who he was, and who he was to be, and what he was capable of. He died with so much purpose.

Right now there's a King Herod targeting many of you. A man/woman, family member or close friend. Herod's attitude was one of hatred and hostility. Why? Because he knew greatness was coming. They see the blueprint for something beautiful.

What's happening now is, they are seeing your identity when you don't quite yet know your identity yourself. So they are trying to bury you alive before you can get knowledge of who you are and what you are capable of. Here is the true fact; if they can bury you alive, then they can eventually smother you to death. Taking all life from you. Giving up on trying to live the plan God created you to live. Many obstacles, people, family, circumstances, and situations will come to try and destroy you. Even your past will raise its head at some point to remind you who you once were, but you don't have to listen.

Listen, I have been in that place where I just didn't know who I was. As a matter of fact, I can honestly say since I was a 5-year-old kid, I felt this way. That's the age I remember my father leaving. He was that one person I believe that could have shown me, helped me, and told me who I was, and who I would become; instilling that confidence.

Instead, I spent many years trying to be who everyone thought I should be while hearing others tell me who I couldn't be. I had my own visions and dreams that God was giving me. My biggest dilemma was that I didn't know what to make of them or know how to go about making them happen. When I did decide to share with my family and friends, it turned out to be more costly than if I had just kept it to myself. So I found myself shutting down and eventually just keeping quiet all together. That's the one thing you don't want to ever lose…is your voice. If you lose your voice, you can no longer speak to your circumstances, acknowledge your greatness, or communicate with the source of your visions and dreams. You will no longer be able to cry out for help. Yes! We all need help at some point. That help is God. This is where your relationship with Him is so important. Your communication with the creator is so important for your success and your peace of mind. Looking past the doubters, and the haters. Many will not want to see you successful, but God always want to see you at your best, after you have been through your worst. It brings Him glory.

It wasn't until my late adult years that I began to focus on learning Robert's identity. I needed to know whom this man was that so many were speaking about, seeing greatness in him. Learning my true identity as not just a man, but as a father, and a son. Why was I created? What am I here for?

I realized the only way for me to finally get the answers I so desperately needed, that I so desperately wanted, is that I had to learn more about God, my Creator, the Architect, if you will. Yes, we are a creation, a unique, and beautiful design.

As I began to learn more of who I was, the more desire I had for life. I once desired death…but God. I saw these great passions begin to grow inside me, which has lead me to my purpose in life. I knew I wanted to be the best man I could possibly be. The best father, the best son, the best brother. If you find yourself wondering about your purpose for life, start by doing something you are passionate about. Most likely that is where you will start to see the greatness of you start to grow.

It's taken me many years to learn my identity. Understanding why my fingerprints are different from everyone else's and how it distinguishes me from the world. I love the man I have become, and so will you. This didn't come without a price. A lot of hurt, disappointments, loss of family and friends, but I understood it was a process. A process that was not easy but necessary. As I sit here and think about it, my process should have been easy, but it wasn't. The process!

First, I had to ask the question, "Why was I created, and what was my purpose?" Secondly, I had to really put forth an effort to learn about God, my Creator, so I could answer the first question of "Who am I?" It's like when a son or daughter is born he/she learns about the parents that gave birth to him/her, therefore giving him/her an idea of who they are and where they came from. They watch and listen to their parents very closely, forming habits and words. Recognizing and getting familiar with the person that looks over, feeds, and holds close. The first word most children basically learn or speak is *Da Da*. The same concept goes for learning about the Creator; I'm learning and getting familiar with my Creator, the one who provides all my needs. Who is my Da Da?

Many of you grew up missing a parent, a mother or a father, so this is very important. You didn't have that one person you needed to tell you who you were, who you are, and who you are to become. You're not the only one who has been in this place; there are so many more right now going through this. Fella's, if you don't know who you are, learn all you can about your designer. You are like no other.

God made you specifically with one thought in mind and for a purpose. There really is a plan for your life. You are not a mistake! I felt this way for many years until I learned about my Creator. God can't, and He does not make mistakes. Period!

Lastly take the information you have learned about your Creator, and apply it to who you are. Take those visions and those dreams and make them a reality, know that all things are possible. Keep telling yourself you are destined for greatness.

I never once believed in my life that I would accomplish all that I have, and that I continue to accomplish, because of my self-doubt and the lack of confidence in myself. I hid it a long time behind smiles and sports. I was great in sports and succeeded greatly in it, but I never truly knew who I was. That was my safe place of hiding my flaws. All everyone saw was the great ball player. Then I grew up to be this singer, still hiding behind a mask. In one of the largest ministries in Southern California, and I was still behind the mask. Then death came for me, attacking my mind. I just wanted it all to end. But God! (So I can personally understand what so many men are going through in their mind not knowing who they are.) My story? The Creator and lover of my soul not only breathed life into me, but also told me who I was, and is still showing me who I am to become. All I had to do was read the fine print on my birth certificate.

එංඑංඑංඑං

Fella's, don't keep this knowledge you have gained, or your experiences solely to yourself. Share with other men who need to hear from you; your children, your wives, and even your father. Learn to forgive, because he may not have known what he was doing, just as you didn't know. Share your life experiences to help someone else. It is so desperately needed for us to find out who we are, to come from behind the mask. Check your fingerprints. Do a DNA check and read the fine print on your birth certificate. God has all the answers you need to be a better husband, a better father, a better brother, and an all out better man. Men lets disciple other young men; in doing so, we can change the tragedy that is happening to so many of our young men. Help them to see that there is a plan; a wonderful plan for their life.

✌✌✌✌✌

Ladies, love the men in your lives with no conditions. Pray for them. Encourage them. Stop talking negatively about them, downgrading them, but lifting them up. Your words do play a major part in how far a man can go. A man or a son will not always feel like it's possible, but you can change his mind with your words, your encouragement, and your love. But having said that...be discerning as well, because you can also find yourself just getting in the way of what God is trying to do to save their life. He may be wanting to get that man's attention, to get him totally dependent on Him. Just a thought.

✌✌✌✌✌

Ladies and Gentlemen, we all need to know our identity. The Bible talks about it so much. You just have to follow the instruction manual, the Bible, to see how you work. You came with instructions from the one who created you. Only He knows how you, each individual person works.

Now I ask the question. Who are you?

God Bless you!

My Father, I am

K.L. Belvin

"The Soul of a Man 2, will grant each reader a clear and defined understanding of life through each of the contributions of the talented men of color assembled."

~K. L. Belvin

My life changed at the age of thirteen while living in New York. I walked in my grandmother's apartment from playing basketball to find out from my mother and grandmother, my uncle Joe in New Jersey had passed away. My uncle was the closest thing I had to a father at that time in my life. I was devastated. I went in my room and stared at the picture I had on my wall. A leather bound picture which held a full portrait of my father with a baby picture of myself in the corner. I would look at this picture and wonder why he left when I was three. My father was like many men who had children they didn't plan on taking care of. He would call when his guilt reached a point of spill over. He would get on the phone and it would sound like this.

"Hello, Son," he would say with a hint of booze on his voice.

"Hello, Dad," would be the same response over the years. It was the line I rehearsed each holiday week or days before a birthday. My sister, Renee, my younger sister, would love these calls. She would get excited and fall in love with our father each time he called and lied about what he was going to send us or do for us. You see, he lived in Minnesota and we lived in South Jamaica Queens, New York. As far as I was concerned it was light years from each other. He was simply a lying drunk on the phone who wasn't going to keep his promise no matter how convincing he thought he was.

But this year was different. My uncle Joe was my role model. I was named after his son, Keith, who passed in the first week of life. So I was given his name and inherited his father as my own. My uncle lived in Penns Grove, New Jersey. A small two light town in southern New Jersey where everything seemed to move slower. I lived there from age five until eleven. Those six years my uncle would groom me for manhood. He showed me how to shine my shoes, press my shirts and pants, and how to ride and fix a bike. As I said, he was the father I never had. To walk in and find he was no longer with us sent me to stare at that picture wondering why it couldn't have been my father and not my uncle.

My grandmother came into my room. She was the prototypical southern grandmother. She was brash, tough and loved her grandson. She was only 15 years younger than my mother and my mother was only 17 years older than me. Often folks thought my mother was my older sister and my grandmother was our mother.

That day she came into the room to see me sitting on the edge of my bed with the picture of my father in my hand, crying. At that moment she called out to my mother, "Child, get in here and tell this boy the truth. Tell this boy who is real father is."

My grandmother, may she rest in peace, had no inner filter. She would say anything, at any time. Looking up at her from the bed and feeling confused, I listened to every word of their conversation.

THE SOUL OF A MAN 2

I didn't understand what she was saying to my mother. Yes, I heard the words but what did she mean, "My real father"?

From the next bedroom I could hear my mother screaming back, "Mom! Do we have to do this now? Leave the boy alone. Just let him be."

Before another word could come out of her mouth, my grandmother fired back.

"Get your ass in here and speak to this boy and tell him the god damn truth. Now!"

c/oc/oc/oc/o

I am sitting on the bed listening to this dialog between mother and daughter while glancing down at both pictures within the frame. My pain has turned into confusion.

Inside my head the same questions kept circling; what are these two talking about? Why do they feel they need to have this conversation with my uncle having passed? What does my grandmother mean "real father?"

My mother came into my room and asked my grandmother to leave. She sat down next to me and looked me in the eyes. Her round brown face was looking so sad. As a child you know something is wrong and you're waiting to have the rug ripped from under you. As I stared into her eyes I am thinking first my Uncle Joe and now whatever my mother is going to share with me. My mother placed a photo in my hand of a man in uniform.

She said, "Keith, this is your real father. They call him Dap." My hurt was stunned. I wasn't hurt, I was confused and angry.

"If this was my father, why did you have me listening to the lies of this man in the picture?" I shook my head and looked at my mother trying not to show my anger. "Mom, why would you lie to me? Why would you have me thinking this was my dad and he wasn't?" My mother began to cry and each drop from her eyes hurt my soul, but I needed to hear the truth.

"You see Keith, your grandmother didn't like your real father, so right after I had you, He decided to leave. When I started dating who you thought was your dad, we didn't want everyone in our business so he took you in as his own and named you after him. He changed your name from Watkins to Belvin." Watkins is my grandmother's last name. *Since I am the last of her namesake, I use the name Watkins in many of my written stories.*

My mother explained the man I thought was my daddy decided he too wasn't going to stick around and he left when I was three and my sister a year and half. Since I had no memories of him, his phone calls were all we knew.

I had no idea my life was going to be pushed into a direction it would take years to unravel.

A few years after this bomb shell and my Uncle's funeral my mother moved to an apartment close by but I remained with my grandmother since my friends and school were closer to her house. With my grandmother working from three to eleven, I had the apartment to myself every day. You can imagine what a teenage boy got into with this type of freedom and no male role model to speak of.

THE SOUL OF A MAN 2

As the years passed I grew into an angry young man who stayed in and out of trouble. The streets were my focus and school of choice. I was reckless and uncaring with much of what I did away from my grandmother and mother. Sex became the thing I sought and I learned a man can get places when he has a strong sexual rep in the streets.

Over the years I would look at that picture and wonder, "Who Dap was. Why didn't he care enough to look for me? Where was he?"

As I grew into a man, I would have family member after family member say to me,

"You look just like your daddy."

I never understood which daddy they were talking about. Then the words became more direct, "You just like Dap. You look just like him."

Each time I heard it I grew angrier inside. Why do you keep saying I look like a man I've never met?

I had conceded I would never see this man and so I left it alone and lived my life. Over the next twenty plus years I would get married and divorced, have six children with five different women while becoming an educator and author. Some would call me a success, some call me sad because of the way I lived my life and the number of children I created.

Well things took a turn at age thirty seven; this was the age I gave my life to the Lord. Here I was attached to a beautiful woman who I planned on marrying and it was time to change my cheating and reckless ways. As that year passed, my fiancé Tiffany and I were working towards our marriage. It was 2006 and we had set a date to be married in 2007. With my life changing for the better I got a call from an aunt I didn't know. She said her name was Jannora and she was my father's sister. I asked, "Which father are you speaking of/"

"Your father, Elijah."

"Who are you speaking of, my father's name is Dap".

"I am sorry, nephew; you're mistaken, his real name is Elijah."

This mystery aunt had me guessing but I am intrigued by her message so I continue to listen.

"I am just returning from New Jersey from a funeral and ran into old friends and your father. As we spoke and caught up, one of your father's friends said, "Elijah, you should see your son, who lives in New York. That boy looks just like you."

So at this point I jumped in and said Elijah you have other children. Who is in New York?"

As my aunt fills in the details it wasn't making me feel any better. Actually it was making me feel worse. Since it's clear he knew about me and didn't make a move to close the gap between us.

My aunt continued her story. "I asked your father why he didn't contact you. He said, "I am sure my son doesn't want to have anything to do with me. The way his grandmother ran me off, I am sure they made sure he didn't want to know who I was. Plus with the way I was living in those days, I wouldn't blame him one bit for not wanting to be bothered with a man like myself."

"How can you say that when you've never reached out to him to see or speak to him." My aunt went on and explained the rest of the meeting. She said she spoke to people in New Jersey who knew my mother and was able to get my phone number from those who stayed in contact with me over the years and this was her reason for calling.

"Nephew, you two need to fix this. I am sure you would like to know who your father is and who his family is. I am sure he would like to know you since I've heard such great things about you from friends and family while I was in New Jersey. Here is your father's phone number and email. I told him I would reach out and give you this information. You make the best of it. Remember the Lord will guide you if you ask him to. Take Care"

As I hung up the phone I didn't know what to do or think. I've carried around this anger since I was thirteen. What was I going to do? What was I going to say to make who's been absent from my life for close to forty years.

I sat with my wife and attempted to figure out what to do. The one thing I had grown to learn about my new life as a born again Christian was to listen to my wife and trust in prayer. I asked my wife what I should do and she said, "You should call him. You always wanted to know your father now you have your chance."

I was stumped on what my next course of action should be. Yes, I had always wanted to know my father but the anger I still carried with me. Would it allow me to hear anything he was saying? I took a day to think and pray on the matter. What came to mind was, I am going to send him an email. I'll explain who I am and add some pictures of his future daughter in-law and his grandchildren. This way the next move would be on him. That is exactly what I did.

I crafted an outstanding email, minus the anger, which explained who I was, where I was in my life, and I did not have ill feelings for him. After writing about how I got his information and a few other particulars about my mother not pushing me to hate me, I got to the heart of the email. I told him,

"I forgive you for not being in my life and if you do not want to open this door I understand and respect your choice. I felt it best you hear it from me that I don't hate or begrudge you in any form or fashion. I understand a man is going to make choices and we have to live with the outcome. I have come to know the Lord and he has looked over me for these past thirty seven years and will continue to do so. I love you and I wish you well, Love Your Son, Keith"

I was quite pleased with the restraint I showed in my email. At times the anger attempted to surface but I wasn't going to allow it to mess up this letter. I delayed a minute before hitting send. I knew once I did, my life would change forever. After a few minutes I did. I hit send and off to my father my words flew.

About a week passed and I actually hadn't given any thought to the email. Once the first few days went by I thought things were business as usual. Tiff and I were preparing for dinner and discussing things about the wedding in a few months when the phone rang. I picked up the phone and heard, "Good Evening" a strong masculine voice on the other end said.

"May I please speak to Keith?"

"This is Keith, how can I help you?"

"Keith this is your father, Elijah?"

At that moment my legs were frozen and I felt weak as I heard him say, "This is your father."

I responded, "Good Evening, sir. It's a pleasure to finally hear from you"

"Yes, it's my pleasure also."

The uneasiness of this situation was getting thicker as I sensed it was it was my father who didn't plan this out completely. I decided to attempt to make this a light hardy conversation. I asked, "Are you sure you called the right person?"

My father laughed and responded back. "It better be, I would hate to think I was close to peeing my pants for a wrong number."

We both laughed on queue and sounded somewhat the same. I think it caught us both off guard hearing the same laugh come through the phone. My fear turned into a growing elation. I was on the phone with my father. My real father. I am on the phone with the man in the picture, finally.

My father took the lead and started to explain.

"Listen Keith, I am so happy you wrote that email. I am sorry it took me so long to respond. I must have read it over and over again, close to a hundred times. I went from happy to sad. I didn't know what to do and as the days passed I knew I had to do something."

I said, I can respect that. I am glad you called. We have much to discuss.

He said, "Very true, but I am going to ask something and I hope you don't get offended. But I am straight shooter and I don't hold cut cards, I play them"

I understood his reference to the card games spades being an outstanding spades player myself. I wondered where he was going with this.

He continued, "I was wild when I was younger and I made a few babies in my time. I am sure you have heard. Please don't be offended, but I would like to have a DNA test done before we take this any further. Because I know I was with your mother but she did have another man she married when you were born and I want to be sure. I pray I haven't offended you?"

As I laughed I know it was confusing to my father.

"Man listen, I have no problem with that. If a child showed up and called me daddy, I would do the same. I'll gladly take the test and we can take things from there."

We spoke a little while longer and decided a DNA test would be the course of action. A week later I received mail with the testing materials and information on how to take the test and where to send it. I swabbed my mouth and sealed the envelope and mailed it out. I sent my father an email letting him know I did my part on my end.

The company listed information with the testing materials on how to get your results online. I waited the two weeks and signed in to learn the results. I was nervous but something said to me, "Don't worry he's your father."

THE SOUL OF A MAN 2

Sure enough when I put in my account info and test ID it said the test was 99.8% positive match. We were father and son.

The next evening my father called and said he got the results and was excited to get that out of the way and was looking forward to getting to know me. We spoke for close to four hours that night. It was like speaking to myself we had so much in common. After three straight days of talking I decided to take things a step farther. I said I was traveling to New Jersey to see some friends, how do you feel about meeting?

The pause on the phone was a little worrisome. He responded, "I would love to finally see you/"

I said that would be great and we set up plans to meet in the coming month. A month before my wedding in August of 2007.

I got to the hotel the night before we were due to meet. I wanted to be relaxed and settled in since I knew my life was going to change. The plan was I would be at the hotel in south New Jersey and my father was going to bring his family to a hotel in Delaware since they were traveling at that same, come over the bridge into New Jersey and come meet me. I think this was his way of keeping his wife and son, my new brother, at a distance until he got a feel for what this was going to be. Again, another move I would have done myself as the protector of my family.

After a few calls back and forth, my father had made sure he got my hotel situation correct. He called and said, "I should be at my hotel within the next hour and then I'll head over to see you."

What I didn't know was that my father was altering the plans. As I sat and watched TV, I heard a knock on my door. As I approached the door and sternly said "Who?" I hear, "It's your father."

What? He's at the door? I gathered myself and put my tough face on and opened the door. Standing 6'3", a few inches taller, a medium built man looking older than the picture but clearly the man from the photo in his uniform. It was my father. His caramel complexion was slightly lighter than my own, but we did look alike. As all those family members had said for years when they would say, "You look so much like your father."

They were correct. He shook my hand with a firm handshake and stepped in. We then hugged and said hello to each other. I was still in a state of denial. I was sitting across from my father. I asked did he want anything to drink as he explained the change of plan.

"I know I changed the plan. However, when I thought about it, there was no reason to keep my family from you because after meeting they were going to be your family. So I decided to check in here to be close to you. Plus I wanted to surprise you."

You did. You got me. I was not expecting you this soon. As my father sat back on the couch in the hotel suite, I could see him looking at me the same I way looking at him. We are the mirror image of each other. He said, "Damn boy, you really do look just like me."

Laughing, I said strong genes, all my children look like me also. He chuckled. He took that opportunity to bring up children.

"So you have six children with a five baby mothers, huh?"

Yes sir, I was a busy young man when I didn't know the Lord." Not sure where he was going with the conversation so I continued to be upbeat about the meeting.

He then said, "Let me share something with you; I have a few children myself. I have seven children with six mothers like yourself. I see you like the ladies."

"Yes sir. I loved the ladies when I was running those streets. Plus I loved them thick, the only way I would date them."

He leaned forward and let loose the biggest grin, "Boy, now you're talking. I only dated thick sisters when I was making my name. My wife now is thick in all the right place."

I responded, so I see where I got it from. We both laughed.

From that meeting we went on to meet my stepmother and my brother, Elijah. We took a few pictures and then I asked him about attending my wedding the following month. I know it was off the cuff but I wanted him to be there. My father said yes and as promised he showed up at my wedding the next month.

Here is what I learned over the past seven years about my dad. I needed him more at close to forty then I did at close to twenty. We have more in common then we realized and we are more connected then we knew.

- With the birth of my daughter, Kayelle, in March of 2014 made child number 7 for me and Tiffany, my wife made mother number 6; my father has the same numbers.

- We both have four boys and three girls

- We had our seventh child at the age of 46

- My father is nine years older than his wife and I am nine years older than Tiffany.

- We both love full figured women.

- We both has sons named Elijah.

- We both have been married and divorced and remarried.

- We both found the Lord late in life and it saved our lives.

- My mother's name is Katrina and one of his daughters was named, Katrina. (Rest in peace)

My hope as you read my story you'll see the beauty of fixing the kinship when it comes Father and Son. The Lord wants to see families fixed and fathers and sons are the key. If more fathers would return to take their place with their sons, we could solve the problems we see in this country. God Bless.

K. L. Belvin

The Soul of a Man

Adrian Milan

"Regardless of your skin color, culture or personal experiences, we should all make it our priority to ensure that our souls are being shaped by human compassion, love and dignity, for ourselves and everyone else around us. It starts with you."

~ Adrian Milan

My name is Joseph Miller and I've been an EMT (emergency technician), at New York Presbyterian Hospital for two years now. You'd never know it by looking at me, because I spend my days doing 12 hour shifts riding around in an ambulance chasing the back end of various disasters trying to save lives. But believe it or not, I had an Ivy League education. I was a straight A student my entire life because my mother had always stressed to me the importance of education; which meant nothing to me personally, but the pride and the joy that I would see reflected in her eyes every time I brought my report card home was a constant inspiration for me to always strive to do better in the next semester than I had done in the previous one before. I loved her just that much. How could I not? She was the only person in this life that I knew for sure truly loved me unconditionally. And growing up on the hard streets of the Bronx, New York, "love" was a precious commodity that you simply did not waste. A plain and simple fact that I had learned at a very young age, that somehow over the years, I had managed to forget.

I could have been a doctor or a lawyer or an engineer with my own firm by now had I chose to go in that direction. I found myself reflecting on that now as the smoke and dust from the small fires in the building were beginning to clear out. I was still holding on to the now lifeless hand of the man who an hour ago was a total stranger, but who I now regarded as a dear friend. I've never had a father, but had always imagined that if I ever did have one, that he would have been my hero, like the hero that I wanted to be for my own children. That's who this gentleman had become…my hero. My conscious mind was aware that I needed to clear the area so that the other emergency responders could do their job, but I just couldn't find the will to let his hand go. I felt like if I did, that I would be abandoning him, even though he was already gone. And somehow that just didn't sit right with me.

৩৩৩৩৩৩

One hour earlier

I found myself getting angry with the doorman. Once a week I received a package for my medications. That package is always too big to fit in my mailbox and is always left with the doorman. Every week for two years when I come in, I check with him to see if it's arrived, and he always asks the same questions:

"What's the name and apartment number again, Sir?"

"Joseph Miller, apartment 18-B, Virgil." I shook my head in frustration. "How is it that you can never remember that? Five days a week for the last two years I have been consistently coming to you at this desk to check on my package, and every single time I come, even though you see me and speak to me every single day, you still have to ask me for my name and apartment number. Am I really that insignificant? Or would blessing you with a little financial gift help you in the memory department?

"Well, I can't rightfully say I know, Mr. Miller," he smiled up at me. "You've never given me a tip before, so I couldn't say one way or the other how it would affect my memory."

"Oh, you can't remember my name or apartment number, but you CAN remember that I've never given you a tip?"

My chest was beginning to tighten, that's my cue to cut the conversation before I let my anger get the best of me and I lose all control over my mouth and my ability to shut it before I say something foolish that I can't take back or recover from. A little something I learned from my marriage counseling sessions with my wife, Chelsea. We were separated at the moment and going to counseling to try and salvage what seemed to be a doomed marriage. I don't wait for Virgil to check on my package, I see the elevator door about to close and I make a bolt for it.

"Hey! Hold the elevator please!"

Mrs. Stevens, my next door neighbor, stops the doors from closing and I make it onto the crowded elevator. There are eight people already inside, and all of a sudden I find myself wishing I'd waited it out with Virgil. Mrs. Stevens looks at the expression on my face and immediately gives me a knowing smile.

"Don't sweat it, the elevator is non-stop express until we hit the sixteenth floor."

I fake a smile and turn to stare up at the numbers as the elevator begins its trip up. I'm tired. I've worked a full 12 hour shift and haven't even had time to stop and eat a decent meal. My stomach was letting me know just how unpleased it was with that fact, and I found myself wishing that Chelsea was back home already. That woman kept me fed and would see to my every need as soon as I walked through the door. She was a good woman, a damn good woman; she was just stubborn and didn't know when to stop pushing when she was determined to have her way. And there's only so much grinding against the grain that any relationship can take before things begin to either wear thin or break all together. We were two people who truly loved each other, but found that we disagreed on issues more than we agreed. What do you do when you can't see eye to eye with the one that you love? That's where we were. And it was more than just frustrating, it was eating away at the very fabric of the love between us and destroying our marriage.

I was still in uniform and noticed that the gentleman to the left of me was staring at the name plate on my chest. He seemed to be admiring my uniform with a half-smile on his face when he looked up and realized that I had caught him staring at me. He gave me a friendly smile and waved in greeting. I smiled back to be courteous, but was a bit creeped out. So I went back to watching the numbers as the elevator continued its climb. Feeling a bit embarrassed, the gentleman to my left decided to strike up a short conversation.

8th *floor;* "Have you been working for the hospital long?"

9th *floor;* "A few years now."

10th *floor;* "How do you like it?"

11th floor; "It's a job, you know? It pays the bills."

12th floor; "Oh come on now, it has to be more than that?"

13th floor; "Trust me, it's not."

ↄ∕ↄↄↄↄↄ

He stared at me genuinely shocked. And the look on his face was so alarming that it made me realize just how bitter I was beginning to sound. Before I could change my answer he made a statement that I immediately recognized as him trying to give me some food for thought;

14th floor; "If what you're doing now doesn't bring you the joy or contentment that you know you should have by doing the thing that you love, then maybe you should consider quitting so that you can actually pursue whatever it is that you believe you were called to do."

15th floor; I stare at the stranger who is still staring at me with this knowing half-smile on his face. He's an older gentleman. He looks to me to be about 60 years old, but in fairly good health. He was about six feet tall with a medium build, I'm guessing about 170 pounds. He was clearly an African American with light brown skin but decidedly striking features. High cheek bones and almond shaped light brown eyes that almost seemed hazel. That's what caught my attention the most, his eyes. They were bright, clear and alert, and right now they seemed to be completely focused on only one thing…me. My first thought was, "Is this guy a psychologist or life coach?" Whatever the case, in just a few seconds he managed to assess my entire demeanor. And it occurred to me that we were about to hit the 16th floor, which was probably his stop, and he was making an effort to give me a nugget of wisdom that I myself was already aware of, but maybe just needed to hear again from a different source. Because for some reason that I cannot explain or put into words, though I had thought the same thing a million times over, though Chelsea and I had argued over this issue time and time again, the thought of entertaining the idea seemed ludicrous. We have bills that need to be paid, children that need what they need as soon as they need it, quitting my job to pursue any thing seemed like an unnecessary risk that was nothing short of fool hardy. Yet somehow, when this stranger who was old enough to be my father spoke the words, my soul seemed to be more accepting of the wisdom that laid within them. I smiled at him as the elevator doors opened to let out the passengers getting off on the 16th floor.

16th floor; "Are you a doctor or something?"

"No," he smiled back. "Nothing of the sort. I've just lived long enough to know the importance of living your life on your own terms, by your own rules. Life is shorter than most realize, and there is nothing more painful or regrettable than looking back on your life at the choices you've made and come to the realization that the life that you've settled for, was never really the life that you wanted or deserved."

The elevator doors opened and he and I both stepped off so that the people behind us could get off. I looked at Mrs. Stevens who was smiling at me and making that pointing gesture upwards, as if to say: *"That's God talking to you right now!"* I smile back at her, a genuine smile this time. And then I turn to extend my hand to this kindly old gentleman to say thank you, for speaking not to me, but to my soul.

I can't tell you what made this different, I only know that this time, the words were not only heard, but they were felt and they had taken root.

"My name is Joseph, Joseph Miller."

"I know," he smiled again, pointing at the name tag on my chest.

Again, I can't tell you why, but for some reason, I felt lighter. Like a light bulb had come on inside of my head and a burden had been removed. I just nodded my head and stepped back onto the elevator. To my surprise, he did too.

"Still going up?" I asked.

"Yep." He continued to smile.

As the elevator doors begin to close I was sure that I heard someone screaming. I turned to look past the doors but they had shut. I looked back at Mrs. Stevens to see if she had acknowledged the sound, and clearly she had. Her right hand was pressed against her chest as if she had been startled. My instinct was to stop the elevator on the 17th floor and then run back down to the 16th floor to see if I could locate the source of that frightening sound, but I would never get that chance.

Just as the elevator was reaching the 17th floor we heard and felt a huge boom that reverberated throughout the entire building. The elevator itself jolted and banged against the sides of the elevator shaft. It felt as though we had actually bounced inside of the steel box and I immediately felt my heart start to sink. The power went out and the elevator was not moving anymore. Two seconds later, the emergency lights came on, but the elevator was still not moving. The women and children on the elevator began to scream. And that's when the second boom hit and the elevator began to plunge from the 17th floor down the shaft to what we all believed was the undeniable end. I have no clue as to how fast we were falling, I only know that somewhere between the 7th and the 8th floor, the cable holding the elevator stopped feeding us slack, and the sudden stop made the elevator spring back upwards, nearly snapping the cable and sending everyone inside of it bouncing off of the ceiling. I'm pretty sure that I had a concussion. My ears were ringing and it took me a minute before I was able to properly focus my vision. My head was bleeding and I could feel it beginning to swell. I saw a woman clutching at her children and Mrs. Stevens was completely unconscious. There was one more guy there who was banging on the doors screaming for someone, anyone to get us out of there. The gentleman whom I had just met was kneeling beside me telling me not to move.

"Take it easy son. You hit your head pretty hard. We need to get the bleeding under control."

As a medic, I knew that he was right, but as a human being, the instinct for self-preservation had kicked into over-drive, the adrenaline was flowing and I knew that we had to get off of this elevator. Whatever was going on was catastrophic, and in the midst of all of the chaos, people on an elevator would be the last to be considered. I looked up at the numbers to see what floor we were on and saw that both the 7th and the 8th floors were lit up. I took that to mean that we were between floors. All we needed to do was pry the elevator doors open and then we could either jump up or jump down, either way, we would be off of this deathtrap. When I opened my mouth to communicate this to my new friend, my words slurred. And that's when it dawns on me just how bad I've been hurt. My mind is alert, frantic even, but my motor skills are not responding to my thoughts like normal. My equilibrium has been knocked completely off kilter. Panic begins to set in and I can feel my heart racing like a bat out of hell. I'm struggling to sit up, but I keep falling over. My friend is insisting that I lay still and give myself a minute to recover, and I do exactly as he instructs. The guy banging on the door however, is having a complete meltdown.

"Hey!!! Hey!!! Goddammit I know that someone out there can hear me!!! Get me out of here!!! Open the doors!!! Can you hear me?! I'm trapped in here!!!"

The old guy tries to calm him down and he snaps on him.

"You need to calm down buddy, no one out there can hear you, listen…they're all out there screaming themselves. We need to take for granted that no one is coming and logically think of a way to get out of this elevator."

"Who in the hell asked you anything old man?! I don't give a damn what happened out there, I need to get off of this elevator! And I'm getting off right now!"

The younger man looked up at the access hatch in the corner of the elevator which was right above the heads of the woman clutching her two adolescent children. She was a young Latino woman and her kids could not have been any older than 9 years old. The three of them were just sitting there, all sobbing, huddled in the corner and scared out of their wits. The younger man who looked to be in his early twenties with polish features stepped over to the corner, looked up at the hatch and told the woman not to move. He then placed his foot on her shoulder, attempting to use her as a way up to hatch. He actually managed to knock the cover away from its seated position. My elderly friend wasn't having it. Surprisingly, with speed and strength that belied his years, he grabbed the younger man by the back of his shirt collar and snatched him back to the closed elevator doors as though he was as light as a feather. A feat that left even our young aggressive friend speechless.

"I'm going to say this to you only one time. I know that you are scared, we all are; but that is no excuse for you to be rude, disrespectful or a piss poor excuse of a human being. You are not the only person on this elevator whose life is in harm's way. Calm down so that we can focus on what needs to be done to get us out of here, but don't put your hands or feet or anything else on anybody else in this elevator, or I will give you something to really be afraid of. Do I make myself clear?"

The young man was struggling to break free from his grip as the older gentleman was speaking to him, once he realized that he couldn't, he simply nodded his agreement and the old guy let him go. That's when I knew that I was beginning to feel better, I found myself smiling. The old guy really put that punk in his place. Then he took off his jacket and rolled it up into a ball, kneeled down beside me, and lifted my head to slide his make-shift pillow beneath it. That's when I saw it; one of the cables that ran along side of the elevator was beginning to unravel. My eyes were locked onto it in a gaze so intense that it caused my elderly friend to follow my gaze to see what I was staring at. He saw the cable, and without missing a beat, immediately sprang into action.

"Ok, listen to me, the cable holding this elevator is unravelling. We need to get off of this thing right now. Does anyone here have anything that we can use to pry the doors open? A pocket knife? Anything?"

The Latino woman immediately grabbed her bag of groceries.

"I just bought some silverware from dollar store. Will a butter knife do the trick?"

"Absolutely!" He smiled.

I began trying to sit up while he worked on getting the elevator doors pried open. I was concerned about Mrs. Stevens, she still hadn't moved. I slid myself over to where she laid unconscious on the floor. It wasn't until I went to cradle her head in my hands that I was aware of all of the blood she was losing. Mrs. Stevens has long thick brunette hair that fell endlessly below her shoulders. The blood had pooled there, on the floor beneath her hair. I immediately checked for a pulse, her breath and a heartbeat. She was alive, but in very bad shape.

"Dear God," I said, "we've got to get her to the E.R."

My elderly friend looked back at me with a smile.

"Don't worry son, we'll get you both there in no time, I've got my finger in between the doors. Ok, tough guy, help me pull them open."

Together, he and the young polish kid did indeed manage to get the elevator doors open. And just as I had suspected, we were stuck between the 7th and the 8th floor. The younger man tried to bolt, but again was subdued by the older gentleman.

"What the hell is wrong with you old man? I've got to get out of here!"

"There is nothing wrong with me young man, nothing at all, but there is definitely something wrong with you. We have a woman and her children and two severely injured people on this elevator, and I cannot move them all by myself. I need your help. But it's clear to me that as soon as you step off of this elevator that you aren't even going to check to see if the rest of us make it off safely."

"How do you know that? You don't know me like that! You don't know me at all!"

"I don't need to know you. Everything that I needed to know was revealed to me in your language, your choice of words, every single time you opened your mouth."

"What are you talking about?"

"When we first realized we were trapped, you were banging on the doors yelling for someone to come save YOU. Screaming that YOU were trapped in here. That YOU needed help. Then, your selfishness and lack of human compassion allowed you to step on top of this terrified woman who was on the floor trying to comfort her own terrified children. You are self-centered and completely self-absorbed, none of which is my problem or any of my business; but right now, you are needed. You're right, I don't know anything about you or your life, but right now something important is happening that you are a part of whether you like it or not. And you are needed to make a difference in the lives of 5 other people. And whether you like it or not, right now I'm going to see to it that you do your part. Do you understand me son?"

The kid was clearly stuck between fear and guilt, but in the end decided to do as he was told instead of what his instincts were demanding of him.

"What do you need me to do?"

"First we help the woman with the children off of the elevator, then we move the lady that's been unconscious this whole time. Then we move the ambulance guy, and then after you get off, you can help to pull this old man up out of this pit. Deal?"

"Deal."

I laid there and watched as this old guy orchestrated the removal of everyone off of the elevator. Only the top half offered enough room for us to slip through, so one by one he and the young man lifted each of us to the opening at the top of the elevator. First the Latino mother so that she could haul her kids up from narrow opening, then Mrs. Stevens, whom I was seriously afraid for. When they came for me, I insisted that the older guy go first, that I was feeling better and could haul myself out when everyone else was out, but he wasn't having any of that either.

"Son, you get to be the hero every single day that you go to work, saving the lives of total strangers that you will more than likely never see again, without so much as even a 'thank you' for being the difference between life and death. Today, let someone else be the hero. You have a family out there that needs you."

I can't tell you why his words impacted me so, I only know that they did. And without a second thought I was moving towards the opening, allowing him and the young man to lift me up. I grabbed the edge to aid them by pulling myself up, but my strength completely failed me. I was still too woozy to be of any use to myself. They got me up and once my body was halfway through the opening the Latino woman hooked me under my arms and dragged me the rest of the way. When I looked back at the opening I could see the young man being hoisted up and then he turned back around to immediately help the older gentleman. As he was pulling him through we all heard the snap and everyone turned to look at the elevator at the same time. The cable had gave way and the elevator was plunging again, this time all the way down to the bottom floor. The crash sounded like another explosion. The cable itself was being dragged through the shaft. The bottom half continued on down with the elevator itself, the top half began to fly straight up to the roof. What we didn't know was that once it got there it would be free of its constraints and come plunging straight back down directly on top of the elevator. The shaft was full of smoke and debris, so no one could see what was happening beyond it, but the younger man was standing too close to the opening. And when the end of that wildly swinging cable made its way passed the 8th floor, its tail caught hold of something the young polish guy was wearing and he was about to be dragged back down into the elevator shaft that he had fought so vigorously to get away from.

"What the…HELLLLP!!!"

I watched in horror as the young man fell face first to the ground and began sliding back towards the elevator shaft. I was confused. It didn't make any sense to me. How was this happening? We'd escaped the elevator. Was this a dream? Am I hallucinating? What the hell was happening? It was like watching movie. And everything was happening so fast, but I remained cognizant of everything as it was happening.

As he reached the opening to the elevator shaft, his legs being pulled down into the opening, he clung to the right side of the wall. It was taking all of his effort to hold on, that much was clear, his face was turning beet red. The older man made a mad dash for him, diving to the ground and latching on to his shirt again.

"I gotcha! I gotcha! And I won't let go!"

"The cables got my pants! It's tearing into my leg!"

"Ok! Ok! Then you've got to take your pants off! Just let them slide right off of you!"

"I can't...belts too tight...dragging me down....can't hold on!"

"Yes you can dammit! Just hold on!"

And without a moment's hesitation I saw this old man stick half of his body into that smoky hole to try and loosen the young man's belt. Two seconds later we all watched as the bottom half of the old guy, which was visible to us, was quickly and violently sucked into the shaft and gone from line of sight. The young man screamed out in pain and in grief but continued to hold on for dear life. I began staggering my way over to him and tried to pull him up, finding it relatively easy. The old man had succeeded. The young man was liberated from his pants, his leg was a bit mangled, but he would live. The old man however had fallen down the shaft.

I searched for the stairway exit and began making my way down to the bottom floor as fast as I could. There were still people screaming and running from the building. Throughout the chaos I could hear things being said; something about a terrorist attack, multiple planes that had been hijacked, and one of them being flown straight through the Twin Towers, which was just a few blocks away, but I didn't have time to sort any of that out right now. Right now, the man that just saved all of our lives was laying broken, alone and more than likely dead, at the bottom of an elevator shaft. And no one here seemed to know it or care about it at the moment except me.

When I got to the bottom floor, to my surprise Virgil was still there trying to direct people out of the building.

"Virgil! Virgil! I need your help over here! It's an emergency!"

Virgil comes running with a look of complete and total concern. He sees the blood on my head.

"Oh my God, Mr. Miller, are you alright?"

"He remembered my name this time," I thought to myself.

"Listen to me Virgil, the elevator cable has snapped and there is a man who has fallen from the 8th floor to the bottom. I need you to help me get these doors open now if there is any chance at all to save him!"

Virgil simply nods and runs back to his desk and promptly comes back with a crowbar. He wedges it between the two doors and has them open in less than 60 seconds. The top of the elevator is only two feet down, and there laying across it is my elderly friend. His eyes are open, filled with tears and pain, but he's still alive. I immediately jump down onto the roof of the elevator to assess his condition, the EMT in me coming alive.

"Don't try and move," I say. "Help is on the way and I'm going to stay right here with you until they come. We're all going to be ok, thanks to you."

I tell Virgil to give me his doorman's coat, he quickly obliges. I roll it up into a ball, just as he had done for me, making it into a pillow so that he would have something soft to lay his head upon. His legs are twisted all wrong, but that's the least of my worries. Blood is pooling around my knees where I am kneeling beside him and it's not mine. He's bleeding out from an unknown place at a pace too fast for me to make a difference, and we both know it. He grabs my hand.

"How old are you now son?" He asks.

"Thirty two," I reply.

He smiled at me and then spoke the words that would haunt me and inspire me for the rest of my natural life.

"At thirty two years old, you haven't even seen half of your life. You must listen to me now, I don't have much time left. There is redemption and salvation in forgiveness. Today is your proof. I've no idea how many people got hurt today, but you were blessed to survive it, you need to know that it is for a reason. You have one life to live, live it without fear or regrets and know that it is with purpose. If you have dreams to do bigger and better things, stop dreaming about it and go chase after it! And hold on tight to your family. They are more than just the people in your life: THEY ARE YOUR LIFE. The differences that you and your wife are having are NOTHING in the greater scheme of things. Honor your vows and do the work that you need to do to make the marriage work, but bring your family back together under the same roof where you all belong."

"Wait, how did you know…"

"It doesn't matter now. What matters now is that you take this second chance you've been given and promise me that you won't let it go to waste. Hate to think I'd died for no reason."

"Stop that, you're not going to die! Helps on the way!"

He gave me that smile of his one final time.

"Helps already come. I was your help to get you back to your family and to your life, you were my help to find redemption for my own issues. Now everything's going to be alright," he sighed. "Everything's…gonna…be…alright."

And with that, my new friend and rescuer breathed his last breath. Oddly enough I'd thought, with a look of contentment on his face.

e/e/e/e/e/e

It took over an hour for an ambulance to finally reach us. I was still sitting there holding his hand when they arrived. The city's emergency services were slammed. September 11th, 2011 was a day that would go down in infamy as the day that terrorists sought to break the spirit and inspire the fear of a nation. It was a day of great sorrow for a great many of us, but it was also a day of great revelation.

THE SOUL OF A MAN 2

And it provided us, or at least me, with a new perspective on life and the future.

I stayed to help those that needed the help and immediately jumped on the ambulance when I saw my crew drive in. They asked if I was alright, I told them I'd live, let's just get to work. They decided that my injuries required immediate attention and got me to the hospital where I was treated and sedated and informed that my next of kin had been notified. When I woke up, I was greeted by a room full of sleeping people. The Latino woman and her children, Mrs. Stevens, who looked much better than when last I had seen her, the young Polish kid who now had on a new pair of sweat pants, my wife and children and Virgil, who was standing against the wall holding a mid-sized box in his hands. The hospital had become a shelter of sorts as people from all over were being treated for their various injuries, but these people were specifically here just for me. Virgil was the first to realize that I was finally awake, and that woke up everybody else.

"Well now, good to see you with your eyes finally open young man. You had us worried. You've been out of it for 2 days now. That was really something back there with all of that. Gave me a whole new respect for what you do and all. Anyway, most of us ended up here at the hospital and I just wanted to make sure that you got your package, Mr. Miller."

"Thank you, Virgil," I smiled back at him while spinning the package around looking for my name or the return address to make sure that it was the package that I was looking for, but there was no shipping label on it.

"Uh, Virgil, I think you've made a mistake. This isn't mine."

"No mistake, Mr. Miller, that's for you. Your name is written across the top of the box."

I tilt it over and low and behold, he is correct, my name has been written across the top in thick black magic marker. But again, I can't help but to note the lack of a proper shipping label.

"Where did this box come from, Virgil? There's no postage."

"It wasn't mailed to you Mr. Miller, it was hand delivered."

"By who?"

And the look of shock that came over everyone's face is enough to make me sit up in my bed. Everyone in the room seemed to know what was going on except for me. And when it became apparent to everyone else that I was clueless, they all seemed to turn and look at my wife at the exact same time. Chelsea got up and walked over to the side of the bed, where she reached over and gave me the most loving kiss she had ever given me. It was a kiss that said that everything would be alright between us. It was a kiss that said that she still loved me. It said that we were in this together and that I was not alone, to trust her and just hold onto us with everything that I have. I looked up amazed at the wave of emotion that had come over me in this instant.

"What's going on, Babe?"

"Honey, that guy you were all on the elevator with," she stammered.

"He saved us, Chelsea. Saved us all. I had hit my head and was pretty much useless, but he managed to keep it all together for all of us. Got us out of that damn elevator just moments before the cable snapped and crashed to the bottom. We would have all died if it weren't for him. That man is my hero!"

Everyone in the room was nodding their heads in silent affirmation while Chelsea's grip on my hand had gotten tighter.

"I'm just upset that I never even knew his name. He said some things to me Chelsea that really just made me open my eyes to a lot of things. And I just want you to know that I love you. I love us. Our family. Whatever it takes to get us back on path I'm more than willing to do. I just don't want us to be apart anymore. Especially after all of this."

Chelsea's eyes filled with tears and I could tell that it was a mixture of joy and pain, and then I could see that she was actually beginning to fall apart.

"Chelsea…what is it, Babe?"

She wiped the tears away, took a deep breath and looked me square in the eyes.

"That man that was with you in that elevator is the man who delivered that package to you."

I looked over at Virgil who nodded his silent confirmation.

"His name was Charles Miller, and he was your father, Joe."

The words she was speaking to me were surreal and I suddenly understood why she was struggling with it all. No amount of preparation in the world could equip me for this. She goes on to explain that he had been incarcerated for 30 years for a crime that DNA was now able to confirm he had not committed. And he was trying to find and re-establish his long lost family. My mother had died a few years back from a stroke and his parents had long since passed making me his only living kin. He was unsure as to how I would receive him, so as a precaution he had left this box with Virgil with specific instructions and a $100 dollar tip to deliver to me the day after his visit. That way, whether the visit went good or bad, he would still end up getting the last word.

"Charles Miller? My Dad?"

"Yes Babe...I'm so sorry," she cried.

"My hero...was my dad?" I struggled with it for only a moment. And then I smiled. "My hero...WAS MY DAD."

And then I cried. We all did. And it was a good, strong, cleansing kind of cry. I was saddened by who and what I had just lost, but I was happy and felt blessed by what I saw and discovered about the man with my own two eyes. Prison had kept my father away from me for the whole of my life, but it clearly didn't keep him from loving his family, or more specifically, his son. Inside of the box were thousands of letters. 30 years' worth. And every single one of them was addressed to me. He called them his "LIFE LESSONS." The things that he wanted to teach me himself. It was how he held on to being a loving father to the son he knew he could never see, but would never stop loving. His letters go on to explain that these letters are his anchor. They allow him to hold onto his sanity and aid him in his refusal to compromise the moral fiber of his being. He knows who he was when he came in this place, and he vowed, for his son's sake, to be that same man on the day that he came out. He did that.

Its 2015 now. I did indeed quit my job as an EMT to pursue my own dreams and passions. I now own my own business and have found huge success in what I do. My father was right; *"Life is shorter than most realize, and there is nothing more painful or regrettable than looking back on your life at the choices you've made and come to the realization that the life that you've settled for was never really the life that you wanted or deserved."* Chelsea and I have never been happier. I have raised our children with the lessons that I have learned and have been taught by my hero both personally and through the words that he left for me scrolled in pencil led and ink in the letters he wrote to me, and now our children have grown up to start wonderful families of their own. Families rooted in love; love the way my father taught it to me. I'm only half way through his letters now, but the more I read, the more I grow to love and respect not just him as a person, but the soul of the man.

I love you dad.

Rest well.

I'm Still Here

Pastor Andre' Jones

"What an amazing feeling it is to realize that after everything I've been through, every bad choice and decision and even after every negative thought including feeling like I just didn't even want to live anymore, out of my "mess" came a "mess-age". I thank God for Lady Elissa Gabrielle for having the vision to pull together all of these awesome men and giving us a platform to share our souls. I hope and pray you are one who will be blessed in ways you never imagined by reading, not just a book, but truly 'The Soul of a Man'."

~ *Pastor Andre Jones*

Let me get this straight...I've survived being molested on more than one occasion by more than one person and now I'm sitting on the side of our local middle school in the middle of the night after having been beaten to a bloody pulp by my drunk stepfather! All I could think about was the fact that many children grow up facing far greater situations and circumstances than I, so why should I allow growing up with this abusive, ignorant fool and being separated from my closest sister at an early age to hold me back? This broken, abusive and often hidden lifestyle designed to kill a child's dreams, steal a child's hopes, and destroy a child's destiny and purpose. Unfortunately it is experienced all too often in our community and is exactly what I endured as a child and young man growing up in Forest Park, Ohio. However, in spite of it all, every beating, every fight, every negative verbal and mental attack, I was described by my friends as the kid everyone loved in school because

THE SOUL OF A MAN 2

I was always positive and happy go lucky. Always had something good or funny to say and always, always had my signature smile on my face! However, behind that smile was a hurting and very angry child with a broken spirit...

တ္သတ္သတ္သ

Often when asked to describe my childhood and how living in a single parent home without my father impacted who I am today, my voice goes from joy to pain as I recall the hardships my sister and I faced watching our mother struggle to provide for us. My mother did the best she could and even married our stepfather in hopes of providing a more stable family life; that, unfortunately, provided the exact opposite results! While she worked nights at AT&T, our stepfather would beat the hell out of us for any number of reasons: from us not cleaning the kitchen to just because he thought we were spoiled brats and that our mother did too much for us. Man I was mad as hell my biological parents were not still together!!!

တ္သတ္သတ္သ

I turned to sports as a way of escape playing little league football team in third grade. That's where I got the nickname "Ajax." I had a way of running through the line "so clean" that my coaches and teammates said it was clean like "Ajax." I like that. It made me feel noticed, accepted, even loved and somewhat appreciated. It allowed me to be something I didn't feel at home: CLEAN. It felt so good and safe that I didn't stop there. I ran track, played baseball, joined a bowling league and was the only person of color at the time on the Forest Park Swim Club diving team. All to stay out of my house as much as possible and try to find a place of peace and not pain.

Well, I couldn't sleep beside the wall of the middle school, so I went over to a friend's house and knocked on his bedroom window. His dad was a pastor and his little sister was on my diving team so I figured it was the best place to go rather going home to another beat down. I thank God that my friend let me in and allowed me to sleep on his floor until the morning. I remember riding to the pool with his little sister and parents only to have my mother show up right in the middle of my first dive at this huge meet with our call fully packed telling me that we were moving to New Orleans right that minute and we had to leave "now!" Unbeknownst to me at the time, my stepfather had threatened to kill her and me if she ever brought me back into that house again, and being the protective mother that she was, she didn't hang around to see if he meant it. The only problem was she was so upset, that we drove an hour and half north to Columbus before she realized we needed to drive 10 hours south to get to New Orleans. I hated him for doing this to my mother!

New Orleans was horrible for me initially! The only black on my football team at a private school, I was everyone's friend when I did good and "nigger, spear chucker and porch monkey" when I messed up. Thanks stepdad. I spent one year living like that in New Orleans before returning to Forest Park where I was taken in by the former Forest Park Mayor, Brandon Weirs and his wife Patti, who went to court and became my legal guardians so I could graduate with the friends I grew up with and so I could escape the threat of my stepfather. The Weirs were so good to me and taught me life lessons that I continue to put into practice to this very day. With them and their children, Carl, Suzanne and Dirk, I found stability and a true family; however, it didn't fill the void or replace my own parents.

eseseses

I thank God that I graduated from Forest Park high school in 1982 without getting anyone pregnant, going to jail or spending a moment in anybody's gang. Not only that, but went on to enjoy a successful college career. Not only did I run track my freshman year but I was also the first African American to win a diving meet at Tulane University. Then came the blow that was far worse than any my stepfather could ever hit me with; my mother passing away from cancer in 1986. I remember going to the hospital that day and immediately calling my sister to come and see our mother. I just felt like we didn't have much more time with her and once again, unfortunately I was right.

The night before the funeral, "Something" led to write a speech in remembrance of my momma. What I didn't realize is that would become my first sermon. The Priest that was supposed to conduct the funeral was over an hour late, and as family members and guests became agitated, I took charge pulling everyone together and proceeded to tell them that "Time Waits for No One!" Before the service was over, Mr.-I-Couldn't-Get-To-Your-Mother's-Funeral-On-Time that was supposed to conduct the funeral stood up and said that my speech was one of the best he had heard and asked if it was too late for me to join the ministry. "Dude are you kidding me???" I was so angry with the Priest for being late to my mother's funeral, I wasn't trying to hear anything he had to say about anything, let alone ministry! However, 10 years later I finally accepted the call into ministry.

Jeremiah 29:11 states, "For I know the plans I have for you, declares the Lord, plans to prosper you and not to harm you, plans to give you hope and a future." God was molding and shaping me through trials and tribulations. Out of the ruins, a leader full of love and compassion was born, Pastor Andre Jones! Needless to say, I had a undying passion for youth and young adults, especially those who were survivors of molestation as well physical and mental abuse. I felt it was my mission to protect and give life through the power of the word to these amazing young people who could have easily gave up in the midst of their problems. But God!!!

While attending seminary school I worked as a youth pastor at a church that was a 65 mile drive from where I lived and I was there 4-6 days a week without fail. I felt extremely fulfilled in this capacity. I felt I was making a difference to a young boy or girl that may have been struggling with a broken home or life difficulties and wanted to walk in the role for the rest of my life! However, God had other plans. Just two years as youth pastor, I was approached by my Pastor and informed I had to go. With tears in my eyes I kept asking what I had done wrong and what I needed to do to be able to stay only to be told it was because it was time for me to become the Senior Pastor of my own church. So in October of 2002 AMEN Fellowship was founded in Houston TX on the campus of one of the local universities.

It didn't take long for me to see the need as I recall an incident where while preaching a sermon I was prompted to stop and to address the audience. I said, "There is someone here that does not care what is being preached and has an agenda and is in need of assistance now." A young lady in the audience began to cry as she revealed her plan to kill herself that evening because she was unable to complete her degree in Pharmacy! Thank God we were able to minister to the young lady and save her life. Not only did she live but she went on to graduate with a BA in Accounting; has gone on to get her MBA; and is doing very well living a full and productive life!!! Thank You Jesus for ordering my steps through my mess so I could see her blessed!

It wasn't until after my mother and stepfather both left this life and I spent over 38 years mad at the world because no one could give me the answer to the question "Why???" What happened to me in my past happened in the first place and I realized that my pain and past had purpose. I went from unhealthy relationship to unhealthy relationship trying to prove my manhood and that I wasn't gay because I had be raped by men who didn't love themselves. Lessons for me: love yourself anyway and my past pain is no one else's problem so get over it and get over myself! Man that was painfully liberating! God turned what the enemy meant for my bad into something good for someone else. I could live with that! Once the anger, rage and pity party were over, I could see that God had kept me when I couldn't keep myself. I forgave my stepfather before he died. I forgave my mother for dying. Hell, I even forgave the ones that molested me to their faces. Game over! I was FREE!!! Free to become a husband, a father and a grandfather; free to be a cancer survivor, free to get an undergrad degree in Math/Computer Science; free to get a Masters in Math; free to obtain a Doctor of Theology; free to become the Sports Director at several Christian radio stations across the country; free to be the Senior Pastor of the Cullen

Missionary Baptist Church where I can advance the Kingdom of God one life at a time; just FREE!!! Free to encourage someone else with these words, "No matter what you've been through, are going through, or yet will go through, you were not put here by accident! Don't ever give up on you! God can use people that most people would not associate with!"

Proverbs 3: 5-6, *"Trust in the Lord with all your heart and lean not on your own understanding; in all your ways submit to Him and He will make your paths straight."*

My Heritage, My Blackness, My Journey

Memphis Vaughan, Jr.

"The Soul of a Man Part 2 is a compilation of life experiences from black men of diverse and similar backgrounds. Each man shares how they have dealt with their experiences and triumphed in ways that can inspire others. The anthology will affirm that there are strong black men who have met the trials and tribulations of life in a positive and encouraging manner." ~ *Memphis Vaughan, Jr.*

THE BLACK MAN'S JOURNEY

I am a member of the most hated, despised and feared group in the nation. The black man. Being a black man in America has always been fraught with challenges that no other single group faces. From the time that we landed on these American shores, the black man has been treated in such a manner that it's a wonder we have survived. My male forefathers endured the lion's share of the abuse, mistreatment, heartaches, ridicule, scorn and other negative behavior from those who dominated over them. They survived through the love, support and nurturing of the black woman and their own unflagging determination.

Despite the tumultuous past, we still survive. Battered but unbowed.

MAKE ME WANNA HOLLER

I can't claim that I have encountered a fraction of what these brave black men who came before me faced. I am the beneficiary of their sacrifices, suffering and hard work. I stand on the shoulders of these ancestors and that is why it has been so important for me to make the most of the opportunities I have been given.

The most telling part of the pain and suffering that black men faced was not only the physical abuse and oftentimes death, but it was also the mental and psychological abuse heaped upon them by the white man. After 300 years and more of the all-out war against black people, no wonder we still have many malfunction in this day and age. We are a broken people.

Think about the journey that black people in America have endured. Brought to this country against our will. Held captive as slaves to perform the most backbreaking and demeaning work while being treated worse than animals. Separated from our families. Once freed, we had to endure Jim Crow laws, lynching, rapes, disenfranchisement, and constant discrimination. Today we now face killings at the hands of policemen that are paid by our taxes to protect us. Despite society's disdain for us, they still co-opt our culture at every chance they get. Take a look at media and the entertainment industry and you'll see numerous examples of how black culture influences so many things.

Yes, we are survivors.

In dealing with the racism that I face either directly or through the systemic discrimination that is enmeshed in everyday life of American society, I liken my response to the words penned by the black poet, Paul Laurence Dunbar in his poem, "We Wear the Mask." I wear a mask many times in order to keep my sanity and not react violently against the injustices, intolerance, ignorance and just plain hatred I encounter as I go through life. This duality of personalities is often a burden that I wish I didn't have to bear. I know that there are many other black people that wear a similar mask in order to cope and survive.

As with many challenges that one faces in life, some of this has strengthened me to the point that I can endure it. But, the racism still slowly chips away at my soul. I often wonder what it would be like if I didn't have to bear this burden. Would I have achieved more, had less stress or enjoyed life more fully? Only God knows. Maybe some of my energy could have been devoted towards other efforts pursuing my career, helping my family and improving the community. God brought me through some of these things for a reason. Yet for many that don't have a strong faith in God, the burden of racism has caused them to deal with it in ways that are detrimental to their mind, body and souls.

But that's not the story that totally defines who I am. I am who I am because of who God made me to be. I am what I am because of my ancestors and what they endured. I am also a product of strong black men and strong black women that taught me to be proud of who I am. They preferred to focus on the positive aspects of life in order to help them deal with the negative. Why dwell on the past when it can't be changed? We should focus on today and what the future holds. As a lover of history and one who understands its importance, I'm not advocating that we forget the past. We should remember the ordeals we endured through as a people to ensure that we do better in the future and don't repeat it. But, we shouldn't let the tragedies of the past keep us from carving out the possibilities and opportunities of a future that is boundless.

RECOGNIZING MY HERITAGE

When I hear media and others generalizing all blacks as lazy, uneducated or violent, I know that is a lie that they wish to perpetuate. We all have seen how a news reporter will find the most illiterate and disheveled black person to interview on the street. These images are fed to us each night and ends up characterizing a whole race in this manner.

Black people have been the backbone of this country and our hard work and free labor helped to make America what it is today. Yes, they can trot out the few examples of black people getting welfare, handouts and standing on corners doing nothing, but we all know that there are more white people receiving welfare than blacks. What is the excuse of these white welfare recipients and other slackers when they've had greater advantages than any other race?

Even when some white people work side by side with blacks that are intelligent, hard-working and law-abiding citizens, they still have a tendency to think these negative stereotypes are the norm. The media will rarely show the stable black families where there are two working parents doing their best to support their family. That is a story that many don't want the world to know about because it furthers their agenda to keep us oppressed. But I'm going to tell that story.

My ancestors were people who farmed, taught school, preached, worked in factories, served in the military and did other jobs that allowed them to make a living to support their families. When you have so many examples of hardworking people, it is easy to step right into that role because it is an expectation placed before you. They were loving people who helped others around them in the manner that Jesus taught his disciples. To love your fellow man was instilled in me at an early age. But it was not only talk, as I witnessed them putting their Christianity into action. Love, respect, kindness and hard work were the threads that ran throughout all branches of the Vaughan, Scott, Woods and Clark family trees. That's not to say that everyone was perfect and always acted in a Christ-like manner, but the majority of them tried to follow what the Bible taught. That legacy has been passed down through the generations.

I was born during the segregation era in the Deep South state of Alabama. I was the oldest of five children. We were fortunate that my parents shielded us from most of the harsh realities of Jim Crow laws, discrimination and all of the ugly things that occurred to black people during that period. We lived in Detroit during the worst of the 1960's and therefore the bulk of my knowledge of the Civil Rights movement was via television. These events had a personal connection because my mother's first cousin was Coretta Scott King, wife of civil rights leader Dr. Martin Luther King, Jr. I can remember my mother getting upset over the inhumane treatment that Coretta,

Dr. King and others received during the marches and sit-ins that appeared on the news.

It wasn't until years later as a young adult that I realized the full significance of what Coretta and Dr. King had meant to the nation. Hearing about the Scott family from my mother during those years, I learned of the pride she had for her cousin but she was even more proud of their mutual grandfather, Jefferson Scott. He had been a prominent member of his community, a landowner and had a great influence on my mother when she was a child in Marion, Alabama. The legacy of hard work, determination, pride and faith in God was left to his many descendants including myself. If I look to my ancestors on the other branches of my family tree, I find similar examples of strong, influential black men. The combination of my Scott, Vaughan, Woods and Clark genes meant that I couldn't be anything less than a strong black man.

When I hear about all the terrible things that have happened in the childhoods of many black men and women, it makes me wonder if my normal childhood was anomaly. But, many of the people that I knew growing up in my community and church had both parents in the home. Even the single parent homes consisted of a mother or father who worked hard to support their families. Back then, deadbeats and criminals were not as common as they may be today.

Black pride instilled in me by my family and my community has fortified me and taught me how to deal with the challenges in life. I don't recall ever being ashamed of being black. I love my blackness and wouldn't exchange being a black man for anything else in the world. God made me this way for a reason and I am blessed and thankful for being who I am. I continue to work at being my best to fulfill my reason for being on this earth.

୧୬୧୬୧୬୧୬

My family placed a strong emphasis on education. Many of my grandparents only went so far in school due to the lack of educational opportunities for blacks, limited funds or having to work at an early age to support their families. However, many family members did send their children to college. Most of the women in my family were teachers so obtaining an education and going to college was a given. All but one of my siblings went to college. I have tried to live my life in that manner and I have taught my sons to do the same. Now all three sons are college graduates and hard-working members of society.

HARD WORK AND DISCIPLINE

Laziness and idleness wasn't an option in my family. I remember when I was about 9 years old, I asked my dad for some money and he gave me the lecture about hard work. You just didn't get handed money he stated, you had to work for it. From that point on, I may have heard that message numerous times before it sank in and I realized he wasn't going to just give me money without doing chores or some task to justify it. When dad did give us money, it came with so many caveats such as saving some of it and sharing some with siblings that it didn't seem worth the effort to keep asking for an allowance. So, I did the tasks that I could to earn money.

When we moved back south from Detroit in 1969, I was about twelve years old. Whistler, Alabama was a predominantly black working class community in suburban Mobile. My father was a farmer at heart and he made sure that he had a vegetable gardening our backyard. Like most teenagers, we weren't very interested, but dad taught us gardening skills. Although it was hard work that had us up at the crack of dawn, I enjoyed eating the vegetables that we grew. Even during the summer breaks from college when I had an intern job, he still expected me to help weed, water, fertilize and harvest the vegetables in the garden. I also had a paper route and later a job as a janitor at my church when I was in high school. This gave me a sense of financial independence and helped me to understand that there is no shame in doing manual labor. These jobs were additional elements in building my work ethic and developing my character.

Discipline came in various forms from my parents. It was administered with love and it helped shape me into the man I am today. Most of the time, my parents talked to me and punished me when needed by restricting me from watching television or going places with friends. Other times they knew when the belt or a switch was more effective. My mother gave us more lectures than whippings. When she put her foot down, you knew she meant business. Mom would also pepper her admonishments with bible verses and words of wisdom. I remember "you reap what you sow" as being one of her most common statements. Anytime I was about do something that I knew was wrong, I thought about that particular bible verse. It stopped me from doing many things I knew I'd regret.   It works just as well when sowing good seeds. It is a philosophy that I try to live by today.

IT TAKES A VILLAGE

Whistler was the typical black community of that era where everybody knew everybody else. We had neighbors on our street that helped to keep me, my siblings and other neighborhood kids in line.   I was always amazed at how insightful and aware these neighbors were when it didn't seem like they were paying any attention to us while they sat on their porches or worked in their yards. Yet, they knew about everything that occurred on that block. And these were people who were in their 70's and 80's at the time. Our neighbors kept us out of a lot of trouble when our parents were at work or away from home.

Another source of role models for me was the members of my church. My church had many strong black men and women that were the backbone of their families, active in the church and leaders in the community. The pastor, during my teenage and young adult years, took many of the youth on summer trips to Atlanta, Nashville, Disney World and other places. These were opportunities to learn how to conduct ourselves as young adults, learn about our heritage and to have fun. He established the rules of conduct and gave us latitude to enjoy ourselves as long as we followed these rules. These summer trips complimented other trips that my parents took us on that expanded my horizons about the world.

Helping others was a central part of my upbringing. I always saw my dad doing things for family, friends and others in the community. As a schoolteacher, my mother was a person that many people, young and old, turned to for advice, help with studies and other assistance. My dad had many friends and neighbors that came to him for money, transportation and various other favors. Even though I often felt that my dad was doing too much and never seemed to get favors done in return, I soon learned that we don't always get our blessings back from the one that we may have helped. God sends it back to us in different ways.

My parents lived through segregation and dealt with racism and discrimination the best they could. I often wonder what my dad could have become instead of a laborer and janitor if his options hadn't been limited early on in life because of Jim Crow and racism. His viewpoint on dealing with whites were one of caution but he never taught me to hate white people or any group. My mother taught that we should judge each person on how they treated us. Both parents emphasized the importance of loving everyone as the Bible had taught. I thank God for having hard-working and loving parents that took the time to teach us about right and wrong. I observed how my father treated my mother and never once did he raise his hand to her. That spoke volumes and taught me how to treat my wife and set the example for my sons.

⌘⌘⌘⌘⌘

When I look at the problems that confront the black community today, I attribute some of the breakdown in society to children growing up without someone in their lives to teach them the correct way to function in life. Things such as respect, politeness, tolerance and treating others as they'd like to be treated are cornerstones to learning how to survive in life. Being taught these social skills are important in developing self-esteem, self-pride and realizing one's full potential.

ᕲᕲᕲᕲ

Today when I observe blacks behaving badly, it troubles my soul because I remember a time when that was not the norm. Today, we have so many images, especially in media that seem to glorify disrespect, violence, drugs and immoral behavior in the name of generating dollars and achieving "fame." I truly believe that many of these celebrities who do these negative things only do so because of their lack of self-esteem and love. They clamor for attention and adoration whether it is from fickle fans, the media or so-called friends. Most don't realize that having fame and fortune may not make them happy if they don't address the underlying problems in their lives. We've seen too many famous people hit rock bottom or die tragically because they couldn't effectively deal with their troubles.

STEPPING INTO MANHOOD

Getting an education has been the route many blacks have used to realize their dreams and full potential. Without an education it would have been much tougher for me to achieve what I have accomplished today. Learning a skill and obtaining knowledge are critical for many to achieve success. Those with natural talents and abilities still have to work hard to hone those skills. Over the years, I have spoken to students and mentored young people on the ways to reach their goals. I'm a firm believer in the saying, "Those who think they CAN and those who think they CAN'T, are both right."

My years in college during the late 70's and early 80's were the best times of my life. The friendships I forged with my various roommates and other close friends are still strong to this day. The friends I made at Morehouse and Spelman Colleges helped to further shape my outlook on life. Attending a Historically Black College and University (HBCU) such as Morehouse exposed me to prominent professors, dignitaries, events and other sources of black pride. The education and nurturing received at Morehouse enhanced my academic skills and reinforced the black pride that I had already learned within my own family. Since the historically black college included students from across the spectrum of the black community, I learned even more about black culture and history. College exposed me to different people, music, fashions, ideas, behaviors and backgrounds. Students ranged from sons and daughters of many of the leading black families in the nation to those from modest backgrounds similar to mine.

By the time I entered Georgia Tech to pursue my engineering degree, I felt confident dealing with the fact that I was either the only black or one of few blacks in each class. My prior experience with integrated schools had allowed me to accept this situation with less trepidation than others faced. While I was attending Georgia Tech, I lived off campus so I didn't get the experience of living in a dorm with white students. Looking back, I wish I had lived on campus among white students to see what that was like. Upon graduation, I recognized that I had received an education from two of the most prestigious institutions in the nation. The Dual Degree Engineering program allowed me to attend both schools and prepared me with an education that combined the experiences of a predominantly black college and a predominantly white university.

THE WORKING WORLD

Entering the working world as an engineer was one of the biggest tests that I faced in life. I had to prove myself on dual fronts: as an engineer and as a black man. While most of my white coworkers were easy to get along with, there were a few who made it their duty to voice their biased opinions whenever the opportunity arose. Again I wore the mask as I felt I was the representative of the black race to many who hadn't dealt with an educated black man.

As the dominant group in American society, the white male is still the most difficult to deal with and fully understand. One of the things that have baffled me about the white male is their overarching sense of entitlement. Most of the white males I encountered in the workplace always felt that they deserved the best of everything. The newest computer, the top assignment, the promotion, the prime office, the last word on a subject or whatever superlative they could dream up. I started my career feeling blessed to have a job and approached each opportunity as a blessing from God. I've always worked hard at doing my best and doing the right thing. I refused to let the ignorance and pettiness that I encountered make me stoop to their level. I did demanded respect from them and I did my best to respect others.

I am competitive. I won't deny that. But, I like to think that I do it in a way than most may not realize I'm competing with them. It is a well-known fact that a black person has to work twice as hard as white to be considered competent. Many whites expect blacks to fail, and when we succeed, they can't accept that either. We're damned if we do and damned if we don't. Because of our heritage, we've learned to make the most out the little we may be given. So, when we don't leave any room for them to pick apart our accomplishments, many of them grudgingly have to give us our due.

In the 80's, racism had become very subtle and if you weren't careful, you would think it had faded from view. But, just when I'd become comfortable in a situation or setting, a racist remark or encounter would snap me back into reality. We are expected to not feel uncomfortable and out of our element when we're the only black in the office, class or meeting. Yet, watch how uncomfortable a white person will get when the tables are reversed. Because of these type situations, blacks are more adaptable and innovative when times become challenging.

Some of the most unsettling encounters I had were with white males who would smile in your face when others were around but show their true colors when they didn't have an audience. This ranged from encounters with older white males who still had one foot firmly planted in the segregated society of the past to the young white guys that were my age but had been indoctrinated in prejudicial behavior by their parents.

I had a run-in during my first year of work with a powerhouse operator at one of the rural dams who didn't like the fact that I, a young black engineer, was there to work on computer software that would benefit him in his job. I still can see his sneering stare and remember his ungrammatical comments stating that "I'd had enough of you computer-screwer-uppers, you better leave that computer like you found it." As I sat there working on the software, I could feel him eye-balling me with what felt like daggers. Another encounter with this same operator occurred several years later when I was more seasoned and knew how to deal with guys like him. When I gave him instructions on how to operate the dam (which was part of my job to do), he defiantly said he'd do the particular operation any way he pleased. I reiterated the instructions and told him he'd be responsible for carrying them out. I hung up before he could say anything else. I found out the next day that he'd followed the instructions exactly as given to him.

There were a few other examples of white males being belligerent, indignant and nasty when they had to get instructions, direction or information from me as a black male. Other times, I was questioned about how did I get a certain assignment, how did I go to certain colleges or other questions that displayed their ignorance about black people. As time went on, these same guys realized that I wasn't going anywhere and they learned to coexist with me and other blacks in the workplace. I've always maintained an even disposition so I felt their reactions weren't justified since I wasn't being arrogant, cocky or disrespectful to them. They just had a hard time getting used to the changes that were afoot. I also knew that I had to work with these guys, so it made sense to try and get along with them. As my parents taught me, I just continued to treat them fairly.

Not all white people I have encountered behaved in the manner mentioned earlier. I would surmise that most of the whites I've met are decent people that try to treat everyone as equals. I have developed many good friendships with white people at school, in college, at work and in the community. My first supervisor when I was a summer engineering intern was a white male and he became one of my strongest mentors. It was his confidence and faith in my abilities that helped me get through college with the knowledge that a permanent job was waiting for me. For every knuckleheaded white person that said or did something to undermine me, there was another white person that offered their friendship and support. These relationships have contributed to my personal growth because their actions let me know that not all white people are adversaries or racist. Because of my Christian background and the way I have been taught, it allowed me to see the good in all people whether they are black or white.

Outside of the workplace and classroom, I've experienced the same indignities that many black men face over the years. The random stops while driving, the side-eye glances from whites in stores, white people jumping ahead of you while standing at a counter, the reactions in the elevators and on the streets by white women, etc. I've been blessed that none of the encounters with police turned into tragedies. Even now, I am still cautious when approached by the police.

At the time this is written, black males have experienced an upswing in white aggression towards us in the form of murders of unarmed young black men by white policemen, white security guards and other disgruntled white men. In many of these cases, the black victim was minding their own business when they were approached by these white men who didn't like what the young men were doing. Instead of using an approach to peacefully communicate with them, they chose to murder them under the guise of self-defense or doing their job. Again, I attribute this to fear based on hatred, jealousy and the belief the black man is a violent beast that should be eliminated. But white society will have to deal with their misguided issues by being honest with their racist attitudes and their guilt for the treatment of blacks and other minorities over the centuries. Until they stop buying into the misconceptions, stereotypes and lies that society has ingrained in them about black people, they will never find peace.

PROMOTING BLACK CULTURE

Next to my passion for traveling, writing is an activity that I enjoy. I created the TimBookTu website, a site featuring fiction, poetry, essays and other forms of writing in 1996. I tapped into the power of the Internet to create the site as a way to interact with other black writers. I wanted to establish a site to highlight black culture and display the writing talents that I knew existed. I didn't really know what I was doing but the site soon attracted aspiring writers and poets. Eighteen years later, the site has presented the works of more than 2,500 writers and continues to attract new writers. I have met many talented, creative and versatile writers that are now well-known names in the literary field. Yet, the site is still a place where a beginning writer or poet can have their work displayed to reach an audience. I feel the success of TimBookTu clearly demonstrates that we are awesome people who have taken our adversities and setbacks and made something great and wonderful.

My journey as a black man in life has been overwhelmingly filled with blessings from God. The combination of black pride, a loving family with many wonderful role models, educational and career opportunities and a wealth of great friends have made the journey amongst racism and other adversities much easier. All of the positive elements I received from my parents, family and mentors helped me to be a loving husband to my wife, a good father to my sons and a productive citizen. My message to others on their path in life is to have faith in God, embrace the love of family and friends and keep your eyes focused on your goals. This is the image of the black man that I want white society to see and appreciate.

Breathing Problems

Maurice M. Gray, Jr.

"Eric Garner's last words before his death in police custody were "I can't breathe!" As Black men in America, we all experience that sensation sooner or later. "Breathing Problems" is my look at the unique difficulties associated with being a Black man in a country that doesn't always welcome us."

~ Maurice M. Gray, Jr.

"I can't breathe!"

I was six or seven years old the first time I said these words. Or rather, I tried to say those words but failed spectacularly due to having had all the oxygen in my body leave dramatically. I remember playing Follow the Leader with my friends (all boys that day). As boys are wont to do, the leader decided to do something incredibly unsafe and appallingly stupid. Naturally we followed him☺. He took the game up into the trees. We were in my backyard, and back then, there were three trees, two of which were close enough together where an enterprising lad could do a passable Tarzan impression.

The leader led us into the trees, and we four or five, like sheep, followed him up. He leaped from the first tree to the second, caught the branch, pulled himself into the tree and climbed back to the ground from there. Those in front of me imitated him perfectly, as I had done a thousand times when playing alone. This day however, I mistimed the jump or didn't push off hard enough from the other tree or miscalculated the distance- I can't remember exactly which it was. I do remember missing the branch and face-planting spectacularly into the grass. Stomach-plant might be a more accurate description, because that's the part of me that hit ground the hardest.

"OOOOF!"

That is the sound one makes when every molecule of oxygen is forcibly expelled from his body by a hard impact. I remember lying there, flat on my face, trying frantically to suck wind and replace the air that had been knocked out of me. My friends murmured among themselves about who should go tell my mother what had happened, and wondered if, perchance, I was going to die. After a few frightening moments, I was able to get enough air in my lungs to where I could stop gasping like a fish out of water. At that point, I was able to get up off the ground and my friends stopped arguing over who had to tell my mother. We switched over to playing football after that; there was still hitting, but at least I got to keep most of the air in my lungs.

I will never forget the feeling of oxygen deprivation until the day I die. It's not something I dwell on, or even a memory that surfaces often, but it's there and it's significant to me. When I heard about Eric Garner's death while in police custody, his saying "I can't breathe!" struck a chord with me. I remembered that day in my backyard. I remembered how helpless I felt, how inevitable it seemed that I would continue not to be able to breathe and how I was sure I was going to die that day.

And it occurred to me that Eric Garner must have felt the exact same way.

I'll be the first to admit that on the surface, I couldn't easily identify with Mr. Garner. He was over six feet tall and over 400 pounds; he had a fiancée and children. I am five feet tall with the right shoes on, 145 pounds soaking wet and single with no children. On the day of his death, Mr. Garner was arrested for selling loose cigarettes, which he and everyone else knew was illegal. It's what he felt he needed to do to provide for his family; I can't judge. I've always had something remotely resembling a job, and everything I have ever done to earn a living was perfectly legal. I was too scared of my mother, rest her soul, and my father to even *think* about doing anything illegal, no matter how broke I felt I was.

And besides, I'm too little and too cute to go to jail.

But, when I heard how Mr. Garner died, it resonated with me. He died struggling for air, vainly begging for relief from the situation that inhibited him from the simple act of respiration. As a child I faced that same struggle. My situation was different though; there was no physical impediment stopping me from eventually drawing breath anew. All I had to do was roll over from my stomach to my back and let the trauma I'd endured pass. In short order, my lungs pulled in enough air to replace what was lost, and all was well again. Mr. Garner didn't have that luxury; once placed in that illegal chokehold, he was not released until he died.

As I pondered the whole "breathless" connection, I began to reassess the way I perceive the world around me. While I've always been on the optimistic side, I also developed enough cynicism to survive in the real world. However, the deaths of Trayvon Martin, and then Michael Brown and Eric Garner so close together reminded me of what I already knew; the world ain't fair.

You're probably saying I should have known that long before these murders happened, and I should. But give me a break- I didn't know I was black until I was eighteen.

Okay, let me clarify. I wasn't that dumb. I knew I was black from a young age. I just didn't find out what that meant until I got to college. It took me that long to learn that being black was seen as a negative by some, and just how cruel those people can be. I don't remember every single detail of that day, but the encounter itself is nothing I'll ever forget.

I was a freshman at the University of Delaware, Newark, Delaware. It was a Saturday morning, and the fact that I was up and about as early as I was tells me that there wasn't a party on that Friday (I wouldn't have been up before 10 a.m. at a minimum). In any event, I'd gotten up early enough (before 9 a.m.) to walk down Main Street and run an errand or two before starting my day. Main Street was where all the action was; stores, restaurants and at the far end, a movie theater. At 18, I could easily walk all the way up Main Street and back to my dorm (about two miles) without getting winded. I was on my way back from wherever I went (I'm pretty sure my stops probably included the arcade for a few video games) when I heard it. "It" was the sound of an engine gunning, really close to me. I remember thinking I shouldn't hear an engine that close because I was on the sidewalk and not particularly close to the street. I turned around to make sure someone wasn't about to jump the curb and hit me, and that's when I heard overlapping annoyingly nasal Caucasian voices.

"Hey! Nigger! Little nigger!"

THE SOUL OF A MAN 2

I couldn't believe what I just heard. Apparently they didn't think I heard them, because they repeated it. "They" were a pickup truck full of drunken rednecks, apparently still juiced up from last night's bender. The driver swerved as close to the sidewalk as he could get so they could make themselves heard, hence the loudness of the engine from my perspective.

Nothing in my experience prepared me for that. While I grew up in an all-black (middle class) neighborhood, I'd gone to schools that were racially diverse from K-12. Even though my closest friends were from my neighborhood, I'd always had friends of all races. None of my non-black friends had ever acted like I was any different from them that I had noticed. My dorm (third floor Rodney Hall B) was diverse, no small feat on a campus with such a small black population. I had a single room, but my neighbors on either side were white guys. Aside from all the white dudes, there were three other black guys on my floor, two Spaniards, one Puerto Rican and even a guy from Iran. We treated each other the same- with juvenile insults, practical jokes and a glorious lack of maturity. None of them ever treated me as less than one of the guys. These rednecks did, and that pissed me off.

I couldn't breathe.

My first feeling was outrage- blind, unthinking anger. As in, I wished I could snatch them all out of that truck, pick the truck up and beat them with it. I then processed thoughts of giving some sort of impassioned oration designed to cut through their collective inebriation and shame them to their cores. I also considered giving them the peace sign, to let them know I wasn't fazed by their insult.

I stopped halfway and gave them the finger.

143

They laughed and zoomed off, but this brief encounter consumed my thoughts long after they were gone. Though I didn't realize it at that moment, this was the day when I learned I was black. More to the point, that was the day when I learned that in this country, race matters.

I didn't realize it at the time, but that was a turning point in my life. How I reacted from that point in part shaped who I am today. And believe me, I had options. I could have called on a few large friends, found those guys who insulted me and had them beaten. It's not like they would have been hard to track down; having nothing better to do with their lives, they "cruised" Main Street every weekend, vainly attempting to attract girls and verbally accosting random Negroes when their sexual frustration got the better of them. When I shared this encounter with my fellow black students, they told me that I wasn't the first nor would I be the last to be harassed by those rednecks (who hailed from nearby Elkton, Maryland).

Failing putting a hit on them, I could have stayed in the anger I felt in that moment and hated all white people from that day forward (dramatic I know, but there are folks out there who do just that for reasons similar to mine). I could have forsaken the faith of my youth (Christianity) for the Nation of Islam's more militant approach to race relations. That's not a stretch; we had someone come to campus once at the request of one of our Black Student Union members to speak, and believe me, that guy was recruiting.

I did none of the above. I got past my initial state of pissed-offedness, but the underlying anger, disappointment, frustration I felt from being called out of my name stayed with me. I wasn't immediately sure what exactly I wanted to do about it, but I knew there was something I wanted to do in response to their ignorance. And that's how I found my way into the Center for Black Culture.

At the time I went there, UD boasted a student population of about 15,000 students, approximately 200 of which, were black. Needless to say, we all spoke to one another whether we liked each other or not with only a few exceptions. It was hard to feel at home when so few people looked like you or understood where you were coming from culturally, and we couldn't afford to be standoffish with the only lifelines we had. As an English major, I didn't have too many of my fellow African-American students in my classes (most of us were in Engineering or Business). I'd joined the Gospel Choir, but that only met once a week. I saw my friends in the dining hall for meals (we tended to sit in the same section whenever we could), but I needed more than that.

One of my friends told me about the Center For Black Culture, and it quickly became my home away from home, just as it was for a lot of us on campus. It was about the size of the smaller fraternity houses on campus, but it was larger than life for those of us who took refuge there. I took to hanging around there between classes, which was more convenient than going all the way back to the dorm or waiting somewhere less comfortable. And somewhere between meeting black folks I hadn't seen yet, watching endless games of spades and observing the never-ending battle for the TV remote control (soap operas vs. music videos- the war that never ended), I recaptured "black" as a good thing.

In other words, I *could* breathe.

I began taking Black American Studies courses for all my electives. I took the first because my friends were taking it, but after that, I was hungry for more. This wasn't the history I learned in K-12, and I found it ironic that I had to go to a predominantly white college to learn black history. This wasn't just "Slavery happened, it was bad and now it's over, then Martin Luther King Jr. came and now there's no more racism." This was Shaka Zulu and Harriet Tubman, Black Wall Street and Rosewood, Chinua Achebe and Zora Neale Hurston. This was the Middle Passage and the Harlem Renaissance, and the discovery of more black inventors, politicians and entrepreneurs than I ever dreamed existed. Faith in Jesus Christ saved my soul, but this information filled the hole in it.

There were the endless debates in the Center that didn't involve spades or the TV remote, the ones that made us all better for the exchange of thoughts and knowledge. Because of those, I became able to articulate why Christianity is not a "white man's religion." White men may have used a bastardized version of true faith to justify holding slaves, but I learned not to blame Christianity for their crimes any more than I would blame fire for burning down a house instead of holding the arsonist who set it accountable.

There were the protests. I have to laugh; we were quite the radical bunch. If a mosquito bit a black student and not a white one, we had a protest organized on three hours' notice. Okay, it wasn't quite that serious, but there were serious issues that we felt the needed to address, and address we did. My first sojourn into advocacy came when the BSU realized how heavily invested in South Africa that U of D truly was. Apartheid was still the rule of law in South Africa in the late 80s, and we didn't want to be part of a university that via financial complicity, indulged a racist regime. We organized, we protested, we made our voices heard. U of D didn't divest immediately, but eventually they did. I'd like to think our protest pricked their consciences and encouraged the powers that be to do the right thing, but I suspect it was on their agenda already. While as many as half of the black population of the campus supported the rally, it doesn't follow that the wishes of 100 or so students could influence how they spent their money.

And, I learned something else from hanging out at "The Center." Some of the older guys shared a story of their encounter with those same rednecks (if not the exact same group that harassed me, their friends). I'm pretty sure the story changed some by the time it reached The Center; the men involved told the story in the dining hall the day after this happened, and a guy who was there to hear the story told it to us the next time he came to The Center. These four gents were walking up Main Street one night minding their business when Idiots On Wheels rolled by and gave their standard oration about eff you niggers, go back to Africa (they probably couldn't even spell 'Africa,' let alone know where it is). Unfortunately for them, they hit a red light as they were yelling. Even more unfortunately for Elkton's finest, these were four *large* Negroes.

As we rolled on the floor laughing, we heard how these four brothers ran up on the car, surrounded it on all four sides and shook the car as hard as they could. They cursed the Elkton crew to the third and fourth generation, questioned their ancestry, suggested that those rednecks had improper relations with their mothers and kindly requested that they immediately vacate their vehicle in order to engage in a scintillating debate on race relations. The second the light turned green, the driver floored it. He probably broke the sound barrier getting them all back to Elkton where it was safe (and they probably had to clean the seats thoroughly when they got there). We didn't hear of any further "nigger callings" for quite some time after that. It wasn't the March On Washington or the I Have A Dream speech, but it was a strong statement made on the battlefield of race relations.

In event, I'm glad I lost my "black virginity" when I did; my U of D experiences helped me prepare for the day when my studies were done and it came time to be immersed in the real world. It was appropriate that my college experience prepared me so well for adulthood in a society that still harbors overt and covert racism.

Fast forward to now. Years after my U of D black awakening and many more experiences dealing with racism later, I believed that nothing else in this country's racial climate could surprise me. I was wrong. Trayvon Martin was murdered, and the racial divide began. We went on an emotional roller coaster, the likes of which I hoped I'd never see again. Tempers flared; social media went from a fun safe haven to a place where anger and mistrust ruled the day. Folks looking like me raged against the dying of the light, so to speak, while many Caucasians I heard from could not understand why "we make everything racial." I wanted to throw up every time I saw George Zimmerman's smug face. It took a while, but the case was resolved to our dissatisfaction, Zimmerman walked free and the emotional healing for us began.

That wound was still open for this year's double whammy. Hearing the Eric Garner decision on top of the Michael Brown incident was like taking a kick in the groin right after a punch in the stomach. And, when the same Caucasians from before sought to justify those deaths by looking for criminal records, it was a kick in the butt- with steel-toed boots on.

Michael Brown is said to have shoplifted not long before his encounter with the police. That is illegal. So is shooting a man multiple times after he's surrendered. So is putting lying witnesses on the stand to testify against the murder victim.

Eric Garner was arrested for selling loosies (individual cigarettes). That is illegal. So is the chokehold the arresting officer put on Mr. Garner that killed him.

Shoplifting and selling loosies are not, the last time I checked, death penalty crimes. Neither are being big enough to look threatening, or being obese and asthmatic. Those men were killed because to the officers they encountered, black life does not matter. When I read the accounts of their deaths (from as many sources as I could, to get a full understanding of what happened), I felt sick to my soul. I felt the same stab wound to my spirit as I did at 18 when those rednecks called me out my name. In college, we joked about people getting pulled over for being black after midnight (or for being black on a sunny day), and said "Hey, they were guilty!" We laughed about it then. Now? Not so funny. For the first time in years, I truly felt "less than."

My Black American Studies courses kicked in, full strength. I remembered the history of African-Americans, how far we've come, yet how little some things changed. I remembered reading about the mindset that enabled slaveholders to enslave other human beings and rationalize it away for centuries. I remembered learning about Rosewood, Florida and Greenwood, Oklahoma (Black Wall Street); two all black towns burned to the ground when their Caucasian neighbors' jealousy over their continued prosperity reached its breaking point. In each instance, all it took was an accusation that a black man raped a white woman to set off rioting that killed many black residents of these towns and sent many others fleeing into the night, forced to start all over with just the clothes on their backs. I read of the ingenuity of black inventors, and of how so many of them did not receive full credit or compensation for their creations. I even remembered a joke I read long ago, in an aptly titled work called Truly Tasteless Jokes.

Q: "What do you call a millionaire Negro physicist with the skills of an Olympic athlete?"

A: *A nigger.*

When nestled among the Polish jokes and the anti-woman jokes and the anti-gay jokes, it seemed innocuous enough. However, that joke says what too many Caucasians still think (and want us to believe as well): no matter what we accomplish or how far we rise in this country, we're still "less than" to them. While it's comforting that back during slavery times and even now, this attitude is not universally shared by all Caucasians, or even most. However, there are too many with this poisoned mindset, and unfortunately, a lot of them have spheres of influence where they can practice their racist ways unmolested.

When I dwell on this too long, I can't breathe.

It occurred to me that I will never be able to change the mindset of a racist. I wish I could, if only to rescue that person from the mind-numbing stupidity that seems to accompany white supremacist beliefs and practices, but I can't. What can I change? The way I react. When I was my 18-year-old mindset, it was appropriate to handle racists by flipping the bird in their general direction. At 46? Fight ignorance with prayer and with the knowledge that prayerfully comes with age.

There are many who advocate all out mistrust in and war against the police. That would be illegal, immoral and short-sighted; it would turn us into the beasts that racist white people already think we are, and we're better than that. One, black people kill too many other black people as it is; we need not start targeting police too. Two, there are many good policemen and women out there who take their oath "To Protect And Serve" seriously. If you hate all cops, who will you call when you need help? Yourself?

I've seen and talked to many fathers who teach their sons what I was taught: respect authority, including police. However, in this day and age, these wise men also teach their sons how to behave around the police. It's galling, but if we want ourselves and our sons and daughters to live, we need to squash the attitude should we have to deal with an officer of the law. It's not fair that we won't be excused for popping off a little under stressful circumstances, but when police are involved, we can't get all in our feelings. No attitude, no sudden moves and a whole lot of "Yes Officer, No Officer" will go a long way toward keeping our families from having to bury us prematurely.

Do I advocate we just sit back and take it? NO! While I haven't participated in a die-in, I find civil disobedience to be a fine way to get the dialogue started. If we don't say anything, white people (especially those who do NOT hold a Ku Klux Klan worldview) will be only too eager to say that focusing on race only exacerbates the problem. I beg to differ- not having any dialogue on the topic and acting like there is no problem is what exacerbates it.

The thing is, those who have never experienced institutionalized racism can't fathom why we're so angry, so upset about current events and so quick to see a racial overtone in everything. If you live like that, you can't help but see it. It shows subtly (an old woman clutching her purse tighter at the sight of a black man, mall cops following a black person around the store while ignoring an equally shabbily dressed white person) or overtly (George Zimmerman assuming a black youth shouldn't be in an affluent neighborhood and taking violent action as a result of his racism-influenced mistake). They can't see that the blatant disrespect for President Barack Obama as the direct result of racism as much as from political opposition.

There is no easy fix to this, nor should we expect one. It took a few hundred years for the powers that be in this country to abolish slavery, and I submit that we are still not seen as equal. Given that, why should we think that race relations in this country will normalize in the blink of an eye?

The situation hasn't changed, but we can. Things may not be perfect, but that's why we have voices and platforms through which to use them. God gave me creativity and fingers that can work a keyboard, so I write. Others organize or speak out or mentor children so they won't fall into society's traps. We don't all have the same gifts and we won't all do the same things. It's good to see so many people willing to do *something*. Each of us, in our own way, one small step at a time.

I *can* breathe.

This is not easy for many of us to process. When we see so much wasted life and casual disregard for us and our children and our neighbors and friends, it's easy to get angry and stay there. There's nothing wrong with getting angry, but when we *stay* angry and allow that to keep us thrown off stride, situations like this keep happening and we are in no condition to do anything about it.

God gave me my breath back that day long ago when I was six or seven, and now, when recent events knocked me breathless yet again, He stepped in again to restore my breathing and to help me get out of my feelings and back on course.

Because of Him, I *can* breathe.

What They Don't Tell You, May Fail You

Marc Lacy

"The magnitude of a true champion is measured by his or her ability to fight through adversity, keep the faith, and stick to their guns. However, being that 'opposition' can come from multiple sources and from different angles, achieving the aforementioned can be a very perplexing thing. With that said, when one strives for success, people can give them instruction, indoctrination, and guidance; however there are some things for which a blueprint does not exist. The person then must learn to adapt, develop a mental toughness, and battle through the unplanned discomfort in order to survive. Ultimately, the lesson learned is, 'what they don't tell you, may fail you...'" - *Marc Lacy*

As a kid growing up primarily in the south with stints in Europe and in Asia, I was blessed to have been in a household with two loving parents, supportive siblings, and also many influential role models in my life. Whether I was involved in something school related, sports, extra-curricular, or church, numerous positive people were right there to guide me. For the most part, all of my teachers in grade school saw something in me and therefore did not hesitate to go out of their way to see to it that I arrived and remained on course to excel. Although there may have been a bad influence or two during certain times in my upbringing, I am thankful having had the opportunity to be guided and assisted mostly by good wholesome, and God fearing people.

THE SOUL OF A MAN 2

During the process of seguing from an innocent fun-loving kid into a young man, many noticed that I was articulate in my speech without me even knowing what "articulate" meant. I was enunciating words and phrases effortlessly, without really knowing what "enunciation" meant. People of all races found this unorthodox and fascinating alike. When I thought about it, it seems I was being judged on how I sounded whether that was good or bad. At the time, I didn't think anyone was ready for a lanky black kid with subject and verb agreement.

As soon as people figured out that I was articulate, they made many assessments. Some folks swore up and down I was trying to be "white." Others automatically assumed that my parents were rich and that I had a silver spoon in my mouth. Folks surmised that my life was just a walk in the park with no obligation of responsibility. Therefore, many chose to treat me like a "softy" or they automatically felt they had to take up for me because of the docile and innocent aura I projected. This is something in which I learned very quickly to just roll with the punches and take it. I didn't think too much of it. It did not necessarily make me feel bad…it was just something I knew I had to deal with. I figured as long as I did not inflict any harm on anyone or try and belittle them, I would be okay. But as time progressed and I got a little older, the range of personalities with which I had to deal, became wider and wider. As I came into contact with more personality types, the more challenging things had gotten for me. This feeling went against everything I was taught because it was supposed to have been "do unto to others as you would have them do unto you" right? Hmmm. Why were so many people appearing to live a blessed life without even a hint of abiding by the rules? Why did it seem like no one was there to oversee the situation when people did not play by the rules? Why did it seem like I was being punished or picked on for the mere fact that I was following the rules? These are questions that would zoom through my mind like a racecar on a track. Nonetheless, I did not fold and succumb to peer pressure, nor was I making an extensive effort to be different; I was just being me and doing what I knew was right. At the time, I would hear people mention things about dealing with jealousy, envy, and insecurities, but my mind was not at a stage in which I could process all of those things. Therefore I could not say what was what. All is I know is that something did not feel right. Again, I still went with it. It was also during this time in which I knew I had faith to a degree. I had an idea of how it was supposed to work; however, I did not know how to apply if fully, despite church, Sunday school, Vacation Bible School attendance, etc.

By this time, my sports participation went from the little leagues to playing for schools. Of course when you play for a school, you get more attention. When you get attention on the field or court, it automatically translates to attention off the field or court...mainly in the classroom. I noticed this and I wanted to continue doing my best because my best was supposed to cause more good than harm...especially if my heart was in the right place. With that said, my family and all outside role models continued encouraging me to excel in the classroom and in sports.

At the end of each season, regardless of the sport, there would be a team banquet at which the team, coaching staff, parents, and supporters were invited. I noticed how much of a big deal receiving a certificate was to the family. Back then, you were taught that it was some form of "validation" or the notion that you had "arrived." That was the culture. At the end of the season, if you were presented with a trophy, certificate, or some sort of plaque, it would register as another stripe on your sleeve giving you a higher rank. For those of us who were still trying to figure the "merit" thing out, we were satisfied because our parents and elders were satisfied once we received recognition for the season. However, I also noticed that somebody had to make the ugly decision as far as who deserved more recognition than the other when certain awards were presented. Although I could not put it in to words back then, I can see vividly now, people were feeling some type of way when they did not receive what others received, whether they earned it or not. I do remember being in situations where the "under-performers" received just as much recognition as the "over-performers" to either emphasize "teamwork" or satisfy inquisitive parents. Then I thought, "Man, I'd hate to be the one to decide who gets what recognition." It sounded like a dirty job.

By this time in life, I began advancing in my academics and athletics. It wasn't uncommon for me to hear things like "teacher's pet" or even "coach's pet." Whenever those words were said, I'd take them in stride. They seemed to mention those phrases in good fun. At that point, I didn't feel any strain or stress, I just went out and did what I was told, and let the chips fall where they may. I wasn't really thinking outside the box, or for that matter, thinking period. I just went directly by the blueprint of what my role models told me. I bought into what they were saying and I automatically assumed that everyone around me would buy into the fact that I was buying in. I assumed the world would not do badly at you if they knew you were trying to do well. I mean, why would they even think about doing harm to innocent me? I said my prayers, worked hard, and tried to treat everyone with respect. With that formula, I knew for a fact that there was not a snowball's chance in hell that I could get any negative energy hurled my way.

So as I made it to and through high school, I realized that there were many people who saw large potential in me. In an environment where certain teachers are pulling for you, you may not get as much support from the student body as a collective. But you will discover a certain contingency of support amongst your peers that hardly ever wavers. High school is a very critical time in that students really need to be thinking about what they are going to do in the next phase of life. And even though you're still a kid, you're still feeling a little pressure to make it big; especially when many around you are overachieving. These are the years in which many things are revealed about each student. Although decision making in high school is typically not a matter of life and death, it does reveal a clear glimpse of the direction in which a person may be headed in life. It does not take a genius to figure out who is serious and who is just going through the motions. However, there is no real way to determine absolutely how someone is going to turn out in life. I must admit, this was a time where some serious relationships and bonds were built. Circles of various friends were automatically formed. Next thing you know, you are a part of a clique you never thought would ever be called an actual clique. Others begin to identify you by who you associate yourself with whether it is a group, club, or a sports team. It's like people are trying to be individuals; but there really isn't too much individuality recognized as the attention is mainly focused on whose flag you're flying. With that said, I felt the high school years were very pivotal in that serious decisions had to be made academically, athletically, and while guys are really chasing chicks and chicks are chasing guys at a high level. I had my crushes; but my main focus was books and basketball. I was somewhat of a square who really wasn't trying too hard to fit in; but I somehow did fit in. However, I was considered the odd man out because I hit the books very hard, as well as the practice floor; but I was still a rather goofy kid still trying to find his way. Although I had great experiences from many dedicated people, I also realized that there were plenty of people who really did not seem to care too much about their future. All they were concerned with was being cool, and riding the wave of those of us who were doing the work. But what shocked me the most was the fact that I ran into several students that really were not overly concerned about graduating. They just wanted to take advantage of the fun of being around peer groups which garnered lots of attention on a routine basis, and just coast along. Although I disagreed with that mindset, I embraced all of my peers as best I could.

When I arrived to college, I was in awe, not only based on the fact that I finally made it; but the level of hype and attention that permeated through the air as I walked the campus was a bit overwhelming at first. But eventually I gathered myself and was able to breathe normally as I matriculated. However, there were people, places, and things that would come into view reminding me of the fact that college life is "big time," especially when you're considered a "scholar-athlete" and knowing the babes were going to flock to wherever the hype was. I also found out very quickly that college was a time in which you could totally find yourself, or completely lose yourself. Regardless of your level of faith and upbringing, you are forced to make quick and possibly life-altering decisions when certain temptations are flaunted right before your eyes.

In the fall, every night is party night. While you're trying to stay focused, you're hearing people in the door of the suite talking about kegs, cheap liquor, and easy women, who apparently do not mind being easy. All of these things are right in front of your face on a regular basis, and you are just an unproven freshman student-athlete with the opportunity to savor the amenities of super stars. It was frightening, yet amazing at the same time.

Grownups would always allude to the fact that college was supposed to be the most fun years of your life. Of course I've grown to realize that it took a grown and mature mind to state those words and form that conclusion. Because when you are a kid who is eighteen or nineteen, you're just doing what comes naturally and not really trying to assess too much outside of what you're immediately experiencing. Young and invincible is how I felt because at that time life really hadn't had the opportunity to get in the way of anything. All's I know is that the only thing I had on my mind was excelling in the classroom, on the court, and whatever attention can be gained from the ladies while doing it, would be the icing on the cake.

Along with everything else that student athletes have to deal with on a college campus, the social activities were monstrous. They were very significant because everyone wanted to be there to see who was who and what was what…especially at the beginning of the school year. But even throughout the year, the social activities were the place to be for students. One reason behind the big enthrallment of the social activities was because on a college campus, money was no obstacle because NOBODY had any. Most student activities back then were either free, or dirt cheap to enter and participate. Everyone wanted to check out the new hotties on the yard, athletes, frats, sororities, and anyone who flexed some sort of mass appeal. Me being an athlete, I heard all of the stories from past athletes about groupies, attention, and temptation. Even though I was not swimming in that lifestyle, I saw firsthand of how easy it was to get caught up. Believe you me, there are many people still seeking to graduate today, all because of getting caught up in the allures of life as a collegian. What made it so bad, "hooking up" with somebody was nothing. If you were a young man who was ready, you could definitely find a young lady who was just as ready. If you were an athlete, you did not have to show that you were ready. Someone was there to take up the slack if you wanted them to. If you were in a fraternity, you automatically had immense pull whether you deserved it or not. Three letters meant automatic props, regardless of how shallow or materialistic it may have sounded. But man, you put those three letters on an athlete, you've got a walking, talking mass appeal machine…no questions asked. So as it was stated earlier, whether you wanted to admit it or not, attention from peers is a major part of the college life.

As I took in everything, I always remembered the things my parents and outside role models attempted to show me: work hard; be thankful; be humble. I swore up and down, in the midst of basking in the attention, I did those things. Even with the attention, things never really got out of control for me. For one, I carried too many hours per semester to even have a chance to really become deeply entrenched in the college life. Plus, during the season, basketball practice and the game schedule demanded a lot of time. But I still did what damage I could do with the limited time I had. But all the while, I never even processed anyone feeling some type of way about the attention they "assumed" that I was getting all because of what they may have seen or how the stereotype played things out in their mind. Additionally, I didn't even think about those with whom I never really had any contact. I mean, if I never had any contact with them, how could they possibly know me, or be impacted by my actions or lack thereof? How could they possibly expect me to understand something that is distant or remote to me? I never thought that I'd have to deal with "issues" caused by conjectural or indirect things. I always thought that if it is a true issue, there will be a concrete reason for the issue; therefore needing a concrete solution…at least that's what the textbook alluded to.

When the time came to prepare myself to graduate, I felt some apprehension. Although I had two prosperous internships, I did not have anything solid awaiting me as far as full time career-oriented employment was concerned, upon my graduation. This bothered me immensely. After all of the honors, awards, accolades, and connections, zero jobs, and zero prospects. In the months leading up to graduation, I had several interviews locally and abroad. But it still was the same result, "We will contact you upon something opening up for us." I called myself happy for my friends who were able to land employment immediately. I was elated that "somebody" made it. In the meantime, I was still interviewing but things were not happening at a fast enough pace for me. I was embarrassed as a national hiring freeze blanketed the entire country that summer. With that said, I decided to take an hourly job which paid just over minimum wage so that I could have some income coming in. It had gotten so bad, that I even did an interview with a local TV station that produced a segment on the difficulty college graduates were having in finding employment in their field. I received some decent exposure for it; but I also had many folks feeling sorry, gossiping, and making snide remarks about it. Then I thought, "Why would someone make snide remarks about it?" I thought we were all in this together; but I guess I was wrong. Either way, I needed to seriously find a career-oriented job so that I could escape the thoughts of being a failure in my mind; but more importantly, shut those up who had something smart to say about me being out of a job. Yeah, I know, I shouldn't have paid attention to all of the negative and messy talk, but me being the competitor I am, I had to show them that it was "game on." But I have to be honest in that I was still perplexed as to why certain people said what they said. These were folks I really did not have a direct connection to. Or maybe I had and "indirect" connection and just didn't know it. Either way, I had to act like it was not bothering me and just push on. The "manual" didn't have a chapter covering this so I just had to pray and continue trying to figure it out.

Well, after a few months, I received a call from corporation about their interest in interviewing me for an engineering job. Well, naturally, I took it. The Good Lord must have been willing because they called me back less than a week later to tell me they were going to extend an offer. Once they extended it, I accepted immediately. My family and immediate peers were happy for me. I was thankful and it was a good feeling. Certain folks at the job who knew me from the community welcomed me with open arms. They were happy to see a young brother coming in doing his thing on the engineering side. I must have been having fun as time flew like a fighter jet. I felt very stable in all facets of life. I wouldn't say I felt my career taking off, but it was certainly off to a very decent start. Things were sailing smoothly and I truly felt that I was on my way to "living the life," whatever living the life meant. But as soon as my happy plane became airborne, I hit a huge wall of turbulence. Somehow and some way, word got out about my salary (which I did not think it was that much for the time, but it was competitive nonetheless). Then suddenly, the energy changed around certain people. The hellos converted into ugly stares and silence. I thought, "Dang is it that bad? I mean, what in the world could I have done that was so wrong?" But then I began to wise up a little and understand that, with some people, it's not what you did or did not do, sometimes it is what someone else did or did not do that was not addressed when it was supposed to be. Thus displaced anger can easily take place. But I honestly did not think that far into it. I just felt strongly that it was an isolated incident and just left it alone. However the strangeness of it and the fact that I was pushed to think deeper into it, definitely stuck to me. As a matter of fact, any subsequent event that bore similar traits caused me to spin my wheels more, but in the form of researching what the root cause was. But I never really could find a logical answer. Again, this was not in the manual. In the music world at that time, I was beginning to hear the word, "hater" but I never even processed it past the song. I'd just wonder why they were using that word. I guess they had some bad experiences with certain people and that was that. For them to put it in a song, it must have been pretty major. But I never thought that I was doing anything significant enough to garner up any so-called "hate."

After I settled into my life in the corporate world, I was inspired to step my game up within the community. Now I was always involved to an extent; but this time I put the pedal to the metal and made community service an active part of my life. During this stint, I remember getting major attention from TV and radio media. Seemed like every other week there was an interview being aired on somebody's station. I was invited to be the guest speaker for many events. Memberships on several boards, committees, and leadership positions in organizations became commonplace for me. Even though I was not necessarily looking for attention...I received plenty. I called myself remaining focused on the ultimate goal...helping others while helping myself. I remained true to the values that brought me to that point. I met many, many people who were of the affluent status, as well as many folks who wanted to get there one day. I also learned over and over again, that women loved dedicated men and men seemingly in positions of power. Dates and dates with benefits (whether you anticipated any benefits at all) were not difficult to come by. The accolades and the recognitions continued to roll in as positive differences were made in the community. My job at the time even recognized what I was doing and immensely backed me when it came to community affairs. Life was not a piece of cake at the time; however, it did feel good to know that I was making a difference.

There were challenges from people within the fold as well as challenges from people who were on the receiving end of our assistance. Nonetheless, I did not expect anyone to roll out the red carpet or make things easy. However, I also did not expect major resistance from people who were supposed to have been on my team. Certain complaints were made about certain issues. So I took it upon myself to track what I thought was the issue. Low and behold, if/when I came close to resolving the issue, another one would pop up out of nowhere and take its place. Although I was perplexed, I never got discouraged. There were times when my energy waned, but it never completely dissipated. But yet and still, something was not right. Even in going through the appropriate diplomatic means of addressing the issues, it still did not feel right. No one ever told me about this "feeling," therefore it was a mystery as to how to deal with it effectively. Nonetheless, time did not stop, neither did the issues; but moving forward was a huge priority. With the way things were going, I did not have any choice but to move forward.

In the early 2000's, I was inspired to explore my artistic talents a little deeper than I did initially. Early on in grade school and through my college years, I knew I had a knack for creative writing, but never really explored it outside of school. Short stories and poetry were my thing. However, there was never really a solid platform for it to influence me to hone my skills. But upon the advent of HBO Def Poetry, myself and many other performing artists were influenced to begin writing and performing at open mic shows and anywhere there was a mic and a stage. Spoken word as an art form had clearly come back into circulation and was hot. People began incorporating it into church services, concerts, community events, and school activities. So any poet with any following was bound to have their following increase astronomically. Next thing you know, I was blessed to become published along with having spoken word cds produced. I then toured the country for many years as a featured author or poet. I became affiliated with many people local and abroad who bore the same interest as I...and that is, do everything possible to uplift creative writing and poetry, and creative opportunities in which artists could get recognized and benefit from delivering a quality product. Things were rolling and the entire movement picked up steam. Of course, the attention piled up in epic proportions. Next thing I knew, my name was in the mouth of every other person whether it was favorable or unfavorable. Regardless, I had no choice but to accept it and move on. This is another thing that no one told me to be prepared for; but after it happened, there was no more preparation, only reaction.

As I'm going about my business trying to stay focused, I noticed something else; people were giving me credit for things that I did not accomplish. I guess they just assumed if they saw my face in a particular venue. However, they were also giving me credit for negative things that I had nothing to do with. At that juncture, I couldn't help but to wonder what Hollywood actors and actresses had to go through because they are very popular for real. Oh, but it still gets deeper and more complex. As I progressed I began to notice that there were many people who wanted to become affiliated for the mere prospect of gaining popularity. Once this was realized, I would think, "Do they really know what comes with popularity? Do they think that popularity was something that I was striving for? Are they really serious about accomplishing a goal?" I would think these thoughts because I would have encounter after encounter of people "wanting to be down." And it seemed the more people I would meet, the more feelings I was suddenly responsible for. Even if the encounter was a very light and brief conversation. Everyone became super-sensitive overnight. I would think, "What in the world? Do people think that this is an easy-money cakewalk? Have people really thought about what comes with it?" I really don't think so. All they want is an end product and not deal with all of the obstacles along the way.

At any rate, through all of the clutter, I still felt like progress was being made and that I was growing in my craft while helping others grow. In using resources and connections, I was blessed to be a part of high-level movements in which artists and writers were showcased and given a platform that could provide them with the exposure and experience for serious career enhancement. So regardless of what was going on in the peanut gallery, the train was still moving and moving in a very positive direction. But still, the more I realized any type of advancement, the more I felt an undertow. There were constant whispers in my ear about "so-called" problems. However whenever I inquired about specific problems…crickets.

After talk of the first problem died down, now there's yet another problem…and a third and a fourth. I felt that people wanted me to address the problems; but I couldn't because I could not get a good read on what the problem actually was. The feeling went from eternal problems to me somehow being the catalyst of those problems. Funny thing, in growing up, when I was on a team, we always trained with an "us against them" attitude. All of what we were taught was team first and that's it. The guys in the other locker room are the bad guys. The guys in this locker room are the good guys…so I thought. When I began slowing down just to try and see things clearer, I noticed that there were not too many suspicious looking strangers. In essence, I realized that it's hard for someone to be concerned about you from a distance…whereas up close, they can see all of your tools and attributes. They know what you are capable of and know that you can rub off on them, just as they can rub off on you. See, when I was trying to find my way, no one ever said that I needed to lookout for the so-called good guys. All's they said was to be on the lookout for the known bad guys. But based on my experience, there's nothing more de-energizing than having to deal with friendly fire, but not knowing it is friendly fire until the damage from the explosion is realized. Someone is telling you about a fire just to see you scramble; but what they do not tell you is that they are the one who started the fire. Why did they start the fire? Well, initially, you're made to think you've done something wrong; but the only thing you've done wrong is being successful. And that's it.

People spend many hours shaping you and molding you to be successful; but no one tells you the truth about what comes with it. All of the isms, subjectivity, contentiousness, politics, and conjectural issues, are not in the success playbook. I can only imagine the amount of people who stopped striving simply because they were not prepared to deal with the aforementioned items. I can also only imagine the amount of people who would not strive period, because of the grim and dim expectations of the actions of others. If I knew back then what I know now, I would probably bypass my own locker room and walk straight up into an enemy's. That way, when the fire is received, it will be EXPECTED; but probably not as severe.

Now I'm not even blaming anyone for not telling me something I should have known. Heck, maybe they did not know…or maybe they did and did not know how to explain it. The blueprint can only entail so much data. However, if you want to grow and evolve, there are some things you're going to have to find out on your own. With that said, I'm proud of my upbringing and elated to have had the people in my life to shape and mold me. It was up to me to use my faith as best as possible, and handle all hurdles and obstacles. But yet and still, regardless of the outcome, I stand firm with the assessment of the fact that what they do not tell you, may fail you…hands down.

Purposefully Black

Shakeim Edmonds

"It's something that I want my brothers to adapt in the concept of their minds and that is, "Look at your failures, disappoints, disabilities and downfalls as the workouts that were created to strengthen your purpose. YOUR PURPOSE IS STRONG, therefore you as well have to be. Being born black came as a birthright, hatred came as an inheritance, poverty came as a projection but God trumped it all when he gave you a PURPOSE."

~Shakeim Edmonds

"I'm black...but I'm black, On Purpose"

"OH, LORD... OH, GOD," she bellowed, both pain and the hankering of her soul battling for dominance.

"YOU'VE GOT TO PUSH," The doctor shouts, as if to galvanize the young winsome woman to victory.

Again, she yowls with perseverance in her spirit that will not waiver, hesitate, stall or stumble. She knew/knows that there is and will be a purpose for your life and she has committed herself to ensuring that the plan of the Most High be fulfilled.

The doctor stabilizes his position and shouts once more... "PUSH!"

THE SOUL OF A MAN 2

Mercifully, there you are/were breathing, kicking and crying. Everyone is relieved. The doctor has done his job... he's allowed the results of his education and training in his specialty of the medical field to manifest so that your life could be attained. Your mother has done her job... she's long labored, sacrificed and at some points even suffered, to ensure that your opportunity be awarded. "EVERYONE" has done their job... but the inquisitive question remains, *WHAT ARE YOU GOING TO DO, BLACK MAN?*

The reality, though inevitably present, is that you had not yet had the opportunity to experience the trials and the tribulations that came with being a BLACK MAN, however... you're black... but you're BLACK, *On Purpose*, which causes major issues even in your infant state. Your adversaries didn't even know your name yet, but they knew you were a black male, and instantly that made you a threat. More importantly, the fact that you were Black, *On Purpose* gave birth to hatred, your mere existence was already being threatened and somewhere somebody was already laying the groundwork for the nonfulfillment of your purpose. The question again pops up, WHAT ARE YOU GOING TO DO, BLACK MAN? The question alone causes a war of contradiction; on one hand you bare the weight of your ancestry, heritage, and culture. Everyone that looks like you, talks like you, lives like you, or even has a genealogical connection to you, wants to know...will you rise up to the occasion of which our expectation alludes to, will the spirit of Dr. Martin Luther King Jr. reside upon you, will the zeal of President Barack Hussein Obama inhabit within you, will the perseverance of Thurgood Marshall shine through you? In silence and with a loud cry what we want to know is, WHAT ARE YOU GOING TO DO, BLACK MAN? Even as an infant, we hold steadfast to the possibilities of your life, prayers for your success and over your life never cease, because as a people we believe in you and we know you have a purpose.

On the other hand, the opposition has the same question. WHAT ARE YOU GOING TO DO, BLACK MAN? The opposition doesn't want another strong black man in power, position or authority, so they plot and compose political ensnarement's that are uniquely designed to guide you off the purposeful life you were destined to live. Within their bowels it hurts them to know that there was even a purpose for you. The opposition is fed up now with even the potential thought that you could be and become everything that God created you to be. They say Martin had his marches...Obama had his terms, Thurgood had his seat...in silence they are saying... "We will never let another black man live out his purpose, before we do...we'll shoot him dead in the street."

As time passed, each day you became older...they became more fearful. The fear was not derived from the sense of your physical being, but the adaption of your intellect. A State of Emergency was declared by the opposition in secrecy, and something had to be done. You had made it thus far, and you were heading in the direction of your purpose. Something had to be done. The first thing that was thrown at you was the deprivation of your education. Our ancestors learned to read and write, but the opposition was still on a quest to keep you from remembering and retaining. Suspension and expelled, kept you derailed from reaching your purpose, thereby preventing you from knowing your true potential. The opposition's plan seemingly started working. You were barred from the same institution that was awarded grant money to build the facility for you.

Using behavior, non-compliance, disabilities and disorders as a cover up, they snatched your education from under you. Symbolically their plan has you slipping further away from your purpose, of being purposeful. The next thing that evolves is the solidification of their plan. You as a black man are now...uneducated, which is also a direct connection to employment; you're unemployed and you're tracking right along with the plan to make you uneducated, unemployed and soon to be...unavailable. No education, no job and no view of your purpose. The streets become refuge, an unrealistic and unstable source of your livelihood. The neighborhood, in which you live, has in the shadows become identified as the battleground. Their plan has materialized and the second that they are able to slide the bars shut, is their silent moment of felicity. There is a concealed smirk when the gavel knocks, twenty to life they recite while the injustice is costumed under this process we were taught was law. It is at this point that the opposition thinks that your purpose will be buried with the freedom that they have managed to manipulate away from you. To take it a step further, there are times when the confinement of the prison cells, are not suffice. It is at these moments that your life becomes more vulnerable and fragile as ever. They replace the targets from the gun range with your black skin, discredited your credibility by using the lack of education and claiming that you have no substantial contribution to society.

Nonetheless, even though the odds against the black man have been aggressively stacked against them, many of them have still been able to accomplish their purpose and are still forging ahead with the purpose of which they were created. The beautifully ironic part about the set up to set them back is that the black men who have achieved being purposefully black, haven't abandoned their purpose.

All has not been lost. Purposefully Black, men who are fulfilling their destiny have picked up the torch and catapulted themselves through the adversities and obstacles that were strategically placed to tear them down. Look around the executive boardroom, check around the halls of Harvard, scan the Forbes 500, and you will see that we are living our purpose. At birth, the modern day Herod's wanted to kill us because they knew the heights of our achievements come. They knew that God's plan for our lives had infinite limitations. In some cases its jealousy, in some cases its envy, in some cases it's fear, but no matter the reason…they knew they did not want us to get where we are today. It's bigger than having a black president, it's bigger than having a black congressman, and it's bigger than having the best athletes, because living your purpose that God gave you is bigger than anything in this world. That's why they wanted to kill you at birth, that's why they wanted to strip you of your education, that's why they wanted to blind your vision, but they didn't do it. You made it. You made it to living out your purpose.

It's one thing that I must inform you. You were also equipped with a gift, not a talent but a gift. The most important thing to understand about the gift is, it's not about you. The purpose isn't about you, the gift God gave you isn't about you. It is now time to make an intimate connection between the gift and the purpose in order to reach the utmost capacity that God intended for your life. It sounds clique (cliché?), but the saying is true, "It you want to see change, be the change that you want to see." I write this neither as chastisement nor a declaration that we have failed as black men, because surely we have not. I write this as a degree that we won't let the people who created a blueprint for the collapse of our purpose snatch another black life from our grasp. I am not talking about bearing arms, I am talking about reaching arms. Before the officer has the opportunity to extend his arm to aim, we have to already have extended ours arms to embrace.

It is in this moment that I would like to take my opportunity to be a Purposefully Black Man. I would make an ignominy of my life if I did not take this time to do what God created me to do. The first thing I want my Purposefully Black brothers to know is, regardless to what you may have been taught, regardless to the plan of those who wanted to see you fail, regardless to what you've done, God has a gift and purpose for you; there is/was a purpose for your life. Not just the opposition, but people in general may try to tear you down, but this one thing I know to be true...there is a purpose for you. My desire is that this reaches into the prison cells, to every crack street and backstreet, into every school, college and university, congress to Compton and what I hope reaches to my black brothers is, you're black...but you're Purposely Black. From the time you breathed breath into your lungs, God had a purpose for you. There are people who will try to attempt to tell you that because of the color of your skin, because of what you've done and because of your level of education, your purpose is over. The true fact is that they see the purpose for your life and they want to steal your opportunity to see it through... yes, you are black, but you're Black, On Purpose. You're a black man with an assignment and you are here to fulfill the cause of which God created you to do. Contrary to what they want you to believe, you've got a gift. Inside of you there is something God gave you that he wants you use. Like everyone else, I love to watch Lebron, marvel at Kobe, chant for Curry because those brothers have a gift. But inside of you, you have the capacity to do something greater.

We glare at the flat screens trying to see if our favorite player is going score 50 points in four quarters and if he does, it's impressive. However, I'd like to inspire one black brother to find 50 young black men and save them from the entrapments that have been strategically placed for their failure... that would be a marvelous accomplishment. I'd like to inspire one black brother to find a felon who thinks that because of his past he is irrelevant to society and let him know that the derailments that were placed in his path did not eliminate his purpose. Will it be tougher...yes,; will his journey be longer...yes; will he have to work harder...yes; but as a purposefully black man I am compelled to let him know he is not purposeless. The time is now, no excuses can be accepted. Political America has an agenda; they are killing our dreams, killing our ambitions, killing our motivation, killing our opportunities of education which set's them up them to kill us.

Don't you find it funny that they won't educate us while on the outside of a prison wall but will provide the opportunity once we're incarcerated? From the outside it looks good, and in many cases the education is helping our brothers. However, look a little closer...you educate us while incarcerated, free us and tell us to thrive in society, but as soon as we fill out an application there is a tag on us... *Have you ever been convicted of a crime or a felony?* The question alone keeps you in prison systematically, enough though you are free, even after you've paid your debt to society. It's another plot and ploy to shelter your purpose and your destiny. I want to challenge every black man to look in the mirror and see themselves for who they truly are. You are black, but you're Purposely Black. You might be a felon which causes a hindrance but it's not an excuse. If there is not a job for you, create one. Young black brother, if they won't educate you, educate yourself, or find someone who will. We've got to keep reaching for our purpose.

We've come too far, we endured too much, to allow the opposition to take and trample the dream that was fulfilled. My personal aspiration is that we all grab the hand of another black man and walk with him into his purpose. It shouldn't matter what his past is, but as long as he has breath in his body, he's got a future. It is our personal responsibility to police each other, if we allow the system to do it, there is going to be more caskets than we can carry. We should have no issues abiding by the law, but we should have issues being buried because of the law.

Uniformed officers, who swore an oath to protect and serve, have become cold blooded killers but you won't see their faces on crime stoppers, no most wanted posters, not First 48 nor any forensic files episodes. The blue uniforms and badges have become the new camouflage for the white hoods, and the high powered pistols have replaced the high pressure water hoses…but the injustice of the black man has remained the same. To conceal the wrong, the report is that "he was reaching for a weapon" but the truth is that they saw him "reaching for his purpose." The shameful truth is, there is a new crime not listed in the law books of America; that crime is being "Purposefully Black" and if black lives matter, we've got to make these so-called lawmakers, politicians and people of America administer justice for that.

My prayer for you black man is that God's purpose for your life be fulfilled. I wish you peace and prosperity, Amen.

"Breathe and Stop"

Isaiah David Paul

"THE SOUL OF A MAN 2 will allow readers to understand that men come with complexities and identities that are unique. Everyone has their challenges and the way they strive to overcome them makes each man stronger."

~ *Isaiah David Paul*

CHAPTER ONE

How much off the top?" My barber inquired, as pieces of my hair fell from the side.

Truthfully, I resented the idea of cutting off my Mohawk. I'd grown attached to the way my hair formed a sharp peak at the top, and fell into a fade at the side. For a man in his early thirties, my hairstyle shaved off a decade in my appearance. I'd pass for a college freshman on a good day.

Whether I wanted to admit it or not, I needed to look young in order to accomplish my latest goal.

"How much?" My barber's tone was a little sharper. I didn't mean to ignore him. A plot idea for the ghostwriting project I was working on for a well-respected celebrity captivated my attention like an action packed movie. I didn't want to let it go. I hated that I couldn't write it down or pull out my iPhone and record it. Yet I didn't want to waste my barber's time either. I could see that it was standing room, and even with four barbers and two beauticians, they didn't look like they were going to get through all of the customers they had. I'd have to get back to the story later.

"I got to cut it all off," I finally answered. I looked in the mirror. My fade was sharp and all he had left to do was bulldozer over the style I had maintained for almost half a year.

"What's going on?" He turned his clippers off. I could tell he'd sensed my hesitation. The choice to obliterate my style hadn't completely been by choice. "Somebody die?"

Yeah, me, I wanted to reply. If I had my way, I'd just straighten the 'hawk.' Played with the idea of dying the peaks to match the first gray strands strategically forming at my temples.

As an artist, I was always eclectic and experimental with my self-expression. I didn't mind standing out from the crowd either.

"No one died," I answered as I inhaled the airy mint fragrance being forced out of the aerosol can being applied to the gentleman's hair who was sitting in the next chair. "I got a job interview tomorrow."

And there it was. I was officially a sellout. I'd sold my soul to chase after a job I may or may not get. Of the hundreds of applications I filled out in between writing books, this would be the first interview I'd landed all year.

"What kind of job?" The man proceeded to destroy the monument on top of my head.

I didn't want to answer the question. Admitting it was for a shirt and tie job further confirmed that I had failed as a writer. That none of the twenty-seven books credited to my name, or the other twenty I'd written or contributed to as a ghostwriter, did well enough to sustain my family on the income generated from those books alone. Ever since I was sixteen, I had at least one job while actively pursuing my literary career.

I'd studied all the great writers—and I didn't feel bad. Majority of them, even the New York Times Bestselling authors held down a 9 – 5 somewhere. Most of your medical drama and crime novelists either worked in the medical profession, were law enforcement or at one point in their "past" life might've been criminals. Being a teacher and a youth advocate helped me formulate my teen series—having a teenager I was responsible for didn't hurt either.

The goal this time was to find that *one job* that would take over the two full-time and two part-time positions I held. That *one job* that would allow me to make at least $40k a year while being the sole breadwinner for a house of three.

"You not looking to add to the collection of jobs you already got are you?" My barber knew too much of my business. And the two inch peak that once crowned my head found its new home on the floor. The little boy who looked too much like the man cutting my hair anxiously waited to sweep my remains from under my chair, adding them to the others being collected inside his square dust pan.

"Nah," I replied as I watched him dump the hair in the trash can. "It's time to consolidate."

I didn't want to make it sound like I was being ungrateful, because I knew plenty of people who wished they had one of the jobs I held. The men I worked with once they left the state or federal correctional institutes would suck their lips when I mentioned having problems at one of my jobs. The young women who held down two or three jobs of their own would tell me I needed to man up. However, I've grown tired of going to work at six o'clock in the morning, getting off at ten. Then going back to work at two in the afternoon and working until about eight. Only to have to be back to the third job an hour later that night and pray that my coworker came in on time to relieve me so I could go home at five.

Folks just don't understand but it is possible to work twenty four hours as long as you strategically aligned the shifts to where one doesn't conflict with the other. I mastered that the second year into this madness. By my fifth year, sleep and I barely knew one another. It was a luxury I couldn't afford. I barely had time for any of my other passions, like weight lifting, hanging out with friends or going to the movies.

"Yeah man," my barber agreed with me, "politics and conversation is just not the same without you."

Who is he telling? I thought to myself as he continued to shape me in the image that the masses preferred the black man to be. With the shootings of innocent black people all over the country, I wouldn't be surprised if the low cut, bald fade or going completely bald would be the only three choices we'd get. Pretty soon, we'd have to walk around with three-piece suits and winged-dress shoes just to prove we weren't a threat to the "typical American." "Yes, Massa" and "no, sir" would become required phrases of inferiority.

The maintenance of this haircut I'd have to keep up with would require that I have to wear wave caps at night to make the curls appear to grow in naturally. I would have to choose the right oil or grease to give my hair that glow. And every two weeks I'd have to carve out money and time out of my schedule to keep up with a style I could barely afford.

Once the hair was taken care of, I'd take my button up out of the closet, pull the plastic from the hanger that my pressed shirts from the dry cleaners came in. Then the big decision, was I going to tie a Windsor knot or fashion my tie into a bowtie. Either way, I'd make sure the color of my tie coordinated with my socks and if I had them, the right pair of underwear. The black slacks with black shoes would be mandatory.

After I dressed appropriately I sprayed myself with the appropriate body spray, making sure I wasn't overbearing yet subtle for those with fragrance allergies. Then I get in my old Honda Accord, fight rush-hour traffic to get to a job 25 miles away. And pray I get there early enough to get a good parking space, so I wouldn't have to walk what seemed like a quarter of mile from the edge of the parking lot to the front door.

Politics and conversation, would be checked at the door. Other than my attitude, the only outward appearance that I was a godly man would be the cross that was in the middle of my wedding band. No Post-it notes with daily scriptures for me to absorb and placed on walls or calendars throughout the day. Pretend I didn't hear the conversations bashing Obama although personally I thought that for the most part he was doing a good job. Act like I didn't get offended when an off-color racist joke casually flew from the lips of my "not racist" coworker. Then I'd have to smile and say "it's okay," once these lying jokers insisted "they weren't racist."

Yeah, at the new job, if I got it, I'd sell out. Look so much like Uncle Tom, we'd be able to question my paternity.

I guess in exchange, the perks would be worth it. Guaranteed weekends off, clock in at ten in the morning and be able to leave by seven at the latest. Health insurance, 401(k), discount at the local YMCA, just a few of the perks that neither of my jobs afforded me right now. Not to mention that if I showed how great an employee I was, I'd be able to rise into higher managerial positions. My status determined by my merit not by who I was relating to or who someone I knew was sleeping with.

Rent would be paid on time before the first, not working things out with the landlord to pay on the 10th or the 15th. I would flip on the light switch and pray that the power was still on. I'd be able to afford my own wireless internet connection, and not have to ask my neighbor for the password every time they felt the need to change it. I could get from under the title loan I'd gotten on my car again, just to tide me over.

If I got this job, everything in my life would be right. It would be nice to come home to my wife and be able to spend more quality time with her. I wanted to drive out of town to visit my children and grandchildren on a more frequent basis. I could even afford to treat them and spoil them the way it seemed like my grandparents had done me.

As my barber handed me the mirror, I looked at myself. The bald fade looked nice. No visible signs of gray. No sideburns, goatee trimmed at a respectable length. Hairline razor sharp.

I looked young again.

I gave my barber his fee and a $10 tip. That was standard for me. I pulled out the phone and looked at the time. I had thirty minutes to get to my next job. Thank God I remembered to pack a snack and a lunch because I wouldn't have time to stop at a fast food restaurant to grab something hot to eat. Before I got in my car, I can see traffic piling up. I need to get on the road. The last thing I needed was to get another write-up and possibly terminated for being late.

In fairness, I didn't outright "hate" either of my jobs. At one job, I had enough flexibility and free time to work on my books, write my music and pursue leisure time on the computer. What I didn't like was that I wasn't white, lesbian or kin to one of the supervisors to get a fair shot at a promotion.

The other job was a challenge. My boss knew my aspirations for advancement and liked to dangle it in front of me like a carrot to get me to do "extra work." I didn't complain because my coworkers gossiped so much that if I recorded their drama, I could come up with two books a day. Truthfully, I stayed busy, not because the cameras were watching, but I couldn't trust too many people. If I opened my mouth and said "hello," I'd be in the bosses' office being asked why I cursed out half of the staff. Admittedly, this was a toxic situation I prayed most about because I knew that somehow, some way, I'd have to find a way out.

THE SOUL OF A MAN 2

The third job was okay. I enjoyed the work even though it was difficult. There was always a level of danger and excitement. I never knew what I was walking into when I came to work. I loved the staff at this job because we all seemed to get along. Many of my colleagues hung out together after (or before) the shift. Even though I couldn't, we found ways to find things at work I could participate in. Of the set of employees I worked with, this set made me the most comfortable and most likely had my best interest at heart.

My last job was seasonal—closer to my dream job. One that reflected what I'd spent eight years and well over $60,000 pursuing in undergraduate and grad school. This job depended on the number of customers we had in the interim. Ironically, this job was the one I could get all three of my other jobs to revolve around. Probably the one I had to fight the hardest to get—four applications and three years to get on board. The wait was worth it and now, I'd face the battle of making it a permanent part-time job at least until I worked long enough to become full-time.

I didn't hate any of my jobs—or my employers. I hated the unfullfilment that to a degree each of them left me with. My ambition and drive didn't seem to match two of them and at this moment in time, irritated another of them. The lack of opportunity for long-term growth and expansion forced me to look elsewhere.

Between all of this, I maintained a literary career. As technology evolved, I learned to text myself portions of the book as I thought about it. I dictated scenes and dialog on my way to and from another job. My lunch breaks, if I got them, consisted of me editing books and articles on the calendar for publication. I fielded phone calls and emails between jobs and during slow leisure periods away from work. Ultimately, my business was the "job between jobs" because I worked hard to build the residual income and to come up with ways to make one of the books I had in print become more noticeable. Also, I had to figure out how I was going to reapproach one of the majors about a set of books I felt would be perfect for one of their mainstream imprints. I had yet to land an agent, but I'd learned enough since I was sixteen to handle certain things on my own.

I got out of my car, grabbed my change of clothes and my personal bag and walked into one of the jobs. Instantly, she noticed the disappearance of my Mohawk and had her twenty questions and speculations ready. She and another co-worker asked why'd I get my haircut and if I was going to a job interview soon. I hated that they knew me so well—or made up stuff they thought about me. One asked me if I was going to "finally" become supervisor. I vaguely answered questions knowing that what I'd say would get flipped into something else I didn't say that I'd be asked about later on.

Before I walked into the bathroom to change and freshen up, I looked at the clock. Amazingly, I had seven minutes to change and get into the groove of this workplace.

Superman had a telephone—I had three minutes to strip naked, wash over and wash up, dry off and change into something I typically wore at this job in the bathroom. Once I got that out of the way, I brushed my teeth, sprayed some body spray and slipped back into my tennis shoes. As I was getting myself together for a very short shift before I headed back to my other job for the night, I noticed a packet of pills fell out of my travel bag. I recognized the pills as being one of the gag gifts the job down the street had given me. I smirked as I realized my co-workers there were telling me to relax again.

The phone buzzed on the sink and I saw that my ghostwriting client was sending me a few notes for the changes they wanted in the book I had finalized for them in two days. I'd wished they'd given me the whole book, but they only wanted me to write a few chapters and to redo the dialogue for a particular subplot. I nodded my head as I scanned the numerous text and stored the instructions in the back of my mind.

Quickly, I refocused on the job at hand and I picked up the pills and tucked them at the bottom of my travel bag, which was going back to my car. I looked in the mirror and was satisfied with my presentation. After ensuring I had all of my belongings, I hurried out of the bathroom and flew back to my car. I had about 90 seconds to secure everything and clock in so I could start my day at this job.

I made it back in 45 and after my identification was accepted, I eased to the back of the growing crowd around my desk. The floor boss was giving an update and I caught his subtle pause to make eye contact with me.

I was good.

CHAPTER TWO

"Jay!" I could hear the woman frantically calling out my name. Yet my eyes were closed. I didn't quite remember where I was but I did remember I was struggling to get up. My eyes seemed like they have been shut with superglue. "Jay!"

My body rocked back and forth like I was sitting in the middle of a boat going exceedingly fast downstream. I looked around for the paddles and found nothing inside. My fishing pole had become the victim to a school of fish that stole the bait and dragged the hook attached pole up the stream. How I let that happen had to be anybody's guess.

"Jay!" My name exaggerated as the violent shaking continued.

An eye popped open and I could barely see. I brought my hands to my eyes and rubbed them. I wasn't in the middle of the boat caught in the middle of a fast running stream. I was on the right side of the bed I barely slept in.

I could hear Issac Caree and Mary Mary glorifying the Lord on two different devices. Some may call it confusion, but for me, that's how I wake up.

"Jay!!!" My wife yelled so loud I thought my eardrums are going to pop.

"Yo, I'm up!" I yelled as I struggle to lift my body off the mattress. It had been days since I slept in my own bed. "I'm up!" I yelled again.

THE SOUL OF A MAN 2

My bare feet hit the floor and I looked down to find where my pants ended up. I rubbed my eyes and then when I looked down again, I found the black and red striped pajama pants crumpled up at the foot of the bed. I quickly put them on and underneath found the black T-shirt I had worn too.

My phone was still replying, "Go Get It," and I swiped the touchscreen to the right so the song would go off. I looked at the clock. I needed to go get ready for the interview I had in about two hours.

I have been called back for a third interview for a supervisor position I had been pursuing for the last six months. This was the fourth time I'd applied for the same position in the last 15 months. The second application I had interviewed for.

I probably should've had Littlejohn and the Eastside Boys playing in the background instead so I could get crunk. Nevertheless, I walked across my thick, plush light brown carpet to the bathroom and turned the shower on so that it warmed up. I walked back to my closet and pulled out another starch dress shirt and some black slacks and lay them across the bed. I found a nice blue and black tie, then walk to my dresser drawer and was glad when I saw that I actually had an undershirt and underwear that matched the dark color of my time. I wasn't superstitious but always believed that the color should match from top to bottom inside and out.

Let my grandmother tell it, I should always be caught dead in a clean pair of drawls. For me, it was a slight rebellion against the white undershirt and or underwear I've been forced to wear since I was three. I was on my own now to pick whatever colors I wanted.

Satisfied with my selection, I got my pajamas and walked straight into the bathroom. The minute I hit the shower curtain, I could hear my wife yell something inaudible. I cursed myself, not wanting to break my stride or to go see what she wanted. I had half a mind to step into the shower anyway in between my daily cleansing, but I didn't want any drama.

So I turned around walked out of the bathroom, "yeah." I was hostage to make sure there was no agitation in my voice. I hated starting something and then having to stop, to address anything I wasn't doing at the time.

"What would you like for breakfast?" She asked.

I appreciate the fact that she thought of me. "A few slices of turkey bacon, a bowl of fruit would be fine."

I cut up watermelon, cantaloupe, and honeydew melon during one of my off breaks the day before. It would've been faster for me to buy everything precut and pre-sliced; I couldn't afford the luxury.

After answering her inquiry, I returned to the bathroom. The water was warm enough and I stepped in ready for the heat and the stain to relax my body. Unlike the bird bath I took at my job the day before, I'd be able to loosen up a little. I grabbed my wife's lavender body wash squirted a little on my towel. The flowery scent allowed me to ease my mind and think of nothing as a scrubbed my body.

Now I wish I had someone to massage me as soothing music played in the background. There I was laying on top of a mat getting my back rubbed and my face pressed. The tension leaving my body and the only thought I had was the chapter I was working on while recording on my phone on my way to work. The daydream gave away quickly and I tried not to get frustrated thinking about the luxuries I couldn't afford. As I rubbed the towel across my stomach I prayed to God I wasn't developing with my friend called "Dunlap's disease." The Freshmen 15 were more like the Freshmen 50. I walked into undergrad shaped like the Wimpy Kid, I walked out looking like I could've carried my ex-girlfriend's baby.

I missed exercise. Lifting weights allowed me to take my aggression, anger, and other life ills on the barbells and not catch an assault charge. I doubt that if I didn't get this job, I'd be able to return to the gym and get my body back.

Turning off the shower, I stood in the fragrance and steam again. The water rolling off my body took the nervousness away. I didn't just want to ace this interview, I wanted the job. It wasn't a dream job, but it would allow me to get rid of one of my unfulfilling full-time jobs and minimize the time spent at both part-time jobs. This position looked better on both my resume and my LinkedIn profile.

I picked up my iPhone and touched my recorder app. An idea had just come to mind that I wanted to fix after I did my job interview. Once I confirmed that the application was on, I started speaking as if I were addressing a meeting in a conference room. As the words flowed from my lips, I quickly dried my body, threw the towel in the hamper and reach for my foot spray. I wanted my feet to be cool and the harsh, mentholated smell jolted my nose. In an instant, my mind woke up, and I got dressed with a sense of urgency. The pacing of my voice changed as I felt like I was rushing to get my idea out. I made sure to lightly apply the body spray to my skin and my clothes. I wanted the fragrance strong enough to be inhaled but not overbearing to leave a bad impression.

❧❧❧❧❧

My LinkedIn profile. My mind wandered as a raced to the iPad sitting on the dresser next to the bed.

I was doing it again. Obsessing about what someone may or may not have connected me to my social media profiles. Of all the ones I had, my LinkedIn profile should've been the safest. No one could post pictures of me casually drinking hard alcohol with my friends. Nor could they ask me to confirm or deny whether that was me they saw pleasuring the woman I didn't marry on a sex tape. Those two blackmail pieces would haunt me forever.

Distracted from the story I was working on, I turned my recorder off. I would have to connect it to my iPad and let it dictate to the ghostwriting file on my break.

I looked over my profile. The picture of me in a side profile, black leather jacket over a red and white striped button up. It was one of very few pictures I'd posted publicly aside from the ones that appeared for the book signings I participated in or the literary events I attended. I read the details in my profile quickly and decided I didn't leave anything out. I was pleased with my work accomplishments and was ready to head into the interview and settle into a life with my future employer.

THE SOUL OF A MAN 2

CHAPTER THREE

I barely made it to the interview on time. Traffic was atrocious, and the only reason I didn't have road rage was because I remembered to turn on the recorder on my iPad and continued to narrate the story from where I had left off in the shower. In between my story, I reminded myself to incorporate the idea that my client had requested.

Balancing my literary career and my "jobs" was the only way I could do this double life I'd grown accustomed to. The frustrations I couldn't go into and vent at in my jobs came out in my books or those for my clients in one way or another. Not always violently, but the release seemed to keep me from going ape when things didn't go right. I always remembered I had my writing to get back to.

I got in the door for the prospective job about five minutes early.A short, brown-haired lady eyed me above the rim of her glasses. A smile formed on her lips.

"Mr. Imes," she addressed me by my government. Very few people outside of my classroom addressed me as mister. Took me by surprise. "Kendall will be with you shortly. Have a seat and enjoy a refreshment, if you'd like."

Kendall was not the lady I'd interviewed with at my last interview with this company. My last interview was with an older lady who'd been my supervisor for a few months before she accepted a different position. I hadn't heard from her in a while so I didn't know if she retired, moved up or moved on.

I eyed the small bowl of prepackaged nuts and took one. I also grabbed a few of the mints that were next to it.

By the time in I finished my refreshment, a tall, slender and youthful woman opened the door. A small portly man nestled a black portfolio under his arm as he left the office. I noticed he didn't shake her hand or say goodbye.

I didn't assume anything one way or another so I waited until she turned her attention on me. Her smile revealed bright white teeth. "Mr. Imes, this way," she welcomed me with her hand extended.

I got up and made sure no salt had made it onto my outfit. I felt the mint getting smaller as I swiftly swirled it under my tongue.

"Ms. Alexander," I shook her hand and noticed how firm her grip was. I looked in her eyes and saw warmth.

I dared not travel lower than her neckline because I had a wife at home. Even if I didn't, I'm about my money. Business over pleasure.

We walked into her office and I got a whiff of the cheap cologne the guy before me had on. I tried to sneak a cough.

"Welcome to Alexander Jasper, Inc," Ms. Alexander invited me to take a seat. "And please, call me Kendall."

"Okay," I smiled as I followed her directions.

Lowering my body into the chair, I noticed the seat sunk in a few inches. I tried not to make the descent noticeable.

"You know what we do here?" Kendall asked as she moved my resume up to the front.

This was my time to shine, I thought. Before I could get a word out of my mouth, Kendall continued. "I looked at your LinkedIn profile and I did not see any relatable experience there."

Oh God. I tried not to panic. I was losing the battle before I could get a word in. In the few seconds she had looked over my profile, she probably decided her screeners had made a wrong decision in giving me the interview.

"My profile is a work in progress," I admitted. Who knew being slow to maintain my profile would be used against me in an interview? "I will be mindful of making the updates after the interview."

"Go ahead and do it now," Kendall had leaned forward and then back in her chair. She looked over to her left and pulled out an iPad that was encased with the OtterBox protective covering. "While you get that done, we'll continue our interview."

I'd never experienced that before. I knew then she was testing me. She asked me general business questions I was ready for as I figured out which work experience I'd add or modify.

"What other goals and hobbies do you have?" She asked as I started to hand the iPad back to her.

Should I put them on my profile or nah? A part of me started to ask for the iPad back, but I knew I would risk presenting myself as unprepared.

"Reading, writing, playing Phase 10 and monopoly." I gave my standard answers. I wish I could add working out, playing tennis and jogging to the list. Those were things I hadn't done since high school. Hobbies I missed.

"What do you write?" She asked.

In the back of my mind, I wondered if she discovered which books I wrote. *The safe answer*, I reprimanded myself before I answered, "I write young adults and for myself mainly."

"So the Jarold Imes books are yours?" she inquired as she pulled out a copy of *Worth Fighting 4*.

My eyes wanted to bug out like I was a cartoon character, but I kept my cool.

"Yes."

"I'm on page 60…I love this book so far; how much of it is true?"

Yeah, definitely not like any of the interviews I'd been to before. I'd made it a policy to only reveal that I wrote books *after* I got the job. I'd found that mentioning I was a business owner and any relative experience concerning building my literary brand almost assured me, an instant rejection letter. Not even jobs dealing with youth would give my application a second look. When I reapplied to some of those same jobs without mentioning the books, I got interviews with half of them.

"I'd say about 40 percent of it is true or things I've witnessed."

"It's good to have a well-rounded candidate that can do other things besides light nursing assistant work. I know you've been in the field for almost ten years, and this would be your first supervisor position right? At least the title would match some of the work you've done?"

"Yes," I answered honestly. The reminder made me feel like a failure. It was like I was always the groomsman, never the groom. Upward mobility and career advancement were goals I thought everyone shared, but as I stayed in this field, I found that not to be true. Contentment, drama, and mess seemed to make taking care of those in need take a backseat.

"Have you pursued management positions with your previous employers?" She asked as she scanned my resume again.

"Yes," I answered as I reflected. At one of my jobs, I'd been passed over for various positions at least fifteen times. And as many times as I said I was going to quit, I'd keep applying. Somehow believing that one day a "no" would turn into a "yes." At another job, I'd keep getting promised a "fair chance" to pursue the position, but every time it was "time to start," something would happen and the position would be on "freeze." More lies. One of my other jobs was at least honest enough to say it would not happen in the foreseeable future but offered me the opportunity to work with management to develop skills needed should the opportunity arrive.

The lack of hope—I liked that answer the best because at least it was true. And as for the fourth job, I knew I didn't have the education or experience yet and that normally, one would have to be in the field at least ten years before some serious consideration was given. I was on year two so I had time to get the education at least.

Kendall pointed to one of the jobs listed on my resume, "As you know, we're similar to this job, but our houses are smaller. You would be managing a team of nine on rotating shifts with another supervisor and the house manager, who would be your direct supervisor. You would be expected to give up the full-time position here," as she pointed to another job, "should you be offered the position and accept. And the other jobs would have to be kept to ten hours a week maximum between the two. You would be expected to work ten to fifteen hours of overtime each week, and you would be on-call two days a week in case someone called out."

I expected this. At least I got an outline of the expectations of the job. I prayed this was a good sign.

"What time do you have to be at your next job?" She inquired as she moved her phone to the center, sent a call to voicemail and checked the time.

"In about two hours," I answered hoping it wasn't a trick question.

"Well, if you don't mind, I want to talk to you about another position we haven't posted yet."

Whoa!!! That caught my attention. I wasn't asleep, but if I was, I was definitely awake now.

"Another position, I'm interested," I hoped that had come off as *I'm interested in your company* and not, *I'll take any position you offer.*

"We would like for you to come on staff with us as a regular nurse's assistant if you aren't offered the supervisor position. It would give you time to get to know some of our people better and get used to our culture. We're in the process of taking over another managed care organization in the next two months and you would be groomed to take over a house there. With your background and education, we could even consider you for an administrative position once the merger was complete."

Here we were—the dangled carrot. The "if you take a lower position now, we promise to make you a supervisor at a later time." I'd fallen for that trick twice in my youth. Came to work, did everything I could think humanly possible above and beyond the call of duty, only not to get the promised job because I wasn't white or lesbian.

"That would be something to consider." I didn't feel like lying. No need in getting my hopes up for another pipe dream. I'd fallen for too many of them to take this one seriously.

"Well, we want to thank you for coming in," Kendall stood up and extended her hand. I remembered the guy before and I made sure to give her a firm handshake.

"Thank you for having me." I extended the courtesy.

She reached the edge of the table and took her business card and handed it to me. "We'd really like to have you. Please consider our offer to join the team."

I smiled and I waited on her to step around her desk and we walked out together. I put her card in my shirt pocket.

When we left, we made small talk about the business and she wished me well on my journey to my other job. The older lady who I met when I came in was assisting another candidate for the position. I recognized her, we both had to be at work in almost an hour and a half. We smiled at one another as I made my exit.

CHAPTER FOUR

I remembered to send Kendall a thank you card and I confirmed that I would consider joining the team as a nurse's aide.

Two days later, my coworker who'd gone to the interview the same day and time let me know she hadn't gotten the position. Admittedly, she would've been good. She had told me earlier that she wasn't going to take the regular nurse's aide position.

While on my break and finalizing the ghostwriting project I was working on, I got a call from Kendall on my phone. I said a short prayer in hopes that I wouldn't get the same news and offer my co-worker got.

"Hey Jay," she was informal which helped me loosen up a bit. I made sure I was in a corner away from the people I was serving so that I could have some level of privacy.

"Hi Kendall, I pray all is well," I replied.

"It is. I just wanted to tell you personally that we did go with another candidate for the position, but we did want to let you know that the offer for the nurse's aide position still stands. If you want to start out part-time as needed with us, that's fine."

So there it was—I didn't get the job. No staff to lead, no networking opportunities and I'd still have to work almost one hundred hours a week to make ends meet for a little while longer.

"Thank you for the opportunity to interview with you," I put on the brightest smile I could and hoped she could hear the happiness in my voice. "I pray things go well for you and the new supervisor."

"Me too," a pregnant pause. "By the way, thank you for the card. You were the only one that sent me one. I really hope you get the position you are pursuing one day and don't give up. It will happen for you."

"I believe it will," I thought my face was straight.

"I will let you go and let me know if you are interested in the position. I'll give you another day or two and we'll go from there."

"Okay, I will," I replied and I heard her hang up the phone.

I didn't have time to reflect on what I'd done wrong or what was wrong with me. I wouldn't find out for another week or two who got the position. I always found out. I'd only prayed that it wasn't something I'd done, hadn't done or said that cost me the spot. These days, I never knew.

I pressed the recorder tab on my phone and got a few quick ideas before I returned the work. As I spoke my mind and re-read some of the pieces I worked on, I wondered what it would take for me to make about $40k a year from writing. Back when I was growing into a well respected young adult author, I got a few thousand for speaking to teens, but I often reinvested that money back into marketing the Jarold Imes name—and gave away books to teens who couldn't afford to buy the books.

I wondered if I could ask my ghostwriting client for more work—or even more boldly if they knew someone else who could benefit from my services. And that's where I was at now.

I couldn't let the fact that I cut off my Mohawk for "nothing" go to waste. I'd grown tired of going to interview after interview after interview and not landing the position. Maybe the answer wasn't in pursuing another management position or another position period. It was possible that my answer was in starting my own business.

I had a little know-how when it came to managed care organizations, but I didn't know if I wanted that to be the non-profit I'd start. I was learning how to write grants and had read that I could become a grant writer. Squeezing in the classes and paying for them seemed to be a punch in the gut too.

Before I could think anymore, one of the person's I was serving was calling my name. Reminding me that I was at work and that I needed to serve them. I answered and put my phone away so I could care for their need.

I followed them to their room and once we got inside, I closed the door and took a deep breath. I had to pretend I wasn't disappointed that I didn't get the job and figure out if I was going to let my Mohawk grow back out or not. Next, I had to help the person being served run one of their programs. And try to remember a modification to a subplot I wanted to present to the client in case they asked for it.

Until then, I'd master the craft of acting and praying that one day, I'd see God's purpose for my life fully manifests in me.

Finding the Courage to Own My Place on the World's Stage

Cyrus Webb

"An anthology like Soul of a Man reminds us all that everyone has a story that deserves to be told. We all matter." ~ Cyrus Webb

T wo of my favorite quotes that have been guiding forces in my life have come from William Shakespeare. The first is "All the world's a stage," and the second is "To thine own self-be true."

As I look back over the past 40 years of my existence—the highs and the lows—I have come to understand that by appreciating my truth and playing my part in the world honestly have served me best, and it is these things that I hope will be the makings of my legacy.

The truth is that all of us know what it's like to experience trouble. Sometimes it is brought on just by living life and being in the world that is less about others and more about itself. In other cases, the troubles we face and the adversity we experience have to do with ourselves: learning and growing and reaping the results of the bad choices we have made and the course we have taken.

I believe, however, that success can be found regardless of where the root of the adversity comes from. It just depends on what you choose to do when it comes to pursuing it. The life I have been blessed to enjoy at this point is one that may have seemed unlikely to many—even at times to myself. I tell people that I was born at just the right time in just the right place to be just the person I was meant to be, yet none of my early years, in my opinion, gave any clue to the person I would become.

Some look at the Cyrus Webb (or C. A. Webb) of today: radio and television personality; Editor-In-Chief of a magazine; president of a co-ed book club; publicist to over a half dozen clients; brand consultant and Top Amazon Reviewer---and they make assumptions that are not always based on facts. Many have no idea that when I was born in Mississippi of all places some 40 years ago that no one would have dreamed that this would be the life I would enjoy.

The oldest of two born to a single mother, hard work was always encouraged. Even before my step-father joined the family when I was just 5 years old, I knew that nothing was going to come easy for me. I was going to have to work for each and everything I wanted. I was raised primarily under the care of my grandmother, a woman that would be my biggest inspiration and cheerleader until her death in May 2014—and I grew up to believe that anything for me was possible if I was willing to do the work. She and the rest of my family could have never imagined I would be presented the opportunities I have been, but they always made me feel as though nothing was off the table. They believed in me, at times even more than I believed in myself.

THE SOUL OF A MAN 2

You see I was an awkward child. My father had a speech impediment, and though I didn't know a great deal about him, it was one of those things I also inherited. This made me withdraw into myself, not wanting to encourage the taunts that sometimes children can hurl at one another. Books were my refuge. I studied hard, and I was fortunate enough to have teachers that saw this and took an interest in me.

One Caucasian teacher that I had in elementary school saw something in me and took it upon herself to work with me after school to help me with my speech. That was the beginning of my understanding that your present situation doesn't have to dictate your future. She helped me learn how to take my time and focus on the words I was seeing and speaking. She, in many ways, changed the trajectory of my life.

After that words took on a new meaning for me. I began to realize their power. Sure I sounded different. Some would say I was trying to "talk white" or "act white". That used to bother me until I realized that what they were saying (whether they realized it or not) was that one race had the monopoly on speaking, dressing and conducting themselves well. I didn't believe that, and so I learned early on not to let those things bother me.

I found a certain amount of strength, but I was still a black man living in Mississippi, and not everyone believed as my family did when it came to my being able to truly be successful regardless of my race and where I lived. I would hear things on television or read things that would make me feel as though I was inferior. Though I excelled publicly, there were insecurities that surfaced in me that would haunt me for quite some time.

The arts were and have always been a saving grace for me. I discovered my love of drawing and writing very early in life, and it seems as though I was the most alive when I could immerse myself in that world. I was told, however, that although I was good I would have to find a "real job." Even my family who loved me told me that I would never be able to "make it" doing just art. I would have to pursue another course and just do that art on the side.

Things were different then. Though I don't feel as though the arts have the respect they deserve today, it was a lot worse some 20 years ago. Here I was this kid who really didn't like anything else. My brother was the most athletic one. I played in the band and excelled in art, but here I was being told that this would not be enough. What I heard was that who I was and what I was (a creative) wouldn't be enough.

Thoughts of suicide began to plague me as early as the age of 15 and would linger for the next 5 years. Others didn't understand why I was unhappy, and the truth was that it was all in my mind. I allowed outside forces to seep into my consciousness and poison the possibilities that I was brought up believing were there for me.

It wasn't until a suicide attempt at the age of 20 that I came to better understand that my life had a purpose. I was here for a purpose, and it wasn't about me. I was simply a vessel. Today when I visit schools or do speaking engagements I share that with others because it was an important "act" in the play that is my life. Those feelings of despair and doubt I came to realize were from the Enemy. Not God. Not those who loved and cared for me. By listening to them I was giving them power, and I swore to never allow that to happen again.

Does that mean that the next 20 years of my life would be perfect? Not at all, but I learned that to be true to myself meant that I had to accept who I was and realize what I had to bring to the world. This became clear to me again in 2005 when I left my career as a General Manager of a hotel chain in Mississippi and decided it was time to pursue what I saw as my true calling in life full-time. At that time, I had been hosting a local radio show called Conversations with Cyrus Webb since 2003 and a television show on our ABC affiliate by the same name since 2004. Those two things coupled with the art shows, poetry readings, and speaking engagements were where I felt the most alive, and it seemed that my "real job" was in the way.

My family didn't understand the decision. To them, I had it easy: free rent at the hotel, a company car, and very little personal responsibility. I realize now that they saw where I was as a safe place. What I knew, however, was that it was also a prison. As long as I was content doing for someone else, my goals and dreams couldn't be fully realized. It was a gamble for sure, but it was one I was willing to take. Stepping out on faith I made the leap, and though the first few years were difficult, I saw it as necessary if I was going to truly get to where I was supposed to be.

By 2006, I was interviewing so many interesting people that I wanted another platform to showcase their stories. I began Conversations Magazine that year, profiling mostly wordsmiths and visual artists. I realized that the gift of words I had been given could be used to touch the world in other ways, so I began to blog and even posting reviews of music and books that I enjoyed. It was that year that I had another experience that would completely change my life.

I had interviewed a certain author on my radio program and happened to see in our state newspaper that a book club in Jackson, MS was going to be discussing the book the author and I had conversed about on the air. Wanting to share with other readers and network with them, I attended the meeting. It wasn't until I got there that I realized that the reading group was all women.

I was greeted with some curious looks, and though they were cordial, I knew something was off. Afterward I asked what book they were discussing the following month, and after telling me the title the book club president quickly followed up the comment by telling me that I couldn't come. When I asked why, I was told that attending two meetings qualified individuals to be members, and they didn't allow men as members.

To say I was confused is an understatement. We hear all the time that men don't engage, that men don't participate in conversations---yet here was a group that made it a part of their existence to exclude men from their discussions! I began looking for other reading groups in the Central Mississippi area, and it was at that point that I realized something that had never occurred to me before: NONE of the book clubs in the 7 cities around me had male members.

I knew that men read. I talked with men all the time about books, but it never occurred to me that there wasn't a place where men could come together and discuss books. Since it didn't exist, I decided to create the opportunity. In Nov. 2006, Conversations Book Club was formed with three members: my good friend Stanley Clark, librarian; Laura Turner and myself. Word got out about the group and soon we began to grow. To date, we have had hundreds of men and women of all ages and races attend our free meetings in Mississippi, Louisiana, and Tennessee, and we have hosted over 200 authors over the past 8 years, either in person or through conference calls with the group.

Like anything else there have been growing pains, but never enough to make me want to quit. Conversations BC has become all about partnerships, and through those partnerships we have done things that others have never thought possible.

One of the best partnerships that came out of the work I have been able to do the radio show, television show, and the book club was with Platinum-selling recording artist and bestselling author C-Murder. Not growing up a big fan of rap, I had only heard about C-Murder as an artist. I wasn't really familiar enough with him, but in 2007 that all changed. I was introduced to his book DEATH AROUND THE CORNER (published by Vibe) and was amazed at his literary skills. As is my custom when I read a great book or hear about something of interest, I like to share the experience. I looked for ways to connect with Cee, and it was at that point that I realized he was on house arrest in New Orleans. Knowing that he probably knew LESS about me than I did about him, I emailed him one day, telling him that I read his book and would like to discuss it with our reading group and have him join us by conference call. He responded back in less than 3 days with a yes.

Now, I knew I had a real opportunity here to not just attract readers who would appreciate his gritty novel with a surprising supernatural twist but other artists as well. I began to reach out to the press, letting them know that we would have C-Murder join us via conference call at the Medgar Evers Library and that the public was invited to participate. I made flyers and had them shared at clubs. The response was overwhelming. Not only did we have a great discussion, but Cee was so impressed by the work I had put into it in spite of his circumstances that we kept in touch.

Months later I had an idea: I wanted him to come to Mississippi and meet his fans there. He was excited about it but told me it might not be possible considering his legal predicament. In my opinion, that was just another opportunity. I connected with his lawyer and wrote a letter to the judge stating I wanted permission to have C-Murder visit our reading group and audience in the state. I stated that he would be in my care, and I would be responsible for him during the three-day visit. I mapped out schools, bookstores, and events for him to be able to meet his fans and discuss his book. It was a long shot, but I knew that the only way it definitely wouldn't happen is if I didn't try.

Less than a week after my letter I got the ok. C-Murder came to Mississippi in October 2007, and our unlikely alliance was formed. His fans went crazy. The press—both local and national—ran stories on the event, but most of all it showed a side of the gangsta rapper that few had expected.

I learned so much from C-Murder. I learned that you should never judge a book by its cover. Though we looked so different and had different backgrounds, we were connected by our passion for what we loved. It was that passion that allowed us to come together and promote reading, encourage audiences and gain some real satisfaction by doing so. After the visit, we formed a chapter of Conversations in New Orleans together, and during our first meeting we had just as many men attend as we did women.

That alliance with C-Murder—and my showing that I am no respect of persons—continues to open doors for me today. People know that I come to them with no judgment or no perceived notion that I am any better than them. I come to them as a fellow work in progress.

The success I enjoy when it comes to Conversations the brand is really built on the principle of respect. I go into every interview and discussion with the goal of allowing my guest to be really heard. It's not about me. I prepare in such a way that I can allow them to shine and be the best of themselves. That is what people see, hear and read when it comes to our conversations. That is what the guest feels afterward. That is my purpose.

Today as I continue to build my brand, I continue to focus on the power of words, especially with the increase of power through social networks. I made a conscious decision back in 2009 that regardless of what the situation I was not going to use my power with words for anything but building others up. We are bombarded daily with messages of darkness, and it all begins with words. People feel as though they have the right to say anything, not realizing the consequences of those words or the lasting impact they can have.

My life has shown me that what you choose to dwell on becomes a part of who you are, so I choose to dwell on the good. That is a choice we all can make. Regardless of where we come from or what we are going through, we can make the choice to use our truth to make the world a better place.

Remember that quote from Shakespeare: "All the world's a stage"? In Devon Franklin's book PRODUCED BY FAITH, he helped me to appreciate those words in a deeper way. He writes in that book that the world is like one big movie, and our success in our "role" while here is all about who we choose to allow to "direct" us. If we take our direction from the world, we will believe what it says about us as well as what the limitations are on what we can do and who we can become. If we allow our Creator to guide us through and follow the "script" He has shared through His word, there is nothing that can come our way that is impossible to overcome.

As I think about what it means to be a man that is what I truly believe is the answer: to walk in your truth, fulfill your destiny and remind people through your actions that they can do the same. That is the essence of my existence, and that is what I choose to focus on as I walk the stage of life every day.

What Fathers Should Teach Their Boys

Brian Ganges

"The Soul of a Man 2 anthology is a tool to help re-write the narrative of black men. While we are not a monolithic people (as no group of people is), we have been mis-characterized and stereotyped in a negative light for far too long. These stories are an extension of who we are, and many people will be able to relate to our experiences. The Soul of a Man 2 gives a candid look into our souls, and each entry tells the true story and perspective of positive men of color." ~ *Brian Ganges*

I t was the summer of 1992, and racial tensions were high in America because of the acquittal of police officers on trial regarding a videotaped and widely covered incident of police brutality against Rodney King. The system couldn't tell me what I didn't see with my own eyes. They beat that unarmed man (who surrendered and posed no visible or assumed threat) to a bloody pulp, and the system lets those cops off. But at what cost? And what was the other message that the criminal justice system sent to America? The 8th Amendment to the Constitution states that "cruel and unusual punishments [shall not be] inflicted." But what I saw in that video was an egregious form of cruel and unusual punishment, and no one was held accountable. I guess everything was supposed to be square because the City of Los Angeles awarded Rodney King $3.8 million in damages for the attack.

That same summer, after a long day at summer school and work, I decided to drive home one evening to see my folks. From Durham, North Carolina to Trenton, New Jersey was about a seven-hour drive. I was tired from being awake for approximately sixteen hours already, but since I made the drive a bunch of times, I'd figured I'd make the trip with ease. I blasted my music and kept my windows rolled down for approximately six hours to help me stay awake, and it worked until I arrived in Bucks County, Pennsylvania. I figured I was close enough to home that I could make it without that cool air blowing in my face, so I rolled up my car window, fell asleep, and ran off the road.

I awakened to the most terrifying few minutes that I've ever experienced, as I was moving in a car that I couldn't control. I slammed on the brakes. I turned the wheel. But the car continued to follow its course of momentum. Suddenly, I hit something that made a loud "thud," and the car finally came to a stop. I exited the car without a scratch, but my car was a mess. There was no way that car could drive after that episode. So I flagged down some help and soon after my Dad and a Pennsylvania State Trooper arrived on the scene.

My Dad saw that I wasn't harmed, so he was calm, but we still had to go through a period of questioning so the officer could fill out the report. The officer was very cold and uninviting like he had a chip on his shoulder. He was about 5'8" and I assume he had military experience based upon his haircut and his demeanor. I sensed his callous attitude and it set something off inside of me; and while I didn't get belligerent with him, my attitude shifted from my usual calm self to that of a more militant black mentality. I was a product of the 80's and a lot of black youth (including me) took Rodney

THE SOUL OF A MAN 2

King's beating personally. The hip-hop culture that we embraced also absorbed the gangsta rap "F the Police" sentiment and a super-producer like Dr. Dre of N.W.A. created a lot of street beats (along with lyrics by Ice-Cube and Eazy-E) that resonated with my generation. "Boyz N the Hood" was my favorite movie, and again, the themes of crime, thug life, hating the cops, and disrespect were repeated throughout the movie and many of the popular songs of that day. Although I wasn't raised to behave in an unlawful and disrespectful manner, the media and gangsta rap culture were big and negative influences in some of my behaviors outside of my parents' view; and this cop was about to find that out.

Looking back at this time in my life, I can honestly say that I was somewhat radicalized. I don't mean that I was a terrorist, but I was influenced to embrace some extreme beliefs. I really didn't hate anyone, and I wasn't a racist, but I was confused and definitely more in tuned to black vs. white more than anything. Being black and my identity with my blackness was the most important thing to me at that time, and some white man with a badge wasn't about to chump me. Personally, this was about respect, because for too long, white people have hated and disrespected us. Black people didn't ask to come here, and my people have suffered from the white man's boot on our necks for too long. For a few minutes, in my mind, it was like the trooper was representing white people, and I was representing black people, and the lyrics from "Straight Outta Compton" rose up in me:

Don't make me act the mother@uckin fool

Me you can go toe-to-toe, no maybe

I'm knockin nigg@& out tha box, daily

217

MAKE ME WANNA HOLLER

Yo weekly, monthly and yearly

I was down! I was ready to go! This officer was about to set off a time bomb if he said the wrong thing, looked at me funny or disrespected me in any way. In my mind, it was going to be on!

In a cold, monotone, and matter-of-fact voice the officer asked, "May I see your driver's license, please?" This guy had the personality of a shoehorn. Maybe that was his natural demeanor, but he was definitely not equipped to deal with the public. I gave him the license. He looked at it and wrote something on a piece of paper. A minute or so later, I asked him for my license back with a brazen attitude. He halfway looked at me, brushed me off, and said, "I'll give you your license back when I'm through with it." Then he turned, and went back to the police car to do some more paperwork.

I was so frustrated and angry that I was about to bust, so my Dad pulled me to the side and said, "You need to be cool. This dude is looking for a reason. Don't give him a reason." To myself, I said, "Tell that cracker to bring it." I was so angry, confused, and out-of-control during this time of my life. I had an angry look on my face and again, my Dad said, "Just be cool."

The officer returned and issued me a ticket and told me a bunch of other things that I totally ignored. He spoke and I looked the other way while he said whatever it was he had to tell me. He handed me the ticket and my license, I took them, and we all went our separate ways. I definitely respected my Dad as an authority and father, because something about our relationship and the respect I had (and still have) for him allowed his calm and resolve to influence me in a crucial moment.

There were many things that I learned that day; in fact, I'm still learning from that experience. I can't say for sure which was the most important or the most invaluable lesson, but I did learn a lot of profound things that all men should be teaching their sons; and although my Dad didn't necessarily sit me down and teach me these lessons, per se, they are lessons that I learned by being in his presence and by allowing God to de-brief me and give me wisdom years after the incident occurred.

LESSONS LEARNED

First, I learned that I was uncharacteristically angry. Anyone who truly knows my personality knows that I am generally and genuinely a fun-loving, goofy character as my normal and natural demeanor. This anger was foreign to me, so I had to locate the source of this anger, process the situation, and deal with the results.

In this situation, I learned that what you absorb and ingest would eventually come out of you. While my parents didn't listen to or condone the gangster rap culture, that influence was a large part of our rebellious generation. All of those years of listening to disrespectful music, watching movies with negative images and messages and partaking in foul conversations created somewhat of an effervescence on the inside of me that wanted to escape.

Second, I learned that my Dad was a protector and an on-site mentor to guide me through a difficult process: one of the functions of a father. If I would've taken matters into my own hands and handled things emotionally, that cop might have shot me or I might have been in jail. Boys need fathers. It's not an option or a want; it is a necessity. Unfortunately, many young black boys are raised without a present and/or active father, whether by death, imprisonment, abandonment, or some other circumstance. But that doesn't negate the fact that a boy needs an active father to guide and to teach him how to be a man. Thank God for the mothers, the uncles, grandfathers, older cousins and brothers, and other positive male figures who do what they can to fill in the gaps when the biological father is missing. But there is nothing like a positive, strong, and active father who is present and in his rightful place.

Third, I learned that losing isn't always a bad thing. From a young age, we are taught to be competitive and win. Losing is a part of life, but our goal and what is often stressed in life is to defeat our opponent. In my encounter with that cop, he was my opponent, and instinctively I was programmed to win. In retrospect, that was a poor assessment of the situation, and I thank God that I made an immediate and more than likely life-saving decision to follow my Dad's advice. I had to swallow my pride, and not act upon my anger, immaturity, and my subconscious desire to win, to be right, to get the last word, and to "show whitey" that he was going to respect me.

❧❧❧❧

My Dad's words, "Just be cool" were the words of reason that I needed to get me through that situation unscathed. I could have put on the tough guy façade and emulated what I saw in the movies and what I heard in the rap music. That phony façade would have allowed me to take a one-way trip to either the graveyard or to prison. But I gladly lost that day, so that I could win and live to tell this story.

☙☙☙☙

Fourth, I learned that all white people are not the enemy. I know that we can all point to a myriad of examples in world history where a white person or white people committed some sort of atrocity against a person or people of color. But that general narrative is destructive and it's untrue. All white people are not the enemy just like all black people don't steal or act in a manner that is consistently portrayed on television. To say "all" regarding any group of people is not fair or true. These generalizations are very dangerous, and I fell victim to unfair generalizations regarding the officer.

☙☙☙☙

At that very emotional encounter, that cop (in my mind) represented everything bad that white people did to black people. I know that sounds ridiculous, but my mentality was such that I wanted to blame some hostile white man for the hurts that were brought to my people, and that cop was a convenient candidate. It wasn't fair to label him that way, but if you wear rose-colored glasses, everything you see will have a red-tint to it. Well, I wasn't wearing the philosophical rose-colored glasses, but I was wearing the victim and the "get whitey" glasses. But through the process of maturity, education, and Godly instruction, I learned that was wrong. God bless that cop wherever he is. I am free!

Fifth, I learned that having a pleasant and genuine disposition is important and that a soft answer turns away wrath. No matter how ugly that officer acted towards me, I could have implemented the principles of the Word of God (if I knew them at that time) so that God could have intervened in the situation. It wasn't necessary for me to have an attitude and to disrespect an elder person in authority. By my rudeness, I willingly joined that cop in a low-level and classless encounter. I could have and should have taken the high road and defused the situation by keeping my composure. Although I did listen to my Dad and calmed down, my attitude was still wrong. From this incident, I did learn how to be in charge of a situation, or at the very least how not to allow the wrong sentiment to escalate a situation out-of-control. Keeping a level head is key, and that nonsense about demanding respect from people (as many folks in the 'hood believe) might get you killed. I decided to drop the pride and the façade, and live to see another day.

Sixth, I learned that God's hand of protection and favor was and is on my life. I could've driven my car into another car, driven into a concrete pillar, or driven my car off of a bridge. But I exited my car without a scratch on me. The enemy of my soul knows that God has a great future that He desires for me to walk out in faith. So he tried to use my bad decision (to make a seven-hour trip at night with little to no sleep) to destroy me. But God is not done with me yet on the Earth. Praise God for His angels and the plan He has for my life. I will walk it out in Jesus' name!

Seventh, I learned that respect is earned. I didn't respect that officer, even though I should have respected his badge. The law is good, and the person who represents the law should be a good person, as well. But that doesn't mean that the person will automatically get respect. You still have to give and earn respect and that officer didn't earn it. You reap what you sow, and neither one of us sowed humility, respect, compassion, or understanding. Both of us were cold, hard, and rigid. There was no room or consideration given for love to enter. We both boxed it out, and it took a third-party (my Dad) to make sure that things didn't get out of hand.

In the 'hood, some people fight for respect and they demand respect. When I was in that state-of-mind, I wasn't going to let that white man disrespect me. To some people, respect is everything, and if I had to respect his badge, because that's all I respected about him, then he was going to respect me, as well; and in my mind, I was going to make him respect me. I learned that was the wrong way to approach this situation and those foul influences from my youth are no longer in my life.

Eighth, I learned that we should share life with others. Why is this principle so important? It's important because sharing life is a good way to learn and to live the Christian life with accountability. Now, I must admit that I didn't actually learn this principle from the cop incident, but I did process the situation and thought about ways to help overcome the wrong thinking I had. One way to overcome wrong thinking is to check it against the truth, whether it is the written word or the spoken word of a trusted friend. Relationships with solid people are invaluable, and the principle of sharing life with others encapsulates that fact.

I remember seeing the "sharing life" principle in operation to a small degree growing up. People were more intimate with their neighbors and families years ago. As a kid, I knew all of my neighbors.

Today, I barely know any of them, because our culture is steadily changing and with the advent of 1,000 cable channels, lightning fast-internet connections on mobile devices and computers, and busier lifestyles, the need for human interaction isn't as important to this generation as it was to previous ones. Often times, people find it more convenient to stay in their own little silo, while everyone else in the neighborhood does the exact same thing.

The first-century church was different because they shared life with one another. They actually did what the Bible said: they bore one another's burdens. When one person or family suffered, everyone pitched in and provided support. Today, that isn't really the case. Today, there are family members within the same city or area who haven't seen nor spoken to each other in years. That's not what a shared life looks like.

We must share life with one another. I liken it to a cab ride. If a few people are going in the same direction, but not necessarily to the exact same location, why take two cabs? Why not share a cab? It's just a good use of resources that makes sense for everyone involved. The riders get to their destinations quickly and the cab company can service other clients simultaneously.

❧❧❧❧❧

Another good analogy is shipping a package. Do you deliver your own packages? Usually not. You either use the postal service or FedEx or UPS or some other major delivery service. Right? In fact, every merchant who ships products does the same thing. No one delivers his/her own packages, because FedEx, USPS, and UPS are already going that way. Those delivery services have the infrastructure in place. They have planes that are already flying that way, and drivers who are already driving that way. The incremental cost of adding your package to their route is almost inconsequential in the aggregate because they're already going that way. But to deliver your own package to another part of your state or country might cost you hundreds of dollars or even thousands of dollars if you had to rent/use your own vehicle, hire a driver or consider your own time, a plane ticket, gasoline, etc. Why not save the time, money and energy, and simply take advantage of the resources that are already going that way?

☙ЖЖЖЖ❧

This principle applies to almost everything. Most people don't make their own clothes, build their own houses, or grow their own food, because someone else already has a system in place that is far more efficient. Notice that I said most because there are some people who do these things themselves; but it's the exception and not the rule.

What does this have to do with sharing life?

Well, a lot of folks seem to think that the best way to get anything done is to do it yourself. Although that is a popular idea, that isn't always true. The fact is that no individual knows enough to resolve all of his/her problems. So, should every generation and family be set back and required to figure life out on their own? Should they do all their own research? Should they all subject themselves to trial and error? Should everyone re-invent the wheel? It makes no sense, especially since people have been and are going that way. The mistakes that some people are making today, other people have already made those mistakes and learned from them. A clear path to victory is now set for other people to follow. So using the cab or the delivery service analogy, the expert "drivers" have already been hired. The fastest routes have already been mapped out. The "vehicles" needed to get people to their "life" destinations are already in place. People are already going that way anyway. So let's share life together.

The past is simply that, the past. It's not something that can be changed. Things you've done, who your parents and grandparents are/were, etc., are things that are beyond your control to change. But what we can do is learn from our own personal mistakes and the mistakes of others, be open to mentorship, and hopefully (if he is active and present) these young boys can learn valuable life lessons from their Dad or a proxy. I've learned so many things from my Dad as a child and now as an adult, and the lessons and the experiences have been invaluable. I don't live in close proximity to my father anymore, but I do enjoy visits and reminiscing phone conversations about the times we shared in my youth. Even today, I ask my Dad for advice or his opinion on things, because we have that connection. It is important to respect that connection and to never take it for granted. This mutual respect and connection has led to many good times and experiences, including a trip that we took to Pennsylvania, where we learned that our African ancestors were rescued near Cuba during the Atlantic Slave Trade, and brought to Pennsylvania to became free people. My Dad, his brothers, and some university professors actually discovered the information, but I am blessed to have a Dad who shared our roots with me.

Unfortunately, I am an anomaly in the black community, because I was raised by both parents. The fact that I had an active and present father in my life is not something to which a lot of black people can relate. But we must continue to build, to grow, and to reach out to the community, because there are many people who want to do better. Many of the national statistics on social issues puts our people in a bad light, but that can be changed. I do believe that change starts with the role of the positive, active, and present fathers in the lives of their kids, especially their boys. Mothers, grandmothers, teachers, and neighbors can only guide and instruct kids so far. Kids need their fathers, because a father is supposed to be the child's first introduction to authority, and he is to be a role model for protection, leadership, respect, family, and provision. Those are some of the things that fathers should teach their boys.

My Journey of a Thousand Miles: (Standing in the Gap Amid Adversity and Angst)

Alvin C. Romer

"The second installment of The Soul of A Man series reiterates the need for mankind to know how important for men to validate and value digging deep within to command respect. Men of color often have the stories aiding and abetting this while transitioning from mediocrity to magnified success. A few good men has attested to it! Read our stories!"

~Alvin C. Romer

Would you mind if I open up to you and share my thoughts a bit? No foundation is weakened if you truly believe that you can overcome the undercurrents of woe. The purpose of this essay is to share my feelings and give you my assessment of how I finally stood up and fought diligently for change while standing in the gap amid adversity and angst. The spiritual references that reverberates throughout this essay are classic examples of allowing what is seen on the surface to go deeper when we purpose in our minds that God will not disappoint us when we need Him most.

There are quite a few examples of unsurmountable odds against triumph illustrated in the Bible when obstacles seemingly are bigger than life. David and Goliath come to mind in a perfect example of how to slay giants. David had the confidence to let Goliath know that the dawn of a new day was eminent. What giants are in your midst that need to be slain? It seems that when it comes to the DNA of men, we may be prone to hide behind facades, and even not be able to escape the yoke of oppression due to social biases. Or maybe it's because dissatisfaction tends to be broadcast voluminously, while appreciation is whispered before we can rise to the occasion. I speak as a man that have been knocked down a peg or two hoping for that second chance to be viable and valuable to self, family and community.

I was able to claim long ago that success is a doable process, but I had to be broken and made whole again. Whispers in the case of being successful when it counts should be vociferous, reverberating in our souls so that the world will know that we can STILL prevail against all odds. More questions abound here: What if the measure of your success is only determined by how well you adhere to change, how you challenge doubt, uncertainty and fear? Only the rarest of events forces people to change. Even more rare is individuals who can inspire to the core and move to action. I surmise that when faced with any riveting story of overcoming adversity through sheer determination, will-power and setting goals allow the flow of adrenalin to be infectious. It's a journey.

I've heard my father say many times that the measure of any man is how he can overcome and persevere through the roadblocks before him…It's how you rise up against adverse conditions without losing a sense of accomplished value for legitimacy that counts. Not only does this make sense, I've come to use it to validate what has become the hue that colors my soul. Moreover, I consider myself a seasoned traveler having traversed through many of those roadblocks. And what a journey it was! I firmly believe that ascending above diversity through sheer determination would empower being the man my father wanted me to become, and that was the genesis for me to get my act together when I fell without having a better grip on life. For me, the ultimate goal was embracing a testament for my intent to inspire others to rise above mediocrity to magnificence.

In order to understand my mindset, you must see me through clearer lens. I have a story to tell about rising above adverse conditions to be given a chance at God's Grace. I will tell it from three different and congruent scenarios of interpretation. It encompasses the state of brokenness, being a peer support advocate, and playing the part of meaningful activism in the lives of others. Illustrating this, I became a care-giver for a whole nation that's still seeking hope amid the ruins of their lives, helped a friend of mine regain his dignity, and found out how important it was to maintain a healthy lifestyle in lieu of waiting until the body breaks down. Here's my story:

BROKEN, BATTERED, BUT BLESSED!

The subtitle to what you're reading says a lot about unique situations that makes me most proudest—standing in the gap amid adverse conditions while lamenting the why of it all. Brokenness is real, and it effects all of us to certain extents because it's a part of the wholeness that God wants us to get to and realize before He blesses us. When the chips are down, God wants humility and praise for Him where adversity and blatant disregard is prevalent and pervasive. Complete humbleness is a form of brokenness that should be part of the process where pride is stripped away, where self-sufficiency is devoid and where God's shining light is illuminated. To prove this point God gives varied and intrusive examples to allow the truth to shine through. God is always looking for chances for us to validate our choices to step up out of our maladies.

The year 2010 was a challenging one for my family and I. The certain brokenness in my life stemmed from the pangs of developing a wellness recovery plan from a debilitating stroke suffered in that year, where I had to learn how to walk and talk again. Subsequently I lost my job, my vehicle was repossessed and I became temporarily homeless. Despite the grim prognosis of how a stroke can determine limitations and fuel dire straits I refused to be sidelined. Yes, the grueling physical therapy was tough; somehow I knew I had to persevere. It wasan epiphany for me. It allowed me to be in a precarious state to be lifted up and acquire a new lease on life, but not before making sacrifices for myself and others. My sciatic nerves were severely damaged on my left side, including a twisted face, and damaged joints which later developed into a case of gout. Over time I was diagnosed with a severe case of blood clotting in my left leg.

I'm able to tell this story because human nature will find us at times fallible and prone to error when we initially think negatively when you think all hope is lost. We will stumble, sometimes, fall and allow brokenness to define how not to be focused. Nevertheless, as I ponder situations that have given me the most problems in life, I realize that the journey from wrong to right is full of obstacles, as well as being able to get up after being knocked down. God tests us in many ways. I call it standing in the gap where adversity is a willing and able partner to angst. My intent was to close that gap, tighten the strings of salvation, and hold on with a good grip! I will turn back the hands of time a bit to illustrate points in my life where perseverance became much more than wishful thinking while traversing my well-traveled path.

My life took on a decidedly good turn one day when I wanted to study the book of Hebrews while flat on my back going through my recuperative stages. In doing so, I was able to get a better understanding of God and His plan to save the world, and how I could use it to change my plight. Writing this story, coupled with all things spiritual gave me a new perspective while requesting an audience with God to repent and change. As I vacillated between reality and my world of pain, I absorbed the true meaning of how God intended for me to utilize His plan for salvation. I realized remorsefully how much I truly lacked faith. When you don't have a strong hold on Jesus and don't read His Word daily and diligently, you will not have a deep rooted sense of commitment and will end up faltering.

Broken, battered, but blessed? It goes further. My story up to this point is an open book. I've been told that Christians cannot fall into disrepair and forget faith initiatives to be at their best, but dawn's early light caught me dead to rights and exposed me. Before becoming sick, I wasn't too happy with the state of affairs around me and felt that questioning God was the thing to do! I made a few mistakes and feared consequences that were potentially problematic issues that further decimated me. I realized that I was afraid of other things too. Sometimes I wondered whether I would make it through those tough times of recessive dread. Was I destined to die without a chance to get it right? Because it seems like the more I tried to do right, the more Satan would jump me and dwell within my soul. A lot of times, I questioned why I should even be a Christian. I remember going days without reading the Word of God, and I would just lie around feeling sad and empty. I still would go to church and all, sympathizing with the appeal, but then I would sink back into my malfunctioning mode. People who know me and have followed me were surprised to have seen me in that state. Alas, I was able to rebound and felt comfort now in giving you the soul of this man, but it wasn't always a stable situation.

Tooling in the book industry had been a labor of love, unbalanced at times but not enough to deter me from sharing my talent and expertise to those who aspired to write and author books. I dealt with independent and mainstream publishers who didn't think I had the talent to write…this, amid the fact that I'd constantly read authors who've made it and whom I felt couldn't write as well as they thought they could. Nevertheless, I continued tirelessly reviewing books, editing them, publicizing and helping authors to market them adroitly.

As a freelance writer and journalist I wrote too, and submitted many essays and articles galore to publications willing to accept opinionated views on some of the most prevalent issues in our society. Albeit, there were more setbacks along the way. I submitted three novels to three different publishers and was shown the door with my books in tow, which affected my ego. I was even dismissed by a few of my peers who told me on many occasions that my writing was too pedantic, and that readers would not understand me using words they wouldn't understand. I applied for jobs as an Editor, got interviewed quite a few times, and was put on various waiting lists.

Meanwhile, it didn't take long for me to feel the pangs of despair again, and I completely shut down. I was really angry with God for putting me through the pain of rejection time after time. I felt like I was through. Of course people would admonish me, defy my stance of stubborn retreat and try to encourage me anew. They would say things like -- "Try again Alvin, don't give up...you've come this far; stay the course."

As I lamented my plight, the gap got wider and roadblocks stymied me at every step. I was not trying to hear that at all. I knew that they would question my faith and do a great job of allowing the guilt trip to be a worthwhile journey for them to dwell deep into my consciousness. Deep down, I knew what the problem was. Perhaps I didn't stand in the gap long enough. I was afraid of failure, wasn't strong enough to face reality without a full and replenished notion to stay the course. I was tired of the crap. As I read my Bible more and listened to my Pastor preach sermon after sermon on dealing with pulling up bootstraps to get out of the box, but stay in His will, my life slowly turned for the better.

Then I began to look at others—my peers and those that seemingly had weathered storms and had the wherewithal to slap iniquity upside the head and get away with it! I talked to them and I felt that if they could rebound, why couldn't I? I was so thankful to be alive, and grateful for another day of life. Members of my family and close friends never stopped calling me, and as they encouraged me anew not to give up, I kept my eyes to the sky. One conversation in particular with a person who was once homeless but became a successful motivational speaker really inspired me. You all should know motivational speaker Les Brown, who was an erstwhile classmate of mine during the early days of my high school education. He assured me that there were better options, and that the better part of my life was before me. One bit of advice I clung to that he admonished to me was: "You never know who can, and will be influential enough in your life to wrought change, Alvin." His talk fueled me further and I knew that my walk with Jesus was to be pronounced and provoked. I endeavored to become fearless and refrained from worrying about the last days, and my soul salvation. I realized that God's had my back, and all I had to do was conform! As long as I have faith in Jesus, I got through that life and endeavored to get reformed and refined. I repented, made better decisions, let go of those that didn't mean me well and held tighter on the hand of God. The fullness of Christ is knowing what brokenness is, how to deal with it knowing that God is at His strongest in us when we are at our weakest point. We're all at some point or another have been broken and battered, but still blessed!

FROM CORRUPTED TO CORRECTED: LIVING BEYOND THE LIMITS OF HOPE

Now comes my friend, Erich Von Strauss. My involvement with his ability to look up and live is a true statement of wellness recovery at its best. This is the middle passage of my journey, the second leg. If you want further reason for me to foment reasons to believe that triumph over adversity is real, this guy is par for the course. Eric is a German who emigrated from his home country, joined the United States military, but in the interim lost quite a bit struggling to make life good. Mr. Von Strauss is unlike anyone I've ever met who've lost it all, humbled himself and allowed humility to redirect his life for manifested destiny. He was a work in progress and wasn't endearing to make a change in his life when I met him. With low self-esteem he was ready to give up.

There's a message to the madness of his story. Eric is one of an increasing number of veterans through the annals of time away from their military tenure who have either fallen far from grace, or have come to realize a ubiquitous life on the street. As a Vietnam veteran myself, I can relate to the angst of post-military issues when things go awry and you're wondering what can be done to bridge gaps. You find yourself wandering from hither to yon keeping a tight vigil on a sane mind, and having the temerity to stand firm is fleeting. When you couple this with the pressures of life not agreeing to make the right decisions or no decisions at all, it takes its course. I suffered quite a bit mentally dealing with the aspect of not being able to move on my own, but that pales against what I've experienced after meeting a man that has changed my mindset on the homeless and their issues. It gave credence being associated with the who, why, when and where of it all with him.

Mental illness is a serious condition that has special needs that calls for trained personnel to be in place to assist those that need it most. This is why I'm grateful to the Miami Veteran's Administration Healthcare System (MVAHS) for giving me an opportunity to rehabilitate with physical therapy, and to be put in position to meet the Erich Von Strausses of the world, and for peer-to-peer expertise to make me accountable. As such, the center in Miami has a unique series of transitional programs catering to veterans on the brink of despair needing a theater of worthiness to enter back into society and retain a sense of reality. There are more adjunct operatives in place and proposed programs that will address the special needs of our veterans returning from war. Besides treating physical and mental injuries, there are current therapeutic group sessions, vocational rehab groups, and counseling programs. Despite all of this, the Department of Veterans Affairs still expects the homeless rate and the mental state among the nation's newest veterans to rise because of the violent nature of combat seen in Iraq and Afghanistan.

I entered one of the special programs, **Incentive Therapy (IT)**, a vocational rehab program provided by the hospital while rehabilitating after my stroke. The main thrust centers on therapeutic value sustaining capacity to get back to normal without relapsing into a former life of drug or alcohol dependency. This is where I met the subject of this portion of the essay, and it changed my outlook on reaching out to someone who needed it most. It's being obedient to God's dictate of giving something back by volunteering my service(s), for the sole purpose of helping someone get back on their feet.

Erich, a stroke victim also, is a victim of a corrupted life, but is correcting it in perfect harmony to live well beyond what is perceived to be hope with embellished verve. Looking at Mr. Von Strauss, it would be easy to dismiss him if you are one to judge books by their covers. Tall, wiry in a 6'3 frame barely 170 pounds, and years abusing drugs and alcohol left him with a gaunt weathered appearance...but here lies the paradox that defies stereotypical notion when one fails to go deeper gauging the soul of a man. I say this because I've gone deep and have discovered a gem of a man with more resolve than many who have not befallen harder times. I gravitated toward him instantly. We shared common bonds recovering from physical maladies and a few mental ones too.

Erich, I found out, was a scholar and intellectual in many ways. Tunisian by birth, his family later settled in the Hesse region of Germany. He spoke French, Spanish and other native dialects. He later matriculated to Spain and eventually found himself a naturalized citizen of the United States. He knew books, and have shared quite a few of them with me. Well-read and the holder of two undergraduate degrees and a Masters, you wonder how and why fate dealt such a man a cruel hand. Never underestimate God's timing to break us and make us whole again. Erich is a testament to that! First, here's a man willing to do what's right and adhering to a disciplined order. The beauty of this whole scenario is the fact that he made it a mission to change his life...he positioned himself to be helped. This is why I know that God places people in strategic positions where fate, providence and hope all works for the same result. I knew that he was human and weak to temptation where opportunity is in the eye of the beholder. He needed me and I needed him. Sheer will power and with the help of those that care, both of us got that second chance and we made the most of it.

There's a twist to his story, though. He spent a year and a half as an Army mechanic in Vietnam between 1967 and parts of 1969. He saw many of his fellow soldiers killed during attacks on his base and other constant firefights. Suffering from PTSD (Post Traumatic Stress Depression) he found himself in trouble from a marriage gone awry, entrepreneurial ventures souring, and business partners betraying him.

THE SOUL OF A MAN 2

Before misfortune found him, know that Erich founded and operated three successful maritime businesses, employing more than 120 people. His finances were stable and he invested his money and established a strong home base. The downturn in the economy found him robbing Peter to pay Paul, but found out that Peter was broke! Times became leaner and he wasn't unscathed by the eventual fall of his stock index. This caused a strain on his marriage as his businesses all floundered and eventually fell into disrepair. Topping all of this was unscrupulous business partners who were syphoning monies off the top of earnings. Divorced and disillusioned, he filed for bankruptcy which sealed his doom. Broke, despondent and down on his luck, he found better friends in his mind with drug abuse and alcohol.

Homeless since 2004 and labeled as a derelict, he was able to enroll in the Miami Incentive Therapy Program where I was able to meet his acquaintance and mentor him accordingly. Needless to say, with constant around the clock care and much prayer, he was on the road to recovery! He recently moved into a government-funded shelter in Miami Beach and currently has found a job. Until he found the VA facility, he was sleeping on the street, in laundry rooms and washing himself in fast food restrooms until he would be kicked out. He ate from garbage cans, including panhandling for extra cash. Time is now for Mr. Von Strauss. The NEW Erich, if you will. He is on a fast track to respectability and giving his newfound faith a chance to manifest the meaning of real change. Eric and I have prayed together and share a common bond where camaraderie is practiced with frequent phone calls to each other and a visit or two when we feel it necessary to coalesce. I took Erich under the arm, propped him up and never abandoned him as I gave him much of what was given to me when I needed nurturing. I couldn't be the help Erich needed if I wouldn't have gone through what I did to understand his plight. I didn't turn my back on him. Being there and have done it makes all the difference in the world, and the trust he saw in me proved to make any transition just that much convincing. I wanted to make a difference, but do it in ways where it would benefit and not belabor the point of ineffective intent. I can honestly say that the Peer Specialist training I went through prepared me for the task. Erich has a life where opportunities define sparkling rays of hope. The last time I saw him he had command of his life and possessed and air of accomplishment. Not only are miracles part of the fabric of life, they are the ties that bind when Divine intervention manifests corruptness to correctness.

CRY, THE BELOVED COUNTRY

This, the third and last leg of my journey is no less daunting than the last two. The emphasis I place articulating my voice here is about merit and morality. It's also about eliciting change in how and why I wanted my actions to speak much louder than words. Volunteering time to worthy causes forces you to accentuate what's prevalent for not holding back the tide of change. I really don't know which has more relevance—overcoming a stroke or helping an indigent friend. Helping Erich out of his malaise was a snap and I wanted and needed to make a difference in someone's life, but a whole nation? A rude awakening opened my eyes for it's my thought that we individually and collectively, have moved century's ahead inventing new worlds of influence; but it seems we know little or nothing about our own role in the changing world of trials and tribulation when we're down. I don't want to be locked into narrow horizons of oppression as I'm sure the average Haitian feels unable to fend off adversity because of powerful psychological and social chains due to a devastating earthquake.

Change is most difficult when our heads are filled with self-doubt, misplaced anger and an unwillingness to make strides to help those that can't do for themselves. This is where I am, and why I accepted the challenge. I've always needed to actualize my life when I no longer allowed my doubts to control and limit me. An old adage exemplify my thoughts on this about continuing putting new wines in old skins and new patches on old garments. The key for me at this stage was starting a new realm of activism! I've always learned from all of the situations I faced while on the road to respectability with lots of the roadblocks I mentioned earlier. Often it took going beyond any prescribed amount of inertia I got when I went from point A to point B, especially when the circumference around circles of influence dictated time-honored measures. I realized that the issues I took were much more than challenges —they became a way of life. **Lao Tzu**, an ancient Chinese Taoist philosopher once said, "The journey of a thousand miles begins with a single step." I learned this quote on the first day of high school in Honors English, and never hesitated to lend it to the title of this essay. When one is on a mission, it's so hard to count the steps needed to be viable for a worthy vision. My vision at the time had a lot to do with the failure of my health, and the plight of people looking for quality standards of living amid adverse conditions keeping them from achieving it. In doing so, when a friend of mine lived a dismal life, I knew that if he looked up, there was hope. As such, I've embarked on an excursion that has defined how I feel about giving of myself. Mileage accumulated on humanitarian endeavors often can result in numeric proportions real or imagined to justify validity. For the sake of clarity, you'd want to know that a thousand miles in this case is symbolic to illustrate the point I'm making on a personal note. Since I chose this particular number for this essay. It's about the longitude to justify the latitude of completing tasks, and it's as good as any random number to illustrate my point.

What started the whole process was when a colleague of mine challenged me to go far beyond status quo to reinvent myself relative to the aforementioned. He wanted to do his part to uplift my spirits from the stroke. The more I thought about it, I realized that I actually had a lot to offer where the battles of adversity were prevalent. He decided to throw a few curves into this challenge by telling me I had to pick anywhere in the world to venture to where I would make a difference, leaving my cell phone, laptop and none of the technological wonders of the twenty-first century and other amenities of the modern world at home. Anywhere in the world? What a challenge I thought! It meant that there were to be no communication with anyone outside of the place I choose to visit. WOW! How in the world can I accomplish any goal without connectivity to the outside?

Okay, so here we are. I agreed to everything, albeit with apprehensiveness, but no less eager to test what resolve I had par for the task. Without the aid of communication devices, I knew beyond any doubt that the only person I needed to communicate with was God. Praying diligently was part of my modus operandi, anyway. Augmenting my task I knew the key would possibly entail reaching as many people I could to champion my cause, and perhaps lend some sort of assistance; but at the same time, I had to make sure my volunteerism would mean choosing situations that would appease any voice of reason that I could align myself to. Thus, my secret journey's location was easy. The one place that has always been a destined dream of mine is right in my backyard —the country of Haiti and rebuilding an infrastructure leveled by a disastrous earthquake of monumental proportions. It also meant administering to the people outright. It is this enigma that paint the picture that has become my canvas, and the colors I choose to use for vivacity and a vivid vision— and for others to see yet, another example of righting something that went wrong. When I think of the things that are so important to my success, I thought of how I should give back despite my station in life. One of the main questions asked was how would I get to my destination. I got there with my mind, a will to succeed and reliance on He that strengthens me. It's all spiritual, and I did it by making my election and calling surest that allowed my walk to be consistent with faith initiatives to glorify the Man who made it all possible. How long did it take? Surely not as long as it would have taken without hope and prayer. I chose Haiti because God prepared it for me and is was waiting for me! I believed, and everything was just perfect for my journey!

Now I'm on an accomplished mission that's key to my recuperation. My journey is of a thousand committed miles of hope to give myself and others a new lease on life and to help those less fortunate. This is important to me. I speak namely of the people of intrusive hurts and their dreams of rebuilding their lives. Lest you forget people who are confined to wheelchairs, walkers, canes and other methods of assistance don't want to be reminded that they are not where they were in the past. Endured options depend on how strong are the desires to make things happen without sympathy, but full of empathy. Speaking generically, the challenges we face as men of destiny has a lot to do with our health and living the type of life that insure against injury. That means we have to take care of ourselves, take necessary precaution to prevent ailments that wreck our bodies. With me it was high blood pressure, cholesterol out of control, and large consumption of sugar. I'm convinced that the miles between being healthy and unhealthy is something that can be bridged for what we eat. We're all in this together. We cannot ignore the ability to rise up and deal with what is amiss when things go wrong. We struggle with different maladies where triumphs are determined how strong your faith is. I recall a scene in the movie 'Star Man' where the alien character played by Jeff Bridges asks the character played by Karen Allen, "Do you know what I find beautiful about your species?" He pauses for a pregnant moment and tells her, "You are at your best when things are worst." This is how I feel and why I should be an intercessor for those in recovery mode after falling.

I'm exacting my course by continuing to align myself with the means to make bad things good. I do this through my spiritual outreach operative, **Righteous Apples Ministries**. I imagined traversing all roads that would lead to an accomplished end no matter what level of circumstance it would lead to. This is why I took on the challenge of helping the people of Haiti by lending my support in many facets of recovery. I pictured myself walking quickly and alone along the shoulders of roads with purpose and destined value. I did not realize it that day, but my journey would begin sooner than later. Lying flat on my back, a stroke victim unable to move earlier, allowed reality to sink in mighty fast! I was able to develop a passion within me that would change my life forever. I discovered my true identity. It was advocating for youth of this generation helping to bolster the self-esteem of anybody going through the pangs of pain. My goal is to follow through on my wellness recovery plans where they can bolster determination projecting confidence unpeople of all walks of life. In my endeavors during outreach sessions I continue to see resilience and determination from a different perspective affecting Haitians that I don't see in many people that look like me. They stick together forming coalitions. They never give up. They risked their lives to fight for freedom from tyranny, and I wanted to give something back to them. For those who hoped for a better life, they bravely faced the open sea in shabby boats and overcrowded vessels knowing their chances of survival were slim. Before this era, I was able to get a firsthand look at Haitian life and culture when I, at the time, fell in love and married a beautiful Haitian woman. Shewas a darling who gave me further wherewithal to help her and her people. I was able to see first-hand the stigma and prejudices that the average American probably don't know what has been bestowed on them. I witnessed when asked about their background how they would simply lie and say most anything other than where they truly hailed from, to keep from being ridiculed and slandered. Throughout my subsequent years as a youth worker and mentor, it was my prerogative to teach them that they were descendants of a great people whose strength, defiance and courage have enabled their survival despite overwhelming struggles throughout history.

eɔeɔeɔeɔ

There's another profile in courage that illustrate my point. Later, I met another brilliant young lady, Haiti-born lawyer **Gueter Aurelien**, a dynamic personality of ambition and drive with the support of her parents, who established a prestigious education Academy in Haiti, and one here in America. Balls of Fire Academic Academy has gone through quite a few trials and tribulations through the years, but it has not only thrived, but prospered. Why?

Because they knew what it would take for it to make it. They like I, were survivors…perseverance was paramount and the power of belief in God didn't allow it to die. I watched her parents'resolve, and her tenacity, and knew the answer when someone implored, "Why work so hard with minimal payoffs?" She then pointed to her parents and responded, "Because they've always worked hard to make a difference, and I had no choice but to aid and abet the cause." I didn't hesitate to give more to her and her parents. Later on, I was instrumental in giving consultation to achieve accreditation for that new school project in Miami. I gave of myself because the triumph of my soul reverberated with anticipated joy knowing that ambition would prevail over adversity.

Despite the success of the school and the promising future of my own child of Haitian descent, I discovered that unfortunate situations of dismal decades shouldn't be reasons why a people can't survive stereotypical genocide. The tragic aftermath of a massive earthquake notwithstanding, it has left a lasting impression on me why I should be my brother's keeper, which gives credence to doing the right thing. In Haiti, there is widespread belief for those who have not given up. In their minds battling poverty, life does not matter because massive human rights violations and senseless crimes have been committed without investigation or judgment for years. In my mind, even with a nation fighting for survival, there is hope! For a nation that fought fearlessly for liberty over two hundred years ago, being the first predominantly Black nation in the Western hemisphere to gain independence, people should refrain from giving up on this nation. Haiti will rise just like the legendary Phoenix! Didn't the Lord say that, "The first will be last, and the last will be first?" Many Haitians living in Haiti and abroad are capable of making tremendous changes and have prospered, but the fear of crime and corruption seem to take back seats to rebuilding a nation. Dr. Martin Luther King, Jr. once said, "In the end, we will remember not the words of our enemies, but the silence of our friends." Due to my consultation and immediate assistance working with Ms. Aurelian in her quest to help her family, many children have a well-rounded education and hope for a future. Of this I'm most proud. I've witnessed first and foremost how she taught her staff, families and the people she encountered that their life had purpose. Of course, I couldn't remain silent myself!

Even if you have never met a Haitian, or know little of the country's cultural makeup, it should remind you that are all of God's children deserve a place in the sun. There is a popular expression in Creole -- *'Dieu donne'* which literally means 'God gives'. For decades we have witnessed Haitians endure unfair prejudices, ridicule and abject discrimination of the worst kind, especially from the United States' unfair and ridiculous immigration policy. It's a familiar story for Haitians—last in, first out for the hemisphere's poorest, least wanted, and most abused people here and in their own country. Respect not only is due, but demanded from all of us who feel that parity should not be on condition of the color of one's skin. Our mantra should be to make Haiti apparent to the potential that has always been hers. If the goals are to make this a winnable situation, playing a role in the recovery method should be on everyone's mind to not forget those needing help the most. Not only is it daunting, but in my mind to help staunch Haiti's race against time. The silver lining is that the world has a chance to make Haiti right and turn the tables on America's racist Immigration policy toward a positive gain for people of color looking better their lives. It must be rebuilt correctly -- and it can be done only if we all pull together and do all that we can to help. To sit by idly and not care is a sure epithet to misfortune that may be an onus you wouldn't want to burden.

The emphasis I place articulating my voice here is about merit and morality. It's also about eliciting change in how and why I wanted my actions to speak much louder than words. Volunteering time to worthy causes forces you to accentuate what's prevalent for not holding back the tide of change. I wanted and needed to make a difference in someone's life, but a whole nation? A rude awakening opened my eyes for it's my thought that we, individually and collectively, have moved century's ahead inventing new worlds of influence; but it seems we know little or nothing about our own role in the changing world of trials and tribulation. I don't want to be locked into narrow horizons of oppression as I'm sure the average Haitian feels unable to fend off adversity because of powerful psychological and social chains. Change is most difficult when our heads are filled with self-doubt, misplaced anger and an unwillingness to make strides to help those that can't do for themselves. This is where I am, and why I accepted the challenge. I've always needed to actualize my life when I no longer allowed my doubts to control and limit me. An old adage exemplify my thoughts on this about continuing putting new wines in old skins and new patches on old garments. The key is starting a new realm of activism!

It's no coincidence that all through life we embark on personal treks to justify a means. Mine just happens to be a thousand proverbial miles. Destiny is like than when the ends to the means have purpose. People who know me best will tell you that I'm a man with a vivid imagination and a having a knack for completing tasks, but nobody really knows me the way I know myself. I consider myself ordinary and a man of destiny, yet unique with concerns for life's bigger issues and the frustrations of the modern world. What makes me most different from the rest of my peers are due to the heart that has empathy for those less fortunate. It's all about giving and being an intercessor to those who need me. The original premise that my friend gave me, being bereft of communication without laptops, telephones etc. didn't work for me. I kept my head to the sky, which was the best communication I could depend on! Divine order through careful implementation of law and the establishment of a responsible framework for international involvement is possible in alleviating Haiti's perilous and bleak condition. Belief in Him is essential. Great achievement requires more than visions without clarity and willingness without reason…proficiency and collaboration are the catalysts that transform dreams into reality. I walk with faith as I will continue on many more journeys that may require steps to Christ for completion. I don't mind taking more steps to achieve modicums of success overcoming insurmountable odds. As a matter of fact, I volunteer my time for my efforts to far-exceed wishful thinking and complacency where action ultimately will speak much louder than what you read here. I envision winding unpaved roads, like those found throughout Haiti. I walk steadily, and I am not alone. A multitude may endeavor to follow me, and I must prepare to lead the way. I would admonish those who care to give hope a chance by remembering your brothers and sisters as they cope in disaster recovery! The world is on notice and many have stood, reached out and opened their arms for alms. Life is about giving back, and I'm trying today as best as I can to do my part. We only hurt ourselves when we turn our backs on our own. I want to say reverently that I can see farther over the mountain than the man who is standing on top of it. When we learn to thank God in spite of penchant for doing it on our own, I believe that it is then that we are blessed to see the overflow that He has stored up for us. My journey can attest to that! If we can't be grateful for what we have, how in the world can God trust us with the abundance that He has on standby? So for the remaining time I have left, I will continue to give God the praise. Not only for what I have today, but for those things that I know that He will bless me with tomorrow, the next day, and then day after that. Making a difference is something I believe everyone should strive for. First you have to believe you can—then just let it happen!

I'm where I need to be relegating my steps that have begun anew for my next journey of a thousand miles! There's plenty mileage in all of us…a journey if you will. We're all on journeys of some sort. If this story moved you at all, you can imagine how it makes me feel knowing that it perhaps will inspire others to achieve success by thinking big knowing that sheer determination will always be the mantra for success. Know too, that it's more than my will to overcome enormous obstacles to rebuild my life. I did it through survivor mode and a strong will. It was an unbiased testament to my intent to inspire others and help them triumph over roadblocks as well. I gave you three compelling reasons why overcoming ill-will while persevering in spite of anything defying progress shouldn't be labeled an impossible dream. The depths of my being is bottomless where all of those miles wasn't in vain. The soul of this man made it because to give up wasn't an option as it was an opportunity to make a difference. Today, I advocate for the homeless, for the mentally ill, and for giving others a chance at affordable housing...and I'm still writing! All of the angst suffered during my journey explains how I've triumphed through adverse conditions. Haiti is still receiving my help through one of the church ministries I'm involved in. If you didn't read the forerunner to this second installment of The Soul of a Man Series, the stories in this addition are no less poignant, but laced with other stories that gives meaning to why you should go deeper in your soul. Doing so would give reasons why there's always a need to rise above adversity. Listen to your heart, create your own journey of justification, rejuvenate your mind, and reconnect dots to your destiny—it'll happen if you're willing.

RAPital Punishment

Rickey Teems, II

"I'm honored to be a part of a project that articulates the complexities, challenges and triumphs that men of color deal with. I pray men and women of all ethnicities will take the time to read, understand and appreciate the lives we lead."

~*Rickey Teems, II*

L adies and gentleman of the jury, your honor, distinguished guests, I stand before you today, with the unenviable task of prosecuting the very culture and art that has shaped me in so many ways. I am not happy to be on this side of the aisle, but it is necessary." I loosen the knot on my red tie from the heat of intense stares. It's been years in the making, and I'm still no more comfortable than when these ideas originated.

"You see, every generation has long held the music and culture that was squeezed from the fruit of their era forever changed and quenched the thirst of civilization. We read of King David and The Israelites, almost sounds like a band doesn't it, glorifying their Living God as they danced out of their robes when he broke the hottest new psalms of the day. There were the iconic sounds of Motown revolutionizing music and dance at house parties, but adding a pinch of influence to bridge racial divides during the turbulent civil rights era. The garage grunge that bands like Nirvana were able to recklessly introduce by breaking social suburban norms and kidnapping the world's ears is a definite contender. There are numerous examples, but since we are not here to argue which era has had the most impact, let's agree that 40 years later the arguable champion remains that born of Bronx blood, Cali nurturing and southern United States pampering. The looming bass imported from the deepest roots of the original land and the poetic flow of urban experience. Hip hop."

Those in attendance applaud. Most are significantly younger and couldn't possibly fathom existence without the cultural staple. I almost can't either.

"Having the historic honor to share the same progression of the calendar for nearly 4 decades, I've enjoyed witnessing the undeniable evolution of an art that matured from many of the grimiest slums racism in America could produce, to an international top selling genre. Every 'hood and privileged community around the globe has been touched, enlightened, exposed."

"Examining its infancy, that exposure was well needed and regarded. Twenty years before the robotic dial up connection of Internet access began increasing global freedom of expression. Before there were hundreds of useless cable television stations, there were roughly 3 news stations per city and a couple of local newspapers.

"Wait...you mean once upon a time news was printed on paper? How dated was the information by the time it went to press and was actually delivered and read?" A young female intern called out in bewilderment.

"Order." The judge hollered. "Mr. Teems, this is about music, not technology and journalism."

"Is it, your honor?" I shrug my shoulders. "The reality is, hip hop was a form of unbiased cutting edge, journalistic impressions. Only a little more than a decade removed from the communities that had been isolated by Jim Crow laws, impoverished and neglected inner city neighborhoods rarely received any substantial attention from the handful of news mediums. Hip hop quickly recognized this fact, and began to bare the burden of outspoken youth nationwide. It refused to be labeled as strictly entertainment. It was a voice. It was a message.

"No headline was taboo. Drug infestations to dance moves, gun violence to Government corruption, sex to success, rap's direct line to the pulse of its people provided a pride that rivaled Jackie Robinson's debut. Despite record company and radio limitations, the sound refused to be denied its purpose of informing an entire planet that the struggle was real, and African Americans had a much deeper voice than soulful love ballads.   NWA and their derogatory commentary on inner city police. Public Enemy and their expression of resistance to the "power." There was no shortage of diversity and political opinion in the rhymes. A call to arms for community unity was often mentioned if not the focal point, and that often overlooked fact may be exactly the reason that hip hop may need to suffer capital punishment."

The courtroom gasps in echoing awe.

"The only one who needs to die is you!" A young boy with jeans so tight they couldn't be pulled up over his thighs pulls out a gun and aims it at me. Temporary paralysis hits my legs before gaining my wits and diving behind a partition. No shot is fired. I look up. A scroll unfolds from the barrel of the gun that has one word written on it. Pow. Two sheriffs immediately detain the passionate lad and wrestle him out of the courtroom.

"Do you need a minute, Mr. Teems?" The judge asks.

"It's actually the perfect lead in, your honor." I respond to everyone's surprise. "Nat Turner. Martin Luther King Jr. Malcolm X. Fred Hampton. Rap? There is no irony. Coincidence has been ruled out. Outside of athletic endeavors, those that have attempted to bring about change and gained any respectable level of attention, have been silenced with the eternal quiet. Why should rap be any different? Except oppositional critics have learned rather than eliminate the voice, twist it for their gain. So how ever prominent of an existence some may dispute it still retains, I counter that the hollow shell of the genre heard on mainstream outlets these days is nothing more than an entertaining brainwashing technique. It has successfully erased morals and real world conception, and replaced them with the glorified and ignorant acceptance of self-destructive behaviors. There no longer remains a variety to balance the monotonous party anthems, only more parties, violence, and degrading dialect that greatly devalues the women, family, and distant relatives of those narrating. Why was there a need to silence the progressive voice? Why phase out those that spoke about the sense of solidarity every other ethnic group enjoys to some degree? Clearly strange fruit is still in season, except now they have developed a less blatant form of harvest. Now they use GMOs so we no longer see what's hanging on the outside, it looks perfectly fine. It's the corroded and spoiled insides from the meaningless music themes that kill us from the inside out. When police shoot an unarmed black man or politicians publicly oppose President Obama's bills we demand that heads roll! Well, why should we be any more lenient against an entity more reckless and murderous that increases crime, dropout rates, and pregnancy amongst our own? Hip hop must be brought to justice." I give a menacing look to the defense. I know their argument is weak and it shows on their face, but I must be relentless, intelligently and compassionately, and not rely on them to trip up. This is more than just about me and some vendetta against the youth.

"Before you call me insensitive or out of touch, I want to reiterate that I have never known life without rap music. Literally. By the time of toddler hood rap had already gained local, and was flirting with national attention. There are generations *slightly before* mine that were well defined in their likes and dislikes, but were still young enough to choose whether to incorporate hip hop into their lifestyles. There are generations *well before* mine that immediately rejected the art because accepting anything new would contradict the adage of teaching an old dog new tricks, and nobody likes a bad adage. But for me, rap was as natural and normal a part of life as breathing. It was life.

"See, by age twelve, I had Pee Chee folders full of loose leaf paper containing the most dynamic and skilled rap lyrics…my household could fathom. By eighteen I was recording over instrumentals on karaoke machines, and by twenty-three I was wrecking a professional grade booth to the tune of five independent CDs. Radio stations, clubs, contests, blocks and of course the internet were all infected with the sickness of our rhymes, because15 years ago I was already preaching the demise of the culture that was embedded in our DNA. I was the expert because I was standing on the epicenter, not the executives sitting in their plush offices with skyline views. Even then I recognized that something was afoot. If rappers have a voice that can influence their listeners, it could be dangerous to society if that message were to involve a unified front pertaining to education and improved living and economic conditions for America's slave sons and daughters. Imagine a mobilization to fight for the equality guaranteed by the constitution and the unfulfilled reparations other ethnicities have already received, our 40 acres and a mule moment. Where could that movement carry us to? Sure initially it would be repairing the broken down ghettos, but what next? Suburbs? Politics? Economic empowerment? I'm quite sure those with bigotry still in their blood were none to anxious for that sort of reform. So the powers that be did what powers that be do, they enact their way."

"Objection." The defense finally speaks out. "What does race have todo with anything? There are rappers and fans of all ethnicities."

"Sustained." The judge agrees.

I laugh. "For the record, I don't completely blame racially motivated destruction as the culprit for the turning of the hip hop tides. Yes, I absolutely believe there was a calculated effort to squash any possibility of a black unification movement, but there's also business as usual. Other demographics just wanted to party. They weren't interested in the struggle of impoverished black kids, and probably didn't want to hear about the inhumanity of some of their ancestors, so club and feel good songs appealed to a broader audience, which of course translates into more sales dollars. That is a small part of the reason Marshall Mathers was so successful. Not only was he a superbly skilled rapper, but he represented the voice of the majority, and supply and demand will never be put on trial. There is also the reasonable rationale that as younger generations of rappers became more removed from the civil rights era, there were less informed and less concerned emcees who never viewed the music as an art, but a get-rich-quick-scheme, and they were willing to say or do whatever for a pay check. Separate forces, separate goals, yet they all worked together to the detriment of those that created it, and that is why rap must be put to death.

"Rap and culture is not a chicken and egg scenario, at least not initially. Pushed away by racism, and then infiltrated with drug pushing, prostitution and the crabs in a barrel mentality, rappers started off narrating the lifestyles and events in their environments. They were modern day griots. People from around the world were break dancing in battles and twisting their fingers to represent gangs they had never even met. Sagging pants, baggy attire, the black community influenced the world through hip hop. Now, there has been a 180. Hip Hop dictates the standards of the black community. Those with the fortune and fame began to dictate, and why should we be surprised, we are a capitalist country. It was a subtle process. Newer generation rappers challenging the logic of old until eventually the old was drowned out and forgotten, except by dinosaurs such as myself. Captain Save a Hoe gave way to logic like, it ain't trickin' if you got it. Keep it real was supplanted by, fake it 'til you make it.

"And this is where I would like to call Puff Daddy and Rick Ross to the stand." The two moguls make their way through the courtroom to a flurry of camera phone flashes and cheers from the audience. Both icons hide behind their oversized sunglasses.

"You see, unlike other genres of music, rap has a bravado about it that often causes debates over which rapper or neighborhood represents the best. None have ever readily accepted crowning anyone other than themselves, so rap battles amongst the artist has not only become a mainstay, but a new stage for spotlights. Not surprisingly, in order to compete some rappers began reciting lyrics that didn't necessarily correspond to their actual lifestyle. Others tried to hide elements of their past that contradicted the image they were attempting to personify in accord with the cultural norms. However, once exposed, those individuals typically shriveled into obscurity. But the long time dancer and bearded Florida native managed to defy those odds, in a major way.

"Mr. Sean Combs, aka Puff Daddy, aka Sean John, aka Puffy, aka P. Ditty, aka Ditty, aka Ditty Dirty Money, aka I used every blank line on the name change form!"

Surprisingly, the star struck jurors erupt in laughter and even the judge hides a smirk.

"Isn't it true you began your career as a dancer, and grooved your way up the ranks to become an uber successful record company executive?"

The bad boy nods.

I take a breath. My admiration never ran high, but my respect was always unparalleled. "You broke dozens of new artists that owned the Billboard Charts before giving in to the temptation of trying you own hand on the microphone. A few hits later, questions and rumors began to arise whether you were having your rhymes written by other individuals, a practice long frowned upon by the streets. But you resisted answering the naysayers, simply offering the memorable statement, don't worry if I write rhymes, I write checks. That simple proclamation cemented a 180 degree turn from the genesis of rhyming. It was no longer about talent and creativity, it was about money."

I turn my attention to the heavy set entertainer who probably has more hits than Derek Jeter and Pete Rose put together.

"Mr. Leonard Roberts II, whereas most rappers roll with adolescent nick names or assume the names of deceased crime legends or fictional characters, you broke taboo by electing a moniker from someone who was still living, the notorious Freeway Ricky Ross who played a pivotal role in launching the 80's crack cocaine in inner city Los Angeles. This seems rather curious considering you had the one occupation that seemed to negate even your own unlawful lyrics…Correctional officer."

"So what of it?" His gruff response matches his arms folded across his chest. The comment wasn't intended to be demeaning, but I can understand why he is offended.

"So after a feud with another well-established Floridian culminated in the release of photos of you Mr. Rick Ross, in your correctional work uniform," I drop a couple of pictures enclosed in zip lock bags on the evidence table. "History would have suggested a quick end to your everyday hustlin', but history couldn't have been more wrong. Society had changed. Reality shows paying homage to individuals who had little credibility or achievements created a new pop culture where it was literally about popularity and not talent. Dreams of opulence raised the ceilings when MTV Cribs began to highlight how much more the haves really have. And surprisingly, few people cared that the man who had previously been responsible for keeping criminals in tune, was now making tunes about being a criminal mastermind, because it was highly entertaining.

"The floodgates were opened to a new breed of rappers all too happy to claim personalities they had only seen on TV. Gangsters...surrounded by security and police escorts? Players...forever accompanied by the same woman? Rich...but loaner cars and jewelry? Rap was always entertaining, but now it was completely void of truth, except where it mattered most...where it started."

Neither man is happy. That makes three of us. I've had my fair share of drinks and dancing to both of their discographies. "No further questions, your honor." Both men are dismissed and exit with a swag worthy of royalty.

Juveniles stand outside the doors sliding their index fingers across their necks or pulling invisible triggers. Because today scores of youth in underserved communities believe a lucrative rap deal will be their ticket out of the ghetto. They emulate multimillion dollar rappers, ignoring overwhelming statistics that suggest little to no chance they will ever find themselves remotely close to the same tax bracket. They let the lyrics inspire them to homicide and arrest records to boost their rep to be *hard*, despite very few of the mainstream rappers ever actually getting into fights.

They cover their faces with meaningless tattoos, overlooking the fact the rappers have enough money to not worry about job interviews or public perceptions. They frivolously spend the little they have trying to live a music video lifestyle, oblivious to the free compensation and rental treatment that celebrities receive. The unfortunate reality is the actions behind their million dollar aspirations are far more likely to keep them trapped in the impoverished lifestyle they are desperately trying to escape.

തതതതത

Years before it caught on in the mainstream industry and more famed rappers began discussing it, in 2000 my colleagues and I put out an underground rap CD entitled, Hip Hop is Dead. We received fare review on local radio stations and internet buzz, but shortly after the release I committed to living a more positive and progressive life in God. At the time we felt the art of the industry was on life support and needed resuscitation, but probably wouldn't survive. Now, as embarrassed as I am to confess, my feelings have stretched as far as wondering if rap deliberately needs to face the firing squad, and then dragged to an electric chair after being injected by Dr. Kevorkian. Redundant, I know, but necessary.

"Your honor, I am openly ashamed to consider such a harsh sentencing of the music genre that has been foundational in my life. It is almost the equivalent of a parent being forced into the unenviable decision of whether to pull the plug on their comatose child after ten years.

Optimism and hope are always the priority, but reality cannot be denied its reality. Which would you choose?"

"I have never had to imagine a life without hip hop. Even when politicians and activist were working to ban it in the early 1990's there was never really a viable threat to its existence. But from the time I wrote my controversial novel, Regression, I have increasingly began to wonder, what would life be like without rap?"

I open a screen and cue up a PowerPoint presentation. "First comes understanding that hip hop is so much more than the handful of rappers we see on TV. It has created thousands of viable jobs ranging from record company owners to graphic design artists, to TV shows and fashion, and every area would be impacted financially. I'm sure the skills of those professionals could be transferable to other genres, however, there would be more competition and probably less passion. So the question is posed, would the number of those displaced from employment be worth eliminating the destructive messages that are negatively impacting youth? As much as I would like to say yes, the answer is unequivocally, no. Rap music is only a fraction of what ails the inner city. Broken down schools, narcotics saturation, lack of money and resources, gang violence, single parent households, higher incarceration rates, we cannot pretend these woes were not inflicting their damage well before rap was created. Though hip hop culture had done little to address these afflictions, forcing everyone into hard times who have sacrificed and worked hard to make a respectable career in the business would not be fair. The ghetto was the ghetto before rap, and there it shall always remain.

"The next consideration for eliminating hip hop would be the infringement on freedom of speech rights. Would it be constitutional to silence so many individuals? More importantly, should we silence those who spout ignorance at the expense of the individuals who have added intelligence and progressiveness? Unfortunately the logical response to this is yes. For every Kendrick Lamar or J Cole, there are probably fifty untalented, unprofessional, cookie cutter content oriented rappers who offer little of anything with their right to free speech. Sorry Chuck D, Common, and Kanye, I would be heartbroken to never hear your divine logic, but I'd reluctantly bid you all farewell if it meant ridding the world of the countless others who do not even attempt to apply any depth or life improving insight.

"The case could also be made about infringement on people's right to choose. One rapper can have millions of fans spanning the globe, and not all of them are corrupting their lives trying to mimic the rap life. Why should they be forced to live without a preferred form of entertainment because others are out of touch with what's real and what's video set? In fact, I'm sure if we were to dissect the numbers based on sales, the majority of fans are not aspiring emcees, so why should a few bad apples spoil the bunch? This crossroads is where I realize I do not possess the unbiased ability to rule in favor of the masses. As an African American male, that has had the distinction of graduating from the streets and college, and using both unique experiences to work closely with at-risk African-American adolescents and help them see a vision greater than their daily circumstances, rap has become a major nemesis to that process. Smoke up. Party up. Gang Bang. Spend all your money on completely depreciating assets like cars, and of course the rims for the cars, shoes and clothes. Don't save a dime. Disrespect women. Hold no value for them. Have endless sex and don't give thought to the consequences of conception or STDs. Kill anyone who opposes you. Prison isn't a problem. Forget hard work! Any parent would be livid if another adult were to preach these values to their child, so where is the accountability for rap?"

"Objection!" The defense stands. "How can a song be accountable? It's just music."

"Sustained." The judge gives me a glare like the floor is about to fallout from under me.

I nod. "Don't misinterpret, I'm not blaming rap music…directly. I realize there is a much bigger system that was at work centuries before Rapper's Delight. It is my theory that the African-American psyche as a whole, will never completely recuperate from the effects of slavery, civil rights, and the crack epidemic. So desperate are we to find a sense of pride in a country that has continuously belittled us, we are willing to accept the crumbs of the crumbs. We support R. Kelly despite repeated statutory rape cases and payouts. No other ethnic group puts such heinous offenders on a pedestal, simply to be entertained. We voted for Obama in droves, but failed to study and vote for the initiatives that would help him be successful. We've watched and allowed the foolishness of reality shows and social media videos to be the primary representation of us, all the while complaining about why there aren't more African-American films or why our books don't sell as well. And we have allowed, rap music that which we gave birth to, to turn and hold us hostage with a knife to our neck. But fear not. There is strength in numbers and we are the numbers. Rather than killing rap, let's take it back. Let's begin demanding diversity on the radio. Let's take the time to search for and support the artists that know how to entertain, but can also embody the changes we want to see in our communities. Family, spirituality, purpose, education, career pursuits, economic growth, prosperity. If rap had the power to put us on the map, certainly it still has the strength to help guide us where the X marks the spot, right? Rap must die…but only so it can be reborn."

I turn the projector off and the room is completely silent. I look at the jury. I look at you. "I rest my case, your honor."

Soul on Soul Violence

Zach Tate

"Do you want to love a black man? You say you want to love my heart but are you willing to understand my soul? Open these pages and allow me the honor of taking you on the journey."

~ Zach Tate

I come from a poor block, where young hard-rocks played freeze-tag with stray shots. A place in the South Bronx where dope fiends were posted on every block, like bus stops. The introduction of Crack rocks came from corrupt cops who made the projects *their* projecting an intricate plot. The place where "stop" meant to drop it like it's hot because you could never forget how hot those stray shots felt when they hit the spot. It was a time when people ran towards drama, where three generations of "Mama" jumped your ass if you caused trauma. Graffiti on walls, most splashed with blood caused by people who were up to no good. I'm from the 'hood, where neighbors fled for good. So where would my manhood come?

I am not a product of my environment. That would suggest that I'm the sum of fire truck sirens blaring to put out arsonist fires from opportunist landlords who were cashing in on faulty clauses in kosher insurance policies. It would mean, I am Black churches and Arab liquor stores on every other corner, both selling hope in a hopeless situation. Or Latin cabs being called instead of ambulances because medical workers feared coming to the same streets that kept them employed. So, instead of seeing the man who holds an infinite soul, you would see poverty—a lack of resources, less than, and I am more.

Poverty is also violence. Period. With an explanation point. The inner city has an abundance of resources that is controlled by a small kleptocracy that we accept as community leaders. The task of these suburbanites is to balance institutional racism, financial aid displacement, and the redistribution of needed funds to the kids of them "other folks." This paradigm causes a large number of people to fight, kill and struggle for a small number of opportunities, while the stigma of Urban Under-classism keeps many other inhabitants numb. Self-medicating gives way to street business, since the demand to escape hell is high, and the supply of drugs being distributed by people who do not look like us is readily available. This trickles down to the hands of the hopeless, who see a path to use their bursting innovation as a means to end their hunger for more, by way of entrepreneurism. Simply put, people have to eat, and since other people want to get high, and the product is easy to sell, the people who want to eat, chose drug dealing to get paid, and getting paid affords one the opportunity to escape poverty. After all, our community leaders show us that crime pays, and they never looked hungry.

A hungry man is an angry man. Anger leads to lack of empathy, then hopelessness, then callousness, and eventually ruthlessness. The harsh things the poor are forced to witness, shapes and molds them to survive harsh circumstances, often self-imposed, but nevertheless harsh. In my lifetime I've been shot on two different occasions, stabbed, cut with over 200 stiches in my face, beaten by the police and correctional officers on numerous occasions, and personally waged war against my community. This was the 80's where on one street, within a ten block radius, over a million dollars was made daily. There are no victims over here. The wounds I reaped is just a smidgen of the terror that I sowed. And what propelled me to engage in this urban terrorism was based on a simple premise: If violence creates a profit, I will be hungry no more.

My soul was shaped by the moral standards of hard working immigrants who came to America, from Jamaica, in an effort to live better. I was employed and exploited by a family plumbing business since I was seven years old, so the mantra of "working hard, having your own, and building a better future" is coded into my DNA. When I had the desire to participate in sports or entertain WWF wrestling on Saturday mornings, the message I heard was, "Men work. Boys play." So I worked, and worked some more, and then entered the life of crime thinking I would escape work and gain higher income without labor, but I was wrong. Selling drugs to people I grew up with required emotional labor, moral labor and a bustling business took up all of my young energy. So for those who said drug dealing was a non-hazardous occupation meant for the lazy, I would instruct those cowards to kiss my Black, hardworking ass and I wanted to glue their eyelids open to our hopeless reality, and then remind them that only a coward would stand at a feast and starve. My soul is still hungry.

Unlike many others, I could have been anything I wanted to be in this world. Anything, besides be White. All my older siblings are college graduates with advance degrees. My uncles and aunts came to this country with nothing, eventually became multiple home owners and most were self-employed, so I knew how to make an honest buck. I knew that if one worked hard, went to school, and became indoctrinated enough that corporate America had a place for me. But to live in a neighborhood where all the neighbors moved out, only to leave a 'hood filled with resources lacking, every municipal service being sub-par, and an overwhelming majority having honor with having less-than, did not allow me to sleep well at night. Not to mention how the inhabitants of the war zone that I called home, glorified the stabbings, shootings, and were indifferent to death. But the harshest experience of violence I encountered was how being Black meant it was expected for me to be okay with all who were paid to serve me to not care about my welfare. Not teachers, store owners, municipal workers or the police. Then when a white, or wealthy black person had the same exact issues we had, they were allowed to skip the line or given V.I.P treatment. Those acts of discrimination didn't cause me to place blame on the 'system,' it caused analysis and sparked a plot. The question I asked myself at the age of twelve was, "How do I get out of the 'hood for good based on what I know?" The answer was always in front of me, and education was the key, but the institutions who were responsible for nurturing my quest to be anything I wanted in this world were failing me.

The first day that I saw my middle school teacher hiding the track marks that his heroin syringe left behind, I instantly concluded that my schooling was subpar and permanently dismissed all credibility of school. I eventually became more propelled to seek immediate financial gratification once my middle school principle, the pedophile that he was, expressed what his annual salary was. Right then, on a balmy fall day, my ego was born and my plot was solidified. As an overpaid runner who ran to the store for the local drug dealers, my eyes had already seen how fast a hundred grand was made. So for the principal to tell me that he made less than that, and he was in charge of teaching me, it was very clear that the math I was taught, deduced that a hundred thousand dollars made in a week was sweeter than $60,000 made in a year. This was the first act of compromising my soul; rationalizing the irrational.

My poor mother tried her hardest to dictate to me the safest route to survive the ghetto. But her views, suggestions and advice was all based on theory. She had not succeeded. She had a six grade education, was employed as a house cleaning lady, and loved her oppressors. What did she know about not having to budget, eating full course meals, having heat and hot water in sky rise apartments or driving everywhere she had to go? So my afterschool program was spent on the corner of 170th Street and College Avenue in the Bronx where a million dollars a week in heroin sales meant everyone could eat. It meant I could sit around and do a lunch run for the drug dealers and earn a full meal of smothered chicken, rice, vegetables, corn bread, pie and lemonade. It meant washing the newest cars and then riding to Harlem in them to see beautiful girls when I was done. It meant coming home full of food, a pocket full of money and a brain filled with new stimulation that school or my poor mother would never know. Hunger can make you turn on your own mother.

The hunger I need you to evaluate is not the one found in your gut. When you think of poverty, call it what it is. It means poor, lack of resources or less than. In the ghetto, poor means poor academics, poor healthcare, poor sexual conduct where we used abortion as a contraceptive. It means poor policing, poor ethics, morals, principles and conduct. It meant poor politics where the disenfranchised were repeatedly sold out by preachers and community leaders for small tokens like dismissing speeding tickets or a promise to a senate seat in Albany. It meant a poor life was no life and you would never be respected if you tolerated having less than. What poor begets is never more resources, so what is one to do when their soul is in conflict with their innate desire to survive? One will either succumb to having less than and live in a perpetual state of despair, or one will search for a way out. For me, the way out was to make that money, gain some power, and earn all the respect that I could. My power was gained from having a gun in hand.

In America, the gun has always symbolized freedom. It means the one with the power rules the masses who live in fear. It represents a compass to guide one's will over another in order to reach a desired effect. The same rules apply in the ghetto. In the 'hood, fighting went out of style with the availability of automatic weapons. The generation before me ruled with the shotguns they hunted with. Then for urban warfare, they sawed the long barrels off the shotguns so these untraceable lethal weapons could easily be concealed. If a gang war got out of hand, a shotgun blast cleared crowds instantly, but they were often limited to two shots only, and that didn't help much when others were shooting back. So the demand for weapons that had more fire power than the revolver carrying cops, and shotgun carrying thugs rose. The answer was Colt

.45's from Vietnam and Korea, AK47's smuggled from army bases, and eventually the .9mm. When the "nine" hit the streets and one gun could fire sixteen shots in an instant, the demand for that fire power was greater than the need for a pair of Jordan's today.

As teenagers, we had field trips to travel down south, or simply to Pennsylvania—two states over, in an effort to purchase weapons for ourselves and anyone who paid top dollar. We would find an adult who abused drugs, pay he/she $100 and have them buy over twenty guns. By the time we reached the Bronx, we were armed to the teeth. With no idea of how to use these .25, .380, and nine millimeters, we turned to Hollywood for direction. While Bush and the C.I.A helped put crack in America, the film industry, who were historically funded by gun companies, began making films with automatic weapons, and whatever we saw the hero's in the movies do, we mimicked. In the era of *Scarface*, *The Godfather*, *King of New York*, *New Jack City* and an abundance of others, we saw direct images of how to use those weapons and the swagger that came with owning them. The fact that we had VHS tapes—a new invention that allowed you to watch the same movie at home, over and over again, caused us to brand images of violence onto our brains. Slowly the soul of a boy was being compromised, and then the mantra of, "If you're going to pull a gun you better use it," spread faster than the news of a free cheese line. Now it was time to practice the irrational.

"Gunplay," as we called it, starts this way. Say you have Harry, nice kid from a nice home with good honest values. He suffers typical abuse at school or in his neighborhood and feels he has to prove himself in an effort to not be harassed, robbed or killed. Or, because he's considered a bum, is too hungry to focus on education and his siblings are going to bed hungry, he needs money. After one too many scuffles, he either sees with his own eyes how the threat of a gun works to the gun-owner's favor, or he hears war stories of how someone in the 'hood used a gun and earned money or respect for himself. So Harry finds his way to owning a gun. It doesn't matter if it was used in a murder, doesn't work well, is rusty, or once belonged to a police officer. All he knows is that he doesn't want to be abused or hungry and a gun can prevent that. The consequences to his mind, body or soul is the furthest thing from his reality. So with a few hundred dollars or far less, he purchases a gun.

At first he practices holding it in the mirror over and over, convincing himself that he could use that weapon if needed. He mimics the images of others he saw in Hollywood, quick on the draw or pumping imaginary bullets into his imaginary victim. For Harry, this is empowering. He has a tool to keep hunger or bullying away for good, and makes a range of excuses of how he has it to "protect his family," or "rather be caught with it than without it," and how he "rather be tried by twelve than carried by six."

With a new appetite for destruction, Harry feels a new power, liberating himself from fear in an effort to change his circumstances. With the gun he will be feared, respected and finally count for something. The power in his hand gives him hope, fills him with a new ambition and sense of entering a new fraternity of men who were labeled "bad," or tough or gangster, not to mention how Hollywood showed him how every single ethnic group came to America, killed their own people in the streets for the sake of financial gain, and one man remained ahead of the game because he ruled with a gun. The only difference between Harry in the 'hood, and the

WASP, Jews, Irish and Italians that carried guns in the same streets, is Hollywood will never dump hundreds of millions into movies starring people that look like Harry, using guns and staying alive at the end of the movie to be a hero. But none of that is Harry's concern. Harry wants to eat. Harry wants some power over his destiny and the ability to do different things so he could do things differently, like eating.

With his gun on his hip, waist or somewhere on his person, Harry's idea of disrespect becomes warped. He refuses to accept any form of disrespect whatsoever. So who is he going to hunt? The bully, or the man with the money that can help him eat better. To get to the point of actually being ready to use the gun comes in stages. First he has to betray his soul and all the upstanding ethics he was possibly raised with. Then he has to convince himself that he has the power to use it. Harry will aim his gun to the sky and "bust his hammer," until he feels comfortable using it. This is what we call, "A cloud killer." Later he will graduate to shooting objects—garbage cans, bottles, cans, and street targets, like stop signs. For some, an image will emerge. This image is self-created from the owner's wildest imagination. So if Harry watches enough movies or witnesses enough street drama, Harry, or others like him, will rename themselves monikers that signify violence, toughness, or killing. So young Harry with the hungry family or who was seen as soft before, will start calling himself Killer or some name that signifies his image of being cool or tough. Unfortunately for Harry, the moment the 'hood hears about the new name, many candidates will volunteer to see if Harry is really a killer. Either Killer is going to get shot, which can work to his advantage if he survives the wounds, or Killer is going to get beat up and robbed of his gun, or Killer is going to be forced to shoot someone. But shooting someone isn't as easy as it may seem, so Killer will have to graduate from being a cloud killer and turn into something much more dangerous.

Killer will want to, or be forced to, actually kill someone or something. It may be animals, pets or a crack-head from a distance. If he is determined, he will pull his trigger, hear a yell or yelp and watch his victim drop, only to never stand again. From that very instant he will be transformed. Either he will retreat to being good ole Harry, the nice kid again, or he will permanently become Killer, a young boy aiming to kill his true self and live out the image he created. And why does his crime seem victimless? Because the institutions that control his community has devalued the lives. From the politicians who control and refuse to protest the injustice of the police and fire department, to the school teachers and social workers who are employed to empower but fail to do so, along with every single employee at every Martin Luther King hospital in America. Their lack of empathy and concern tells poor people that their lives are worthless. That they lack resources to hold these people accountable, and send the message that the killing of Pookie, Leroy, Earl and Jose Rodriquez will not warrant a major investigation, crime scene or CSI team to come out and take evidence. This continuous mistreatment, and denial of resources that was originally designated for the inner city, but is directed to the people on the better side of town, blatantly highlights to people like Harry in the 'hood that a life taken is no big deal. So what does Harry or Killer do with this info? He rightfully knows the consequences for killing someone who lives, loves and looks like him reaps less consequences, or there won't be none at all if a good 'ole snitch isn't around, so in Harry's mind, someone is going to die if it means him gaining money, power or respect. Soul on soul violence.

When Harry makes the full time commitment to be Killer, he will reinforce his new image with others who will accept, promote, or improve his new behavior. In an environment that's poor, the value of life is low, so finding others who don't care about their own lives is very easy. Thereafter, his crew or partner in crime, will agree that money or power needs to be gained, and his gun will assist him in achieving that. Hurting others won't be easy, at first. But like all repetitive behavior, it will soon become a habit unless one of his soon-to-be victims kills him first, or the law gets involved and stops him dead or alive in his tracks. If not, he will see how his bullets hurt, maim or kill. He may shoot in legs and under the waist the first time. Later his aim will lift up higher, because talking victims can testify or get revenge. Then finally he will see or hear about his gun causing death. He will sit uneasy with the thought that he took a life, but the peers who reinforce his new image and behavior will quickly erase all feelings of uneasiness. Suddenly he matters. His words have weight. Food, money, women and the opportunity to make even more money will come to Killer and those like him. If he gets the attention of the right criminal element, Killer will gain wealth either through robbery, extortion, drug dealing or becoming a "shooter," or gun for hire. And in the beginning, he will enjoy the new sense of power, respect and the fear he instills in others.

Eventually, Killer's appetite will change. The 'hood will fear him, and a chain of events are inevitable. He will make some money. He will start eating whatever, whenever he wants. His wardrobe will change and advertise to the have not's that he now has. He will then invest in his image, purchase jewelry and improve his living situation. Depending on his value system, his room will change until he moves out, or gets kicked out. Then he will want transportation so he can further his pursuit of status, money or women. Killer is officially lost and turned out at this point. His upstanding family will ostracize him while his street family in the 'hood will embrace him. Anyone who's "preaching" legitimacy will quickly be dismissed. His soul is on fire. He has twisted rational as irrational, and the irrational as his place of comfort. This stems from self-deception. The lies he tells himself and the lies his friends who reinforce the image he created tells him, will fuel his ego and cause him to easily destroy others and self-destruct. Long gone are the days when the music he listens to has a positive message. His favorite rapper will suddenly be the most popular one who raps about the destructive life that he wants to live. His movies on killing, gaining money and power will be on repeat on his phone, DVD player or even in his car. Money, sex and violence and the images in the media that perpetuate it will be the only source of entertainment Killer will accept. The fire in his soul will need to be fed, and the more hopelessness, injustice and violence he witnesses, is the further he will be from his true-self. His relationship to love will slowly die, but he will still need affection.

Harry may have had a hard time with the girls. His image wasn't up to par, his ability to afford nice gifts and take a prospective mate on a date was limited due to his lack of funds. Most importantly, he lacked the confidence to pursue the overly attractive women, because most of them were attracted to those whom had success in their environment. This is an issue that Killer does not, and will not have. He can only spend but so much time watching from the sidelines while the male he considers soft or unworthy always get the girl. Like a mating dance, Killer will do all in his power to obtain a symbol of 'hood success. He must acquire a "bad bitch," or a "ride or die chick," to have as his own for the world to see and validate his image. And what exactly is a bad bitch in the 'hood? Generally a female with great looks and a great body is the minimum requirement. After all, a few hundred dollars can purchase fake hair, eyebrows and lashes, contacts, makeup and a cute outfit, and for many females, their souls are for sale if they can go from looking like plain Jane, to Nikki Ménage. In other words, a bad bitch is a female who has her own image and identity issues and can be found looking exactly like any video vixen from a Rap video. So how does Harry get the attention of these females? He may not have to. If he has waged war in his community and his name begins to spread, the females will come to him.

Security in a mate is an aphrodisiac, and in the 'hood, protection is priceless. Poverty reminds the inhabitants of the ghetto that it's playing for keeps. At any time anyone, anywhere can be victimized for their dignity, property or their lives. So when any female, especially one who has to deal with her own dysfunction at home, runs across someone like Killer, the security is a turn on. Dealing with a killer, or someone who is prone to violence, is a way for a woman to live vicariously through her mate. The respect he has is transferred to her. After parading him around and announcing to the world that she is one of, or the main woman in his life, she has put all threats on notice that she isn't the one to be harassed, threatened or disrespected in any way. If Killer has transformed his power into financial gain and he's generous with his spoils of war, suddenly his lover's financial status has changed. Like Killer, at first her appearance will change. With his money or influence she can buy that "good," hair, gain access to that "better" beautician and instead of having outfits, she can finally have a wardrobe. If he has continued success, her home situation will get better, her confidence will grow and then her lifestyle. Finally, her morals, code of conduct and her own image will be transformed all in the act of co-dependency. Now two souls are up for grabs.

The gradual digression of Killer's lover generally develops in this order: The female in the 'hood that becomes the object of Killer's desire has to be one who does not object to the criminal lifestyle. Her moral standards and code of ethics are either already corrupt, or through her own traumatic Ghetto experiences, she's callous, self-centered and in the beginning, Killer is a means to an end. If their relationship blossoms to some form of commitment, the female will have to always be at his disposal. This may mean her moving out of her parent's home, if he's financially capable. For his killer image to be reinforced, Killer must remove any potential interference of her being under his spell. He will isolate her from her family and friends, convince her to skip work and lay in bed one too many times until she quits her job or gets fired, and eventually make her socially, physically, sexually and financially dependent on him. Once she's "his," the fact that she's dependent means she must do what she's told. Even if that means holding his gun during a stop and frisk in the car, transporting drugs "this one time," or getting another abortion because neither of them has the sense to use protection because they are "in love." If his money grows, she will shine bright as a star, but live a lonely life and grow dull inside. The more that she needs him, is the more she will have to prove her loyalty, even if it means providing sexual favors to whomever Killer ask. For some women, it can go as far as killing someone for Killer, or gladly accepting prison time for the man that she loves.

This process of losing one's soul is self-induced. The ability to love is actually an exercise of *liking* something a lot. He likes her sex, her obedience, her loyalty and her looks, but to love her soul is impossible. We can all give various definitions of love, but how can one successfully love someone else when they don't love themselves? How can males like Killer love any female when his day-to-day lifestyle promotes, perpetuates and gives permission to the death and destruction of others? This is a simple question that females who are attracted to thugs and gangstas should ask themselves, but it is my experience that her need for survival, change of circumstances, and the ability to eat well, supersedes her knowledge of consequences. The reality of Killer eventually dying from his lifestyle, him going to prison, dying in prison, or someone killing her in an effort to get to him, does not penetrate her own self-deception. Females like the one above do not want the ride to stop, and if she survives Killer's consequences, she will often pick up the next male who idolized, was enemies with, or whom has the same characteristics as Killer, just so he can finance her new lifestyle. She cannot afford to face the ridicule of falling off or going back to being normal, and if a child is a result of this union between the female and Killer, that child becomes yet another player in the game of dysfunction. That child, based on his parents poor values, morals and decisions, will also grow up poor and devalue their souls. I know this story too well.

Like Harry, I made a quick transition from being "soft," to loving to hurt others with violence. The streets gave me a new sense of power. All of a sudden, I mattered. What I said mattered. And I had followers who did what I said to victimize the so-called tough guys. With victims came fear, with fear came a tool, and with that tool others didn't deny me so my desires were met. Like Harry, I wanted my hunger for more to be removed, but how could my hunger die if my soul was dying and all I searched for was more? "More" never ends. Like my soul, but I didn't know this at the time. What I did know, my neighborhood, social status and lack of finances, wasn't acceptable. I knew that the lives all around me were devalued by the police and all social institutions. If there was a homicide in my community, they didn't call a forensics unit out. They didn't dust for fingerprints, re-enact the crime at the scene, or canvass the entire neighborhood for witnesses. But let a White man, who was from out of town, but came in town to buy or sell drugs get killed in a crossfire or stray bullet? Suddenly news vans appeared, ambulances came on time, the entire homicide detective squad came around, and rewards were posted for the capture of the killer. As a witness to these acts, it was very clear that no one cared about us or our conditions, so if I killed another black person, or if I died at a young age, I would just be another statistic for our community leaders to use as a ploy to get more money to come into our community, but only end up in his pocket.

For decades the poor have complained about Black on Black violence, when the cry should be soul on soul violence. In war, the enemy must be devalued. In order for a soldier to kill, he or she cannot see the enemy as a living soul with a family, loved ones and as a member of a loving community. The soldier must see the enemy as a rag-head, terrorist, Kamikaze, gook, Nazi or some other name that negates the fact that a living soul is inside of the flesh that they will soon blow away. In my 'hood, we took on the language of the experts of devaluing and we call ourselves, "Niggas." The language is the first form of identifying this other person as less-than. If we call him brother, King or family, then we are forced to objectify him as being equal to us. If we disgrace his name, culture, history and soul, then removing him from life just makes him a "body." We used language like, "Yo, I'm a body him," or "They found a body last night." Unfortunately, it is not until we see his mother crying, or the graffiti murals on ghetto walls or R.I.P tee shirts that we associate the life that was lost as another living soul.

In movies and video games they never show the aftermath of what happens when the mass amount of bodies are killed. In rap songs when these soft boys portray to be gangsta's with their lyrics, they hardly ever discuss the consequences of their actions and how the entire community is impacted when someone's life is taken away. In real life, when bullets enter the flesh, it rips and burns away everything in its path, causing the heart or brain to lose blood, and eventually stop working and the human being loses their lives. The loss of life affects the community, his or her parents, lover or spouse, their children and the effect is mass despair. All from one person dying. It really doesn't matter who did the killing, but when the killing is senseless, and the Killer looks just like the deceased, the real fact that one life was lost to death and the other is lost to prison means two or more family's will suffer irreparable damage. So how do we repair Killer and put an end to soul on soul violence? We start with the hopeless gaining strength.

When our community is poor, lacks resources and has institutions who devalue the lives, it breeds boys who transform from Harry into Killer. When Killer is easily given the image reinforcement he needs to practice destruction, and his actions are validated with all the media images he sees, his seed of hopelessness grows. And when injustice on behalf of civil servants, politicians and the court system goes unanswered without massive protest, boycotts and shut downs, lives will continue to be devalued. But when boys are shown that they have a responsibility to themselves, their family and community, they grow appreciating rather than devaluing each other. When an open line of communication between the Killers of the world and the Harry's of the world is created so Killer can show Harry the direct consequences of the criminal lifestyle, more Harrys will be content with being themselves rather than being something destructive. Lastly, when emphasis on the greatness of the soul is celebrated in school, churches and the songs we sing, the anger that leads to violence will dissipate and give more room for love.

There is no one perfect pill to cure social ills. However, the devaluing of our loved ones starts with us. For me to not care about shooting others I had to start seeing them as someone who was a branch of entire families. I had no mercy for those who by agreement knew that once we enter the criminal lifestyle that death is a common occurrence and an occupational hazard. As Outlaws we understood that if we lived by the gun, we would die by the gun, but hopefully we would have attained enough financial stability that our family could feed off the fortune we left behind. Unfortunately, there were masses of boys who observed and idolized from the side-lines, watched our demise and still wanted to be like us. It's a greater misfortune that our destructive, foolish thinking is still celebrated today in music and the perpetuation of violence in the media. It is my belief that this stems from a lack of power.

THE SOUL OF A MAN 2

Power is a force developed through repetitive exercise. The same way a muscle is exercised and grows to endure future stress, is the same activity our communities can emulate by speaking power into our youth. I've seen with my workshops that if you show a boy how he is valuable and how his thoughts matter that he becomes powerful. I've experienced when I give them information, and follow up with the comprehension of that information how it becomes knowledge. And when they know better they do better. I teach them how to get food, money and shelter. I describe commerce, business and why a mortgage is better than rent. I evoke sexual power by showing them the might of a sperm cell and how they are responsible for millions of those sperm by where they point their manhood. And lastly I express the power of weapons, where they fit in during a war and that their lives and legacies are too valuable to jeopardize. Is it all up to me to save our youth? I don't know, and I don't even care what anyone else is doing. What I care about is saving lives now rather than taking them. My concern is being authentic and showing my flaws, my weaknesses and how in situations where I might look powerless, I am not defeated because I press on.

At first it will be just I. Then I will quickly turn into we and then we turns into us. To end the devaluing of our youth begins by giving them value, and the greatest value one can give a young man filled with anger is direction and show him that he matters. From there his soul will be at peace, so he won't have to rest in peace.

Meet the Authors

I would like to introduce to you the contributors of The Soul of a Man 2: Make Me Wanna Holler.

MARC LACY   SHAKEIM EDMONDS   ISAIAH DAVID PAUL

CYRUS WEBB   BRIAN GANGES   ALVIN C. ROMER

RICKEY TEEMS II   ZACH TATE

THE SOUL OF A MAN 2